About the author

Susan Parry began writing when she was a university professor at Imperial College. Her work included forensic studies and archaeological investigations that form the basis for her writing. She lives with her husband in Swaledale, where the views from her house provide inspiration.

website: www.susanparry.co.uk
facebook/instagram: susanparryauthor
twitter: @susan_parry

THE YORKSHIRE DALES MYSTERY SERIES

KILLER LINES

A YORKSHIRE DALES MYSTERY

SUSAN PARRY

Viridian Publishing

First published in the United Kingdom in 2020 by
Viridian Publishing

Viridian Publishing
PO Box 594
Dorking
Surrey
RH4 9HU

www.viridian-publishing.co.uk
e-mail: enquiries@viridian-publishing.co.uk

ISBN 978-0-9567891-8-1

For my readers

Chapter 1

He nearly walked straight past the figure lying on the bench. It was still dark and the lights outside the halls of residence were dim. The motionless form was just a shadowy outline facing away from him. Lewis hesitated before rocking the body gently, assuming it was a fellow student who'd had a few too many pints the night before. There was frost on the lawn and the guy's clothing was cold to the touch. He pulled at the hoodie and the body rolled over onto its back, unresponsive. Believing him to be unconscious, Lewis shouted at him to wake up while he fumbled for his mobile to call for an ambulance. As the woman on the phone bombarded him with questions and issued instructions, a security guy arrived and tried to help resuscitate him. Soon a couple of students emerged from halls and someone cried out that Wilf was dead. Lewis hung around for a few minutes conscious that it was nearly half-past five and he was supposed to be in the kitchens ten minutes ago. He left the small group gathered round the bench and slipped away, anxious not to be late.

Nina Featherstone received the call just after six. She was downstairs in her pyjamas preparing Rosie's packed lunch but left the bread unbuttered to tell Nige she had to go early. He would have to sort the kids out.

'Don't forget to check the boys have got their reading books,' she warned her husband as she dressed after a quick shower.

He was still in bed but muttered something as she left the room.

Outside the street was silent. One or two of the houses had lights on behind their curtains but the road was lined with frost-covered cars. It took a few minutes to scrape the windscreen but, once she was moving, the drive over to the university was easy, with little traffic at that time in the morning. She didn't really need to rush because the lad was dead, and uniform were on the scene. The body would probably have been moved by the time she arrived and witnesses would be dispersing. It sounded as if it was an accidental death and she'd only been asked to attend because the DCI was anxious to show that the force was concerned about the tragic death of a student attending their local university.

The halls of residence were just inside the main entrance of the campus and it was easy to spot two marked police cars parked outside one of the buildings.

'DS Featherstone,' she announced, showing her ID to the uniformed police officer who turned as she approached. 'I was asked to attend by DI Mitch Turner.'

The young man consulted his notebook to give her the few details he'd gleaned from fellow students so far. The lad was called Wilf Marriott. He was a final year undergraduate student, studying chemistry. He lived in a shared flat on campus but they hadn't had any contact with his flatmates so far.

'Any idea of cause of death?' she asked.

'The body's gone off for a post-mortem. No sign of violence though.'

'Any thoughts?'

'Looks like he's fallen asleep on the bench after a heavy drinking session or drugs, or both. It was freezing and he wasn't dressed for it.'

'Hypothermia?'

The officer shrugged. 'Who knows what daft nonsense they get up to. He won't be the first idiot to end up that way after a night out, or the last.'

He started to describe a case he'd been involved in with County Durham Police but Nina cut him short. She was beginning to get cold standing in the wind. In her view it was not a case that should be taking up her time and she would set off back to Northallerton and breakfast, as soon as she'd spoken to the lad who'd found the body.

The officer glanced at his notepad. 'That will be a Lewis Chalmers. He was on his way to work in the university cafeteria when he found the body on that bench.'

'Will he be there now?' she asked.

'I suppose so. We've arranged to speak to him when he comes off shift at nine.'

Surprised they hadn't taken a statement already, Nina sought directions and set off for the main administration block. It was getting light now and cars were beginning to arrive on campus. She was passed by a jogger as she took a path beside a large lake. After ten minutes exercise in the frosty air she felt wide awake and hungry.

The cafeteria appeared to be built to cater for the entire campus. It was enormous and almost empty. A tempting smell of toast and bacon emanated from trays of food on the counter. A woman in green overalls was loading baked beans into a deep metal tray. She looked up and shouted that they weren't open until seven-thirty. Nina checked the clock, it was twenty-past.

'I'd like to speak to Lewis,' she began.

'He's working.' The woman banged the metal container to empty the last few beans and turned to go.

'I'm Detective Sergeant Featherstone.' She waved her ID.

'What's he been up to?' She walked back into the kitchen area before Nina had a chance to answer.

There were sausages, bacon and hash browns. The scrambled egg looked overcooked but she could have eaten the lot.

'You wanted to talk to me?'

The lad only looked about fifteen. He was short and very thin. His cropped hair accentuated a pale face. His accent sounded local.

'Lewis? I'm a police officer. I've been asked to make a few notes about the student you found dead this morning. Shall we sit down?'

He followed her to a table at a decent distance from the counter. His oversized apron bearing the university coat of arms flapped as he walked. Once seated at the table, she asked him to describe exactly how he'd found the body. He didn't know the student or anyone called Wilf, but he was in the first year, studying engineering, and spent his free time working to pay for his course. It soon became clear he wouldn't shed any further light on what had happened but Nina made sure she thanked Lewis for acting so promptly on discovering the body and for being so helpful. He shrugged and walked back to the kitchen without asking her any questions himself.

Tempting as it was to sit down to a "full English", Nina left the cafeteria with a take-away coffee and sipped it as she made her way back to her car. Already there were a couple of items on the bench where the body had been found: a scarf and a hastily scribbled piece of card that simply read "RIP Wilf. We'll miss you mate." It was tempting to find out more about the young man, his friends, his family, but it wasn't her job. She had a quick chat with the young officer as he sat in his car making notes, then rang Nige to check he was on his way to school with the kids.

'No problem, I'm just going.'

'Make sure they wrap up warm, it's freezing out this morning.'

'Will do. Are you at work?'

'Not yet. Just leaving. I've been at the university. A student died. They say he's from the Chemistry Department.'

'So not one of mine, thank goodness. The papers will be all over it.'

'I expect so, that's why the DCI told Mitch to send someone over. Anyway, I must get going, the traffic will be building up.'

On the way back to headquarters Nina couldn't stop thinking about the number of student deaths that had been reported in the local news over the last few years. Suicide rates were increasing in the university sector and it was highest in male students. Presumably the autopsy would establish whether this student's death was suicide although her money was on alcohol poisoning or drug overdose. She didn't think the University of North Yorkshire had a serious drug problem but it would be worth looking at if it turned out to be the cause of death.

Mills Sanderson steered the Mini gingerly down the narrow lane to Simon's cottage. The road hadn't been gritted and she was aware of the stone walls on either side. After spending the weekend in Swaledale, they were driving to the university via Osmotherley to drop off her lurcher, Harris.

'Are you sure the dog walker will come today?' she asked, as Simon gave Harris his breakfast while she turned up the heating.

'Yes, it's all fine. He adores her, trust me.'

Back in the car Simon assured her that the lurcher loved the opportunity to race around with the other dogs. They had a good hour or more out with the dog walker and he came back exhausted. Mills had to agree grudgingly that the arrangement seemed to be working. It meant they could all be together during the week in Simon's place, which was convenient for the university. But she insisted they go back to Swaledale at weekends, to spend time in her cottage at Mossy Bank.

At the university entrance they had to wait to let a police car come out.

'Someone's in trouble,' joked Simon.

'Something over the weekend, I expect,' said Mills as she found an empty space in the car park. 'They need to grit round here, it's quite slippery in places.'

They arranged to meet up later and Mills collected her mail from the pigeonholes before carrying on to the office she shared with Nige Featherstone.

He was already behind his desk. 'Ah, "bore da", good morning. Dr Sanderson I presume?'

Mills had noticed that the Welsh accent made his remarks sound funnier than they generally were.

'Very good Nige. Just because you've arrived first, for once.'

'But am I early or are you late?' He was still grinning at her.

Mills ignored him and opened her mail before throwing it in the bin.

'Have you seen the email from the Head?' Nige asked as she started up her computer.

'No.'

She skimmed through her inbox and found the message. It read: *"It is with great sadness that I can confirm that a fellow student passed away on campus this morning. The family has been informed and we are doing everything we can to support them."* She looked up at Nige.

'Nina says he was a chemistry student,' he said.

'What happened? How did he die?'

'I don't know. I assume it was suicide. Nina came over early this morning. I had to get the kids ready for school on my own and on a Monday morning!'

Mills had an archaeology class so she gathered up a folder marked "Student Assessments" and made her way to the lecture theatre. The atmosphere was subdued as she distributed the marked papers from the end of the term exam.

'Take a few minutes to look through the marks and comments on your papers before I go through the model answers with you,' she instructed them.

There was one paper left over when she'd finished handing them out. It belonged to Alison Steel.

'Has anyone seen Alison?' she asked the class.

No-one responded or even looked up. She put the paper back in her bag and turned on the projector. It was time to go through the assessment paper. It didn't take as long as she'd allowed for since no-one asked any questions. Even the most vocal among them were silent. She had just told them they could go when the departmental administrator popped her head round the door.

'The Head wants everyone to read out this message to their classes,' she said, handing Mills a sheet of paper before disappearing.

It was the same message she'd found in her inbox. It was addressed to staff and students so she was sure they'd seen it already.

'Listen,' she said, raising her voice over the noise of forty students packing their bags. 'Before you go, I just want to pass a message on from Professor Cole.'

The room fell silent and the students stayed where they were. Some were still seated but most were on their way towards the door.

'In case you haven't seen his email message this morning, the Head wants to inform you of the sad death of one of our students.' She then read the full statement out.

There was a lot of nodding and muttering between them. Mills guessed that they knew more than she did about who it was and what had happened.

'And if you see Alison, let her know I have her paper.'

A lad called Martin came over to inform her that Alison knew Wilf and so she was probably too upset to come to class.

'So it was Wilf that was…?'

'Yes, they found him this morning, outside halls.'

Mills wanted to find out more but it seemed inappropriate to be seeking information from the student, so she thanked him and watched him leave. If this Wilf had been a chemistry student, it was likely that Simon would have heard the details. She was uncertain what to do about Alison Steel. If the girl was really upset about the dead student then someone should be informed. She checked in the office to find out whose tutor group she was in and discovered that she was Nige's responsibility. Mills found him at his desk.

'Nige, you need to talk to Alison Steel. She wasn't in my class today and her friends say she's upset about the student found dead this morning.'

Nige looked like a rabbit caught in the headlights. It wasn't his forte to act as a shoulder to cry on. Sharing an office had meant she sometimes witnessed his attempts at empathy and it wasn't impressive, particularly with women.

'Couldn't you see her?' he asked eventually. 'You're so much better at that sort of thing.' He pointed at her desk. 'You have tissues and everything.'

Mills sighed. It was a cop-out but she knew it would be better for her to speak to the girl. 'OK, you win, but you'll have to leave me alone in the office when she comes here.'

He agreed at once.

Nina was biting greedily into a sausage bap while she typed up her report. There was little to say but Mitch was adamant there was to be clear evidence that she had been over to the university and ascertained all the facts. Most of the information had come from uniform, for what it was worth. She could now provide the names of his flatmates, his age, university address, home address and phone number. She wouldn't be able to complete cause of death until the results of the post-mortem came through but she was sure it was going to be incapacity due to drink or drugs, resulting in falling unconscious on one of the coldest nights of the year and dying of exposure. But when she discussed it with her colleagues, they each had their own views.

'He was a student,' said DS Hazel Fuller. 'It's bound to be drugs.'

'That's so stereotypical,' argued their young researcher, Ruby. 'Statistically it's much more likely it was suicide.'

'You mean he took an overdose then just laid down outside to freeze to death? That is grim, Ruby,' said Hazel.

Nina agreed. 'You're right though, we shouldn't jump to conclusions. But it looks to me like a tragic accident so that will be the end of our involvement.'

Chapter 2

'Did you hear about the body they found this morning?' Simon asked as they drove home to Osmotherley.

'The chemistry student? Yes,' Mills replied. 'Called Wilf?'

'Do you mean Wilf Marriott?' He went quiet. 'I heard he was a final year student in the department but that was all. I didn't realise it was Wilf.'

'Do you know him?'

'Yes, I supervise him. I mean I did.'

They didn't talk much on the way home after that. Mills didn't have any more information and Simon wasn't keen to discuss it. But once they'd walked the dog and begun preparing their meal, Mills suggested that the police might need to talk to him.

'Why?'

'They may want to know what he was working on. What *was* he doing, by the way?'

'Just toxicology stuff. He was starting a final year research project with me.'

Mills left it at that. He clearly was reluctant to talk about it, so she changed the subject. 'I was thinking, should I come along with you to the meeting tomorrow?'

She was referring to the last of a series of hurdles they had to pass before gaining approval for their new forensic laboratory. The plans had been drawn up and approved by the relevant committees with a few minor changes to satisfy the Health and Safety Unit. Because the laboratory was going to be housed in the Chemistry Department, most of the presentations had been made by Simon, but the initiative also involved the Forensic Department, where they both were academic staff.

'No need,' said Simon. He was making a risotto and was standing at the stove with his back to her. 'It's only the Finance Committee and I'll be in and out. They've got the written details and I'll only be allowed in at the end to answer any outstanding questions.'

'But they may ask something about the work that only I can answer.'

'Don't worry, there won't be any technical questions at this stage.'

'Or something relating to Brenda's contribution?'

'All they need to know is that Dr Yardley will have a share in the venture. We've made it clear in the paperwork that she is retiring and handing over the insurance money from the fire at Yardley Forensics. We've itemised every single piece of equipment her funds will finance.' He turned, waving a spatula at her. 'We can't do any more.'

'Sorry, but I won't stop worrying until we get the final go-ahead.'

She put two forks out on the large table and sat down to wait. Harris came over to her, laying his face on her lap. The kitchen was huge compared to her own and she had to admit she was spending more and more time at Simon's during the week. His cottage was closer to the university than hers which made commuting easier, particularly in the dark mornings and evenings. She enjoyed having the extra space but looked forward to returning home at the weekends and Simon agreed that spending time in Swaledale was like having a minibreak.

'I still think we should go through the business plan this evening, so it's fresh in your mind for tomorrow,' Mills insisted when they'd finished eating.

'OK, fine.'

He delved into his battered briefcase, retrieved a red file, and placed it on the table after brushing crumbs away. Harris went over to investigate the floor where they fell.

Mills could hardly believe they'd reached this point now that everything was falling into place. She thought it was the end of her work in forensics when the Yardley laboratory was burned down deliberately. She'd been devastated when Brenda had said she wouldn't rebuild the lab but collect the insurance money and retire instead. Surprisingly, Brenda had been quite enthusiastic about the concept of a new forensic lab within the university. She was particularly keen on the idea of an independent laboratory designed to carry out defence work, saying that it was impossible to compete with the large organisations which were part of the police scientific services.

'Are you listening?' Simon was asking. He'd opened the file and his reading glasses were perched on the end of his nose.

'Yes, Professor Pringle, I'm ready.' She grinned across the table at him.

'So, it's a very simple business model,' he began. 'We set up a spin-off company which the university will have a twenty percent share in.'

'D'you think they'll accept that?'

'They should. The value of the space, services and running costs provided by my department is equivalent to less than that proportion of the total cost, in my view. The toxicology instrumentation will come from my major research grant and is worth, incidentally, a million quid. Brenda Yardley will provide all your sort of forensic equipment, worth a similar amount.'

'And you still think that the single technician allocated in your grant will be able to run all that?'

'With our help, of course.'

Mills leaned back and folded her arms. 'I can tell you now that they won't manage. You're even busier than I am and you've got a research group to run. My teaching load is getting heavier and heavier. We definitely need someone else.'

'I can see you've been thinking about this. What have you in mind?'

'Donna.'

'Who is she?'

'She used to work at Yardley's before the fire. She got a job at the police lab in Wakefield. You may have met her down there.'

He shook his head.

'I see her occasionally for coffee and she's really enjoying the work but the travelling is getting her down. She's got a steady boyfriend up here now and she's been thinking of looking for a lab job nearer home.'

He was flicking through the file. 'Are you suggesting we add this in somewhere?'

'I thought it could be part of the running costs covered by the university. Doesn't it come under that?'

After another hour at the table, Mills wished she hadn't suggested going through the figures. The business plan included predicted profit and loss, cashflow and returns on investment. She assumed it would all be handled by an accountant but Simon said they had to understand what they were getting into.

'We have to be confident that we can make a profit or there is no point in doing it at all.'

'I suppose so.'

'And I think these numbers are perfectly reasonable. The figures Dr Yardley gave us are a good indication of what is feasible based on her accounts.'

'She never had an interest in money or much idea of how to run a business, that's why it was going downhill. She was heading towards bankruptcy.'

'Lucky for her someone torched it then.'

'I don't think she saw it like that, Simon. Not when Tim died in the fire.'

'Sorry, I didn't mean...'

'At least something good came out of it. She says she thinks of the insurance money as an unexpected windfall and is happy to simply hand it over. But I hope we can repay her in time.'

'I think she's just pleased that it's being put to good use.'

Mills finally received a response from Alison Steel the following day. The message, sent in the early hours, said she would come in the morning if that was convenient. It suited Mills well, since Nige would be safely out of the way until lunchtime. She spent the morning catching up with tasks she'd put off since before the Christmas break. It had been hard to get back into routine work, particularly now she and Simon were spending so much more time together.

She was almost relieved when there was a gentle knock at the door and Alison came in. The student was normally very neatly dressed but today she was in crumpled jeans and a baggy sweater. Mills noticed how her hair, usually tied back in an elaborate plait, was falling around her face. She dropped a large expensive-looking handbag beside her chair.

'I'm sorry I missed your lecture,' she began politely.

Mills gave her a sympathetic smile and asked how she was feeling. The girl nodded, saying she was fine, but it had been a bit of a shock, that was all.

'Did you know him well?' Mills asked. 'Wilf, I mean.'

Alison was reticent at first but soon she was relating how they'd had their first proper date only a week ago, just before Valentine's day. They'd been to a gig in Newcastle, tribute acts playing music from Dire Straits and Bruce Springsteen. Mills waited until the girl had come to a halt and, after an awkward silence, asked her if she knew when Wilf's funeral would be held.

'I don't know. No-one has said anything. I suppose his parents will be sending invites. They won't know about me.'

She looked as if she might cry and Mills pushed the box of tissues in her direction. 'I'm sure they will want to see his friends at his funeral and the university will certainly send a representative.'

Alison sniffed and pulled a tissue out of the box. Mills had so many questions about the dead student but the poor girl had withdrawn back into her chair. It was more important to ensure she was going to be all right.

'Are you living on campus?' Mills asked.

She took the tissue away from her face and nodded. 'I'm sharing a flat in Pease Hall. That's how I met Wilf, we're on the same floor.'

His body had been discovered outside the same hall of

residence.

'So, you have friends back in halls,' Mills said.

It was a comment not a question but the girl nodded.

'I'm going home for a few days. I'll be back for your lecture next week though.'

Mills felt she'd done enough but added that it might be a good idea to make an appointment with the university Student Support and Wellbeing team, and gave her the number.

'We can go through last term's assessment next week when you're back,' she told Alison on her way out.

As soon as Nige returned to the office, Mills told him about her meeting with the student. 'I've given her the Student Support number but I think you should let the department know what's going on. She was his girlfriend and is in a vulnerable state. You're her personal tutor after all.'

He raised his palms in submission. 'Okay, I hear what you're saying. I'll deal with it but may I eat my sandwiches first?' He indicated the brown paper bag he'd put on his desk.

Mills had wanted to meet Simon for lunch but it was too late now to have more than a quick chat. She rang his office but there was no answer and his mobile went to voicemail.

'Damn. I wanted to see Simon before his meeting with the Finance Committee,' she told Nige.

'Oh yes, it's the big day today isn't it?' He ripped open the plastic packaging and pulled out a sandwich. 'I saw him in the cafeteria with a couple of suits. I guessed they were part of the committee. Is he softening them up?'

'I don't know, but it's too late now. The meeting starts in half an hour.'

Mills spent the rest of the afternoon trying to concentrate on notes she was preparing for her imminent archaeology field trip, but she was easily distracted. When Nige asked for her help with the referral form he'd downloaded from the Student Support website, she patiently explained that he was completing the wrong document and pointed him to the instructions that required him to gain permission from Alison before recommending her for counselling services.

'She did say she would contact them herself, Nige, but I'll send her a message asking if she would like a referral.'

He looked relieved and once again asked if she wouldn't be better placed to help her.

'All right, I give in, but only this once. Next time you're on your own.'

Mills was quietly pleased that he'd asked for her help and sent a sympathetic message to Alison offering to arrange a referral for her. Anything to pass the time until Simon let her know that the Finance Committee had finished its deliberations.

Nige had left and the cleaner had emptied the bins before Simon finally appeared and sank down on the spare chair.

'Well?'

'Well, indeed. That was gruelling. I reckon I was in there for over an hour and a half.'

Mills looked at the time. 'So why are you so late? It's nearly six.'

'They didn't call me in at first. Apparently, some serious financial crisis is brewing. They didn't get down to our item until after four.'

'Financial crisis?'

'Nothing that affects us. I heard it's something to do with an overspend in another department.'

'So, what did they say?' Mills just wanted to know that they had approved the plan.

'They were still discussing it when I left. They said they would let me know this evening. The committee secretary will ring me.'

There seemed no point in hanging around so they headed off. In the car, Mills asked Simon to describe the meeting in detail.

'They asked me to go through the business plan blow by blow, so it was good we went over it all last night because they picked up on a couple of the things we discussed, like the depreciation of equipment.'

'But they were happy with those figures?'

'Yes, I think so.'

'What else did they pick on?'

'They felt the university contribution was rather high but I pointed out that they had already agreed to pay the overheads for my grant equipment so it wasn't really much extra.'

'Did they accept that?'

'Some did, one or two were mumbling about it. I think they'll limit their liability to a period, like five years. That seemed to be the line of thought.'

'And Brenda's contribution?'

'They were puzzled. They couldn't understand why anyone would put so much money into a new business without any strings attached. I tried to explain but they're hard-nosed finance people and they implied they thought she was mad.'

'It wouldn't be the first time someone has called her

that. So, what do you think their decision will be?'

He didn't answer immediately as he concentrated on finding a gap in the traffic to turn off the main road. Slowing the car down he looked over at Mills.

'I honestly couldn't call it. We'll just have to wait and see.'

Which is exactly what they did. The conversation was subdued as they prepared their meal, eating in silence as they waited for Simon's mobile to ring. It finally pinged when they were washing up.

'It's a text,' he announced.

Mills tried to read his face as he peered at the screen. Finally it creased into a smile.

'What?' screamed Mills.

'It's a yes.'

Chapter 3

Nina was surprised to receive the results of the post-mortem on Wilfred Marriott just two days after his body had been discovered.

'Must be quiet at the morgue,' commented Hazel, who enjoyed making jokes in bad taste, knowing it annoyed Nina.

'Wilfred is a very old-fashioned name,' commented Ruby, their researcher.

'He calls himself Wilf,' Nina explained.

She was skimming through the report to see if it confirmed her prediction of accidental death. But, no, it didn't. They had detected MDMA, commonly called ecstasy, and alcohol in the blood and urine but not enough to kill him. The cold weather was a consideration but he was a very healthy young man and his core temperature suggested he'd not been out there more than a few hours. It didn't explain adequately what had killed him.

'They need to do more tests,' she told her colleagues. 'It's possible the ecstasy may have been adulterated.'

Ruby was typing furiously. 'It could be amphetamine, cocaine, caffeine, methamphetamine or ketamine.' She suggested.

'They say they've tested for the obvious drugs but there are more obscure things that are difficult to detect.'

'What about PMA?' Ruby immediately began looking up statistics for PMA related deaths in the UK. 'There were two cases of death in Derbyshire last year from ecstasy containing…' She stumbled over the word as she read it out. '…paramethoxyamphetamine. I guess you'd call it accidental if it is that,' she said. 'If the ecstasy was adulterated and he didn't know, I mean.'

Hazel asked why anyone in their right mind would take a drug that was going to kill them. They knew her views on drug addiction and Nina stopped her before she went on to suggest that Wilf got what he deserved. Ruby, meanwhile, had found cases in America of PMA being passed off as ecstasy.

'Will they get further tests done down at the Wakefield lab?' she asked Nina. 'They did very detailed analysis on samples from that drug ring in Bradford before Christmas.'

'Yes but I guess it will take a while before the results come through,' replied Nina. 'And even if they find a contaminant, it will just confirm accidental death, as we suspected. That's a decision for the coroner. I'm just pleased it's not our call to speak to the lad's poor parents.'

Hazel sighed loudly. 'Someone had better warn the other student junkies before bodies start piling up on the campus.'

It was true, thought Nina. They should warn the authorities if a drug commonly used by students was being spiked. She rang Nige to find out who in the university should be alerted.

'Is it the Health Centre?' she asked him.

'I don't know. It could be I suppose, or Student Services. The email about the death came from the Head.' He paused for a second then asked, 'Is this about the dead student. Was it an overdose?'

'I can't say,' Nina replied.

'So, I assume it was then. What did he take? What was

in it?'

Nina looked across at Hazel, who was watching her, and quickly changed the subject. 'I don't know, Nige. So don't forget Rosie has ballet after school. I won't be late but if I am can you pick her up afterwards?'

'All right I give in, but do you want me to tell anyone here about the drugs?'

'No, I'll do it through the proper channels.'

Ruby was ready with the information as soon as Nina put the phone down. 'It'll be the Student Welfare Team at the university,' she informed her. 'Do you want the number?'

Hazel said she thought they should ask the DI before passing on the information. 'It's still a police matter if the student was in possession of MDMA, even if it's not our call.'

Typical of Hazel, Nina thought. 'OK, so please can you go and ask him then?'

Nige looked up from his computer when Mills arrived.

'I can see you've got something to be cheerful about,' he said. 'Let me guess.'

'Can you tell? Well, it's been approved. The Yardley Forensic Laboratory is going ahead at the university.'

'That's good. So when will it be operational?'

'Not for several months.' Mills took off her coat and hung it on the back of the door.

'That's a shame, I could've put some work your way.'

'Seriously?'

He grinned. 'No, just kidding. Nina told me that the student who died on Monday had taken drugs.'

'Is that what killed him?' Mills sat down and turned her

computer on.

He shrugged. 'You know her, she wouldn't say. I just thought I'd mention it since your Professor Pringle is so hot on toxicology. Maybe he'd like something to get his teeth into. Test if the equipment is up and running.'

'But it is. That side of the forensics is in place. It all came out of his big research grant.' She was already thinking through the possibilities. 'D'you think I should ring her?'

Her colleague looked alarmed. 'No, please don't. You know what she's like. She only told me by accident really.'

'But it wouldn't harm to give her a call to let her know we've got the go-ahead for the lab though, would it?'

Nige shrugged and turned back to his computer screen. 'Be it on your head,' he said. 'Don't involve me in your little schemes.'

Mills waited until lunchtime when she thought it more appropriate to call Nina "for a chat". Fortunately her friend was at her desk when she rang.

'DS Nina Featherstone.'

'Hi Nina, it's only me.'

'Mills? Are you all right?'

'Yes, why?'

'I haven't heard from you for a while and if I ring in the evening it just goes to voicemail.'

'You should use my mobile number. I've been staying with Simon mostly during the week.'

'Oh I see. It's going that well is it?'

'Yes,' she replied, refusing to be drawn on her love life. 'And the good news is, we've just heard that the lab is going to go ahead.'

'Nige said you were waiting to hear. That's brilliant. I'm certain it will be a great success when it's up and running, although I'm not sure if we'll be able to send much work your way, not like in the past. Most things go down to Wakefield now.'

'Perhaps if there's anything, you know, very specialised, we could do it. Simon's research into detection of different combinations of drugs is cutting edge. He can detect drugs down to extremely low levels, much lower than commercial organisations would be able to attempt.'

'Mills, has Nige been saying something?'

'No, why?'

'What makes you think we are currently interested in the detection of drugs?'

Mills had to think quickly. 'I suppose it was the tragic death of the chemistry student on campus this week. One naturally thinks about the possible causes.'

'Well you can stop fishing right now, Mills Sanderson.' She paused. 'So when are you going to bring your professor to meet me?'

'When you and Nige stop calling Simon "my professor", Nina.'

'Talking of my husband, is he there?'

'No, he's teaching.'

'When he comes back, tell him to ring me.'

Mills suspected she'd got Nige into trouble and warned him when he returned. She asked him if he'd told anyone else that Wilf had died of an overdose. When he said he hadn't, she suggested the authorities should be told if it was true. But before she did anything about it, she would talk to Alison again.

Hazel came back from her meeting with the DI looking irritated. 'Mitch says we'll have to wait until we get the results of the detailed drug test before we can give any information to the university. He says it's politically sensitive, don't ask me why. You'd think he'd want to prevent more little darlings keeling over.'

'It could be weeks before we see the results,' said Ruby.

Nina sighed. 'At least three weeks, maybe more. I checked with Wakefield; they have a backlog on the more sophisticated techniques they use to analyse complex combinations of drugs.'

There was a long silence. When Hazel went out for a smoke, Nina decided to tell Ruby what Mills had said.

'There's a professor of toxicology at the university who could do the test. What d'you think?'

'Would it be quicker?'

'I can find out.'

'Go for it. See what Mitch says but if the students need to be alerted, I'd say the sooner the better.'

Nina never found it easy persuading her DI to accept her suggestions. Hazel could fight her own corner but the DI tended to ignore Nina's opinions on most occasions. Perhaps she felt more strongly about it than other issues but he appeared to be listening this time, and at the end of the conversation she had his permission to investigate the possibility of getting samples sent to Professor Pringle, depending on timings and, most importantly, cost.

Back in the office she gave her colleagues the good news. Even Hazel was impressed. Nina immediately rang Mills to get her professor's contact details and found herself explaining why she was asking, despite warning glances from Hazel. There was no point in being secretive when her friend would hear all about it from her boyfriend anyway.

The call to Mills didn't take long. 'Can you get him to contact me as soon as possible?' Nina asked before putting the phone down.

You bet, thought Mills, almost running across campus to find Simon. He was in his office but she could see he was on the phone. She hesitated for a second before walking in. He looked up and smiled but carried on talking, holding up his free hand, which Mills assumed meant he'd be five minutes. It didn't sound like an important conversation and she stood waiting until he cut the call short, saying he had a visitor waiting. He didn't look entirely happy.

'That was my technician down in the lab. He can't find any of the small plastic vials we use and swears we'd just had a new supply delivered. He's telling me they've been stolen. It's rather unlikely.'

'Sorry but this is really important,' she began.

'Then sit and calm down,' he told her with a smile.

She moved a box file from the comfy chair and sat, hoping she looked calm although she was excited. 'I've just had a call from Nina.'

'Nina?'

'Detective Sergeant Nina Featherstone from North Yorkshire Police.'

'What have you been up to?'

She ignored his grin. 'She wants to know if you can analyse some forensic samples for drugs. They've had the common ones done but they think the ecstasy was adulterated with something else.'

'Do you know what?'

'No. Normally they'd wait for Wakefield to process them but it will take ages and she wants to know quickly if contaminated drugs are being sold on campus.'

Simon's face suddenly became serious. 'Is this to do with Wilf?'

'Yes, it is.'

He rubbed his chin, resting back in his chair. 'That's rather ironic isn't it?'

Mills didn't understand and waited for him to explain.

'The research project I gave him was looking at exactly that. I'm developing simple field kits that can be used to test the quality of street drugs. He was particularly interested in typical student drugs such as ecstasy and cocaine.'

'Do you think his interest wasn't just academic?'

Simon shrugged. 'Who knows. He seemed a good student. His work was closely supervised and he didn't have access to any of the original drugs, they were all synthetic mixtures I made up myself. The students only need tiny quantities for the analysis.'

'Do you think you could help Nina? If you can, it will be a brilliant start to the new lab's mission.'

'I thought it was supposed to be a facility to support defence lawyers?'

'Well, we have to start somewhere, don't we? It certainly won't harm to be endorsed by the police.'

'We'd better call her now then,' he said with a grin.

Mills listened to their conversation on speakerphone. Simon was his usual charming self as he discussed details with Nina. Yes, he could turn samples around in a week and he reeled off a list of obscure chemical names that meant nothing to Mills. Nina mentioned one called fentanyl and Simon raised an eyebrow but agreed he would look for that as well. When Nina asked about the cost,

Simon said he would get back to her but would only charge for consumables on this occasion. She was very grateful and before the call had finished, had invited him and Mills over for supper whenever it suited them.

'She sounds very nice,' he commented as he switched the phone off. 'Did that sound all right? I thought it best to do it as a loss leader.'

'If you're sure. We will need to make a profit once the lab is up and running.'

'I know but I hadn't a clue what to charge; you'll have to look after that side of the business. It will be an interesting job but quite challenging. Fortunately my postgrad can help with much of the work but I'll need to work on the fentanyl.'

Mills had heard the name but didn't know what it was so Simon explained. 'It's an opiate, much more powerful than morphine and extremely dangerous. It's added to cocaine and heroin in the States to provide a bigger hit but not round here. I'm sure we wouldn't find it in any ecstasy samples.'

'I hope not,' said Mills. 'It's frightening to think our students could be playing with such highly dangerous substances.'

'That's why I'm working on these kits, so they can check the purity of what they're taking.'

'Isn't that encouraging them to take drugs though?'

'You won't stop them so you must keep them safe. If Wilf died as a result of taking an adulterated drug, we should do everything possible to avoid it happening again.'

'Well, I will be talking to Alison Steel again. She was Wilf's girlfriend so perhaps she'll know what he was taking and where it came from.'

29

Simon looked at his watch. 'I think it's time we went home. We've got two excuses for champagne now.'

They had arranged to take Brenda for a meal in Harrogate to celebrate receiving the go-ahead for the forensic laboratory. It had been difficult to persuade her but she'd finally agreed, provided they picked her up, they ate early and she paid. When Simon said he would buy the champagne, Mills pointed out that Brenda would probably prefer a pint of beer.

Her old boss was on good form when they called for her. Mills noted that she had gone to some effort and commented on how well she seemed. Since losing so much weight after her cancer she'd looked shrunken in her old clothes, but tonight she was wearing a rather fancy blouse that was clearly new. Possibly specially purchased for the occasion, thought Mills.

Brenda had met Simon a few times when they'd discussed the initial plans for their joint venture but, once the arrangements were settled, she preferred to take a back seat. She'd always been polite to Simon but somehow had never seemed particularly at ease in his company. Mills had hoped she would relax now everything was settled, and it seemed as if she might be right because she was now laughing at his silly jokes. She asked him to choose the wine and he was suggesting what she might like from the menu. Mills sat back contentedly, feeling that, at last, everything was going well.

'We should drink a toast,' Simon said when the champagne arrived.

He raised his glass and made a nice little speech thanking Brenda for her amazing contribution to their venture. He assured her that they would be working very hard indeed to make it a world-class laboratory. They all drank to the success of the project, then Simon told Brenda that they had already started the ball rolling by offering to do some toxicological work for the police. Mills guessed that Simon was trying to impress her, but she knew Brenda wouldn't be entirely thrilled by the prospect.

'How exactly will you manage that then?' she demanded.

Mills could tell she didn't think it was a good idea but Simon chattered on about how the equipment was there and he had a postgraduate who could help.

'A student?' Now she looked appalled.

Simon reassured her he would be in control of every part of the work.

Mills, sensing his irritation at Brenda's lack of confidence in him, felt compelled to intervene. 'Until the laboratory is fully functional the work won't have the Yardley Forensics label, will it? It's just a piece of work Simon is doing for Nina, so please don't worry Brenda, I'll make sure the correct procedures are followed.'

She looked across at Simon, praying he wouldn't be offended by her intervention, but he was smiling and nodding.

'Yes,' he said, 'she'll keep me on the straight and narrow. More champagne, Brenda?'

Chapter 4

'Mills, this is Callum, he's going to help me with our analyses.'

She smiled at him. 'Hello.'

The lad who had just walked in had curly ginger hair that was falling into his eyes. He brushed it aside and lifted his hand in an embarrassed wave. Simon had already told Mills that the police wanted to talk to Callum Wallace because he had shared a flat with Wilf.

'But first, Callum, I need to tell you that a Detective Sergeant Hazel Fuller will be here soon to speak to you and to someone called Oliver Hayes, do you know him?'

'We share a flat, the one we shared with Wilf.' He was looking at the floor.

There was an awkward silence then Simon said, 'So, I told her she can use my office. She wants to interview you separately so I suggest you see her first, then we can start to prepare the lab for the arrival of the forensic samples.'

The student nodded.

Mills looked at Simon. 'I'll leave you to it then.'

Callum moved aside to let her pass as she headed for the door. She opened it to find Hazel Fuller about to knock.

'Dr Sanderson!' she exclaimed, stepping back. 'What are you doing here?' She looked quite annoyed, which amused Mills. Their paths had crossed in the past and, for some reason, they'd never been able to see eye to eye.

'Don't worry, I'm just going,' she replied, walking past her into the corridor. She could hear Simon introducing himself as she left.

'This is Callum Wallace,' Professor Pringle said, indicating the scruffy student by his side. 'I thought you'd find it quieter in here. We have a meeting room but it gets booked well in advance, I'm afraid.'

'This is fine.' Hazel took off her jacket and threw it over his chair.

The professor went on hovering. 'So should I leave you to it?' he asked eventually.

'Yes. I've told Mr Hayes that I'll see him in about half an hour.'

The professor asked the student to give him a call when the office was free, then left them to it.

'Sit down,' ordered Hazel, taking the padded chair behind the desk. 'I need you to tell me about your friend Wilf Marriott.'

'He wasn't really a friend,' he replied. 'He had a room in our flat, that's all.'

'How long had he shared with you?'

He paused to do the calculation. 'Four and a half months.'

'I see. Did you socialise with him? Did you go drinking together, clubbing, whatever students do these days?'

'Not really.'

Talk about getting blood out of a stone, she thought. 'But aren't you in the same department?'

'He was an undergraduate. We didn't mix socially.'

She sighed. 'Did he bring his undergraduate friends back to the flat. Does he have mates we can talk to?'

'I don't know any of them.'

Hazel was becoming increasingly irritated. 'He must

have had a hobby, a club, something he did in the evenings?'

'I really didn't have much to do with him.'

'So what about your other flatmate?' She consulted her notes. 'Oliver Hayes. Was he a friend of Wilf's?'

'No, sorry.'

She slammed her notebook shut. 'Can you let Professor Pringle know that I'd like to meet him in Reception. I will need to see the final year chemists myself before I interview Oliver Hayes.'

The student called his supervisor while she left for the reception area.

Callum immediately rang his flatmate. 'Hi Hayes.'

'Is she on her way?' He sounded jumpy.

'No, she's gone to talk to the students in Wilf's year.'

'How did it go?'

'Don't know. She asked about his friends, what he did in the evenings, hobbies, that sort of thing.'

'What did you say?'

'Nothing. I said I didn't know.'

'Well, that's all we can say, isn't it mate?'

'Yeah. Let's hope she's happy once she's talked to his class. Is she meeting you in the department?'

'No way, I didn't want to be seen talking to the police here. I said I'd be in the cafeteria.'

'She's not in uniform.'

'What does she look like?'

'About forty, blonde, jeans and leather jacket. Quite cool for someone that old. But definitely not friendly, mate.'

Meanwhile Hazel was getting nowhere with the final year chemistry students either. She'd interrupted a practical session in a smelly laboratory where about twenty students in white coats and goggles were standing around benches full of complicated looking glassware. It wasn't an ideal setting to ask about their dead classmate. The atmosphere was hushed and no-one would speak up. There wasn't one member of the group who knew him well, he didn't socialise with anybody special and no-one admitted to having spent any significant time with him outside the university. As Professor Pringle was showing her to the cafeteria, she commented that Wilf Marriott appeared to have spent the life of a monk.

'Was he a particularly hard-working student?' she enquired, looking for an explanation.

'His end of term assessments were pretty average apparently.'

'Lacking in confidence, perhaps.'

'Maybe, although he had a girlfriend. She's upset naturally and Mills has been talking to her.'

Perhaps Dr Sanderson should be leading the investigation, Hazel thought. But she smiled at the professor as he held the door of the cafeteria open for her, thanking him for his help. A young man, alone at a table, stood up when they entered and was staring in their direction. He was wearing a very smart black coat.

'I guess that must be Oliver Hayes,' she said, leaving Pringle at the door.

The student remained standing but held out a hand when she reached him. 'DS Fuller?'

'Yes, and you are Oliver Hayes?'

'My friends call me Hayes.' He smiled warmly at her and offered to get her a coffee.

She declined and they took their seats either side of the

35

table. Hazel was surprised by the neatness of the student's appearance and quality of his clothes. He was typical public school, which would normally set her against him immediately, but there was something about him, his manners, politeness, the way he answered her questions that made her warm to him.

'I'm puzzled that Wilf seems to have led such a quiet life,' she confided in him, after receiving the same response regarding his friends or lack of them. 'Although I did hear that he had a girlfriend.'

Hayes looked confused. 'Did he? I never saw him with her. He didn't bring anyone to the flat, at least not when I was there.'

Hazel crossed out where she'd written "girlfriend?" in her notes. Trust Mills Sanderson to get it wrong.

'What about weekends? Did you see much of him then?'

'Ah, now there's the thing. You see I'm always away at weekends so I can't say. Sorry, I really would like to help.'

'What about your flatmate, Callum, does he go away at weekends too?'

Hayes took a long sip of coffee before answering. 'Yes, we both go off every weekend. Look, are you sure you don't want a coffee?'

Hazel had to admit she would and he went to fetch it. She watched him chatting casually to the girl on the hot drinks machine and fiddling with his phone while he waited. He was the kind of lad she'd always hoped her son Liam would become but there was no chance of him ever ending up with a university degree, that was certain. He took after his dad, despite the fact neither of them had seen his father since her son was small. When Hayes arrived with her coffee, she asked him what he was studying.

'Sociology.'

'Yes but what are you studying in sociology?' She was hoping he might be interested in social work, prisons maybe. He seemed to be the caring type.

'Mainly economics and politics,' he replied. 'In fact, if you don't mind… if you've finished with me, I'd like to get back to my studies.'

She thanked him for his help and watched him leave. It was time she was getting back to Northallerton to report on a wasted journey. Young Wilf was a loner with no friends who died of an overdose of drugs. In her eyes that was either a cry for help or a deliberate act of suicide.

Alison had asked if she could go over her assessment results and she was due to arrive at noon. The girl gave Mills a smile when she came in and thanked her for being so sympathetic last time they met. Mills noticed she had done her hair up in the usual complicated plait and was dressed very smartly once again. She sat down expectantly while Mills found her paperwork. She showed her the marks, which were neither good nor bad but average for the class. She pointed out where she could have improved her answers and handed her a copy of the model answers along with her test paper, saying she could keep them until the next lecture. The girl went to leave but Mills asked her to sit down again.

'I wondered whether you had heard, you know, about the funeral?' Mills asked.

The girl shook her head. 'No, I don't think I will.'

Mills made a note on her memo pad to find out for her.

'I heard the police were here today, talking to Wilf's class,' Alison said. 'Do you think they know what happened to Wilf?'

'I expect they're making routine enquiries for the coroner. They will have done a post-mortem already I expect. It's normal procedure in the circumstances.' Mills could see that Alison was close to tears. 'I'm so sorry. I've upset you.'

'No, it's all right, I want to know what's happening. No-one tells me anything and I want to understand why Wilf died. I didn't know him very well.' She took a tissue and blew her nose.

'I think you said you would be going home for a few days?' Mills hoped to lighten the conversation.

The girl nodded. 'I went after I saw you on Monday but I decided to come back here to get on with some work.'

'I'm sure it was nice to have a couple of days with your family.'

'Mum understood when I said I wanted to go to Wilf's funeral, although she wanted to go as well. In the end my Dad got involved. I couldn't stay there with him going on.' She waited until she had control of her tears again then added, 'He said Wilf had overdosed on drugs.'

'Why did he think that?' Mills asked.

'He'd read it in the local paper.'

Mills told her that nothing had been established yet but asked her whether she thought he did take drugs. She expected a vehement denial but Alison looked at her calmly for a few seconds as if sizing her up.

'I don't know, he might have smoked a bit of weed, everyone does that don't they?'

'What about other things like ecstasy?' Mills hoped her question didn't seem as pointed as it really was.

She shook her head. 'I wouldn't know. It's not the sort

of thing you use in the week, is it? Not when you're studying. I mean he was away at weekends, wasn't he?'

'Oh, did he go home?'

'No, he was working, wasn't he?'

Mills was puzzled. 'Do you mean studying or did he have a job somewhere?'

Alison looked embarrassed. 'I don't know. I mean I assumed he meant studying but I suppose he may have had a job, I didn't think. All I know is I didn't see him from Friday to Monday.'

Mills wondered if he had a girlfriend back at home but wasn't going to suggest that to her.

Hazel had been moaning about her visit to the university ever since she'd burst through the door and dropped her bag on her chair with a thump. Students were a load of time-wasting good-for-nothings, providing no information about Wilf Marriott that she couldn't have told them.

'He had no friends, never went out, didn't socialise and yet he ends up frozen to death on a park bench full of ecstasy!'

She pulled a notebook out of her bag and flung it on her desk.

Ruby contradicted her. 'He didn't freeze to death, according to the post-mortem, and he wasn't "full" of ecstasy, just a normal amount. That's why the samples are being sent to Professor Pringle.'

Hazel turned to face the researcher. 'Oh yes, and he's a smarmy character. Did you know he and that Mills Sanderson are an item?'

Ruby went back to her work. 'I think Nina may have mentioned it,' she murmured.

'Well she was there in his office when I arrived. She gets everywhere.'

Ruby kept her head down when Hazel was in a strop. She wasn't going to tell her that Mills had already rung Nina to say that she'd been talking to Wilf's girlfriend. However, it wasn't long before her colleague arrived back from lunch and told Hazel herself.

'But his flatmates said he didn't have a girlfriend,' Hazel objected.

'Perhaps he was keeping her secret,' Nina suggested.

'What's her name?'

'Alison Steel.'

'Address, phone number?' Hazel demanded.

'Actually, I thought I might go over myself.' Nina was worried that Hazel's abrasive style might not work well if the girl had just lost her boyfriend so tragically. She felt her own experience in Family Liaison would help in the circumstances and she also knew that her colleague would guess what she was thinking.

Hazel didn't answer but typed furiously for half an hour, referring to her notebook. Finally she stretched and announced she was going for a smoke.

'I've sent you my notes – for what they're worth.'

Nina and Ruby read her report in silence. Hazel had been right: no-one seemed to know Wilf Marriott well. He would socialise with his classmates in the bar if there was an event on but he had no close friends, not even the people he shared a flat with.

'You know it doesn't fit,' began Ruby. 'He wasn't a party animal. He doesn't seem like a lad who would take ecstasy at all. In fact he sounds like a bit of an outsider. I think he probably meant to kill himself by taking the drugs and lying out there in the cold. It's really sad.'

'You're right. Maybe he was finding the course too challenging.'

Ruby was looking up student death rates and suicides, quoting depressingly high statistics until Nina stopped her.

'I'm going to ring Mills,' she said suddenly, breaking the mood. 'I'm definitely going to have to interview this girlfriend.'

Mills didn't take much persuading to ask Alison Steel for an informal chat with Nina on campus.

'You can use our office, provided Nige keeps out of the way,' said Mills.

'Don't worry, I'll see he makes himself scarce.'

Mills called her back within the hour to say that Alison would be there the following morning. When Nina told Hazel what she'd arranged, her colleague shrugged.

'That's fine, I don't relish another trip to that place to interview a weepy girly. She's all yours.'

Mills eventually found Simon in his lab with the student called Callum. They were both busy washing down the benches, dressed in white coats and plastic gloves.

'Hi,' called Simon. 'We won't be long, I just wanted to finish off the cleaning before the samples arrive.'

'When are they due?'

'Tomorrow morning. We're going to start straight away, aren't we, Callum?'

The student nodded, continuing to spray the metal surfaces before wiping them down with paper towel.

Mills waited in the corridor until they'd finished.

'All done,' shouted Simon, as he removed his gloves and coat before washing his hands at the tiny sink by the door.

Callum followed suit before Simon turned off the lights and locked the door.

'I'll see you in the morning,' he called as his student wandered off down the corridor without a word.

'Is he all right?' Mills asked.

'I think so, just a bit absorbed, it's natural with his flatmate going.'

'Does he know that the samples we're getting are from Wilf Marriott?'

Simon looked surprised. 'No, of course not, why would he?'

Mills shrugged. 'Come on then let's get back,' she said. 'I'm starving.'

As they were leaving, she noticed Callum outside the chemistry building in conversation with a tall lad, dressed in an expensive looking black winter coat. They seemed to be having a heated discussion but when Callum saw her watching, he walked away in the opposite direction.

Chapter 5

'I think you should meet Nina when she arrives,' Mills told Simon on the way to work.

She wanted to introduce him to her friend in the university setting, where they would both be in their professional roles and, hopefully, feel more comfortable. More to the point, the meeting would be kept brief.

'Do you think so?' Simon was concentrating on the traffic ahead.

'Yes. She's bound to want to meet the famous professor who's analysing her valuable samples, won't she?' she teased.

'Are you sure?'

'Seriously, it's important that she sees that you're reliable and trustworthy.'

'In her role as a police officer or as your best friend?'

Mills smiled to herself but said nothing.

There was a large crowd gathered round the campus. The industrial action concerning academic pay that had begun the previous day was continuing, with many students now joining the pickets. There was jeering and waving of placards as they drove through the gates.

Nina was due to arrive with Nige just after nine, so Simon waited in the office with Mills. He appeared a bit distracted and she jokingly asked if he was nervous.

'I am, a bit,' he admitted. 'This is the start of our forensic venture and we've got to get it right. D'you think she'll want to see the lab?'

'I'm quite sure she won't. She's here to meet Alison, that's all.' She gave him a hug then jumped away quickly as the door burst open and Nige walked in, closely followed by Nina.

'I've only come in to collect this,' he muttered, without making eye contact, as he grabbed a waterproof jacket.

Nina came forward and held out her hand. 'Simon, I presume?'

Mills couldn't help giggling as he admitted he was. They stood for a few seconds while Nige announced loudly that he was going to join the picket line, then left the office.

Simon began to follow. 'I must be off too.' He turned to Mills, 'See you later.'

'Well, he's very nice,' Nina said, after closing the door behind him.

'Nice?'

'You know what I mean. Good-looking, smart, polite.'

'I'm glad you approve, Nina.'

'I wasn't given long to get an impression, was I? And Nige hasn't been very forthcoming about him when I've asked.'

'I don't think he's keen on Simon.'

'You know Nige has idolised Phil ever since he saved his life that time he was injured in the snow. He was delighted when the two of you got back together again.'

'We weren't really together; you know that Nina.'

'Well, you're with Simon now and he seems really nice.'

'I think the real reason is the strike. Nige is annoyed that Simon came in today, isn't he?'

Nina nodded. 'He's very wound up about the strike. Of course he was determined to take action but the Head of Department has been putting pressure on him to carry on working.'

'Well Simon's not teaching or doing any uni work; he's busy with your forensic analysis.'

The discussion was cut short when Alison arrived a few minutes early. Mills introduced her to Nina and left, saying she would be sorting things out in the lab if they needed her.

Nina asked the girl to sit down and pulled Nige's chair from behind his desk, to join her. She explained that she simply wanted a brief chat, since she probably knew Wilf better than most.

Alison immediately disagreed. 'I hadn't known him long. And he didn't talk much about himself.'

'Would you say he was rather a private individual then?' She nodded. 'You see, it's quite difficult to build up a picture of how he fitted in to university life. For example, do you think he was happy?'

Alison shrugged. 'He seemed cheerful enough.'

'Not struggling with his studies?'

'I don't think so. He didn't say anything.'

Nina took a deep breath. 'Sorry, but I have to ask. Do you think he might have taken his own life?'

'No!' she responded, then paused as if to reconsider. 'No, he was fine. We went to a gig last week and he was really happy. We both were. It was our first proper date. He said it was an early Valentine's present.'

'And nothing happened afterwards that may have changed his mood. No arguments?'

'We didn't argue but I didn't see him again.' She sighed. 'He said we'd go out Monday night but…'

'It must have been a shock when you heard,' Nina prompted.

She nodded without looking up.

'I hope you'll be honest with me if you can because it will help us establish exactly what caused Wilf's death.' The girl raised her head and Nina looked directly at her. 'Yes? Good. Did he take any drugs when you were with him or did he ever talk to you about taking them? Was it something he did on a regular basis?'

'I've not even seen him share a joint at a party.'

'And nothing stronger? Ecstasy, for example?'

'No.'

'What about Wilf's friends? Have you met any of them, did he have many?'

'Only his classmates and flatmates, although I don't really know them to talk to.'

Nina was running out of questions. She was frustrated by her lack of progress, particularly now her picture of a lonely, suicidal lad was beginning to fall apart. On the contrary, he seemed to have been happy with his lot until the last weekend before he died. Maybe that's where the key lay. She thanked Alison for her help and followed her to the laboratory where Mills was sorting though some fossilised bones.

'So this is what you get up to, Dr Sanderson!' Nina exclaimed when Alison had left.

'How did it go? Was Alison able to help you?' Mills asked, removing her white coat.

'You know what I'm going to say.'

'Yes, I know – don't ask me, because I won't tell you.'

'Sorry.'

'Well, the good news is that your samples arrived by courier this morning, so Simon is starting work on them right away.'

'How long will it all take?'

'Several days, he says. But once you have the results, you'll know how Wilf Marriott died.'

'Yes, Mills, but not necessarily why. I need to find out whether he deliberately took his own life and that might prove difficult.' She looked at her watch. 'Anyway, I must fly, but I do need to pin you down to a date when you and Simon can come over for lunch.' She looked expectantly at her friend.

'But what about Nige?' asked Mills. 'It might be awkward with him being a bit, you know, funny about Simon.'

Nina frowned. 'I'll speak to him about it. He'll behave.'

She suggested Sunday lunch but Mills refused politely. It would be just too long in Nige's company if he was being difficult. An evening meal was more complicated with the kids going to bed at different times and, anyway, Mills wanted Simon to meet the children. In the end she agreed they would go for tea early on Saturday afternoon. Nina would bake a cake.

Simon planned to spend the rest of the day working on the forensic samples but Mills had arranged to meet the Chief Technician to discuss services required for the new equipment. Keen to keep up the momentum, now they'd had the go-ahead, she went without him. The north-easterly wind billowed her coat in a ridiculous manner as she struggled across campus. It was a relief to get inside the warmth of the chemistry building.

The new laboratory was on the ground floor, so equipment could be moved in easily, and gas cylinders could be installed outside the building. They had been

47

allocated three enormous rooms with windows along one side. But the plans showed dividing walls to separate activities such as sample preparation from the analytical equipment. Simon was adamant he wanted toxicology isolated from everything else and Mills had ensured the preparation side was designed to avoid any possible cross contamination of samples. Her experience at Yardley Forensics had taught her much of what was necessary and they also had Brenda to consult when required.

Ted, the Chief Technician was almost as excited by the project as she was, expressing the view that they were very lucky the department had given them so much space. It had been promised to someone else, he divulged, but their proposal didn't have the strong commercial flavour that had influenced the Dean. Mills walked round with him, clarifying the plans and explaining why the instrumentation had to be in a particular configuration. By the time Simon appeared at the end of the day, they were almost finished. When he saw the time, Ted apologised, saying he had to get off, he always tried to get away early on a Friday.

'Seems everyone has the same idea,' complained Simon when he'd gone. 'Callum disappeared at two o'clock to catch a train to Skipton, apparently he goes every weekend. I had to carry on by myself. Anyway I've got the first round of analyses done.'

'Really?' Mills pulled on her coat and followed him along the corridor. 'I thought you had to wait for those little plastic vials to arrive.'

'No, Callum miraculously produced a handful before he disappeared.'

'I told you we needed a paid assistant. You won't be able to use students to help you when we have the service running properly.'

Simon was striding ahead and didn't answer. Mills was fighting to keep up with him in the fierce wind but once they were in the car she tried again.

'I can talk to Donna if you like. I'm sure she'd be interested.'

'It's too soon, Mills. We can't pay her when we've no income.'

Callum and Hayes travelled from Darlington station to Leeds, where they had to change. There was just enough time to grab a drink before catching the train to Skipton, which stopped at every station on the way.

'I hate this part of the journey,' Hayes complained, pulling out his phone and unravelling his earpiece. 'Did you bring those plastic tubes with you?'

'Yes, they're in my bag. I had to leave some behind though. Prof was looking for them today. I was helping him in the lab. I don't think he was very happy when I said I had to leave.'

'I'm glad to get away from the place,' Hayes said, looking round the carriage at the other passengers. 'After the interview we had with our visitor.'

'You mean…'

'The woman who came to see us.'

Understanding that he meant the DS, Callum nodded. 'But it's not like we know anything is it? I thought he went straight to bed when we got back. Did you hear him go out?'

'No but I didn't get in until early morning.'

'I only went to the bar for a pint and was back before midnight. I just assumed he was asleep. So we can't help, can we?'

Hayes agreed. 'As we told her, we've only known him a few months. We don't socialise with him, do we? Exactly. What else could we say?'

Callum hesitated. Most of the passengers were plugged into their phones or laptops. He lowered his voice. 'I just think, in retrospect, we should have told her that he came with us last weekend.'

'It isn't relevant is it? I suggest you have a rest; we've got a lot of tubes to fill when we get there.' Hayes plugged the earpieces in and shut his eyes until they reached Skipton.

It was the same routine every week. First, they went from the station to the nearby Morrisons to buy beer and snacks for the weekend. Sometimes they picked up a few extras, like pork pies, to supplement the food that was provided for them. Once they were stocked up, they made for the fish and chip shop. They chose the one by the canal because they could get bottles of beer with their meal and it was close to the station, where they would get the taxi. As usual, the restaurant was busy, which meant they had to share a table with an elderly couple. There was a wait for their meal and the old woman, who'd finished eating, asked them if they were on holiday.

'Not exactly,' Callum answered.

'I saw your rucksacks,' she said. 'I assumed you were walkers.'

'Yes,' said Hayes. 'That's correct. We're here for the weekend, doing a walk.'

The old man had put his fork down. 'Where are you going, lads?'

Hayes paused. 'We're not exactly sure yet. We're meeting some people, tomorrow…'

He was interrupted by the waitress bearing their fish and chips. The conversation changed to how good the food was and, to their relief, the couple departed, leaving them to enjoy their meals in peace.

Once they were back at the station, they found their usual taxi driver. The journey was a mystery ride as far as Callum was concerned, because he'd never visited the area until he started working with Hayes. The furthest north he'd been before coming to uni was Birmingham for Crufts when his mother's dog had qualified. He'd been abroad for his holidays and the idea of spending the weekend in the Craven Dales was not something that normally would have appealed to him. He peered out into the dark countryside as they were bumped and jostled along a rough track and eventually stopped.

'Is this it?' Hayes asked as he signed the piece of paper offered by the driver.

'Aye.'

They watched the tail lights of the taxi disappearing down the track, leaving them to negotiate the lane in front of an isolated building in the dark.

'This is even more remote than last week,' complained Hayes, using the torch on his phone to light the path to the front door.

He struggled with the doormat until he eventually retrieved a key. Callum followed him over the doorstep and heard a click as his friend found the light switch. They were inside what he assumed was the sitting room. He automatically started removing his boots and shouted to Hayes to do the same. Ignoring Callum's protestations, he carried his bag of groceries through the door opposite.

'The kitchen's in here!' he called and Callum padded

after him.

'You're leaving mud everywhere, Hayes,' he complained.

'Not to worry, we'll be giving the place a thorough clean before we go, won't we?'

Callum watched him unpack the snacks and retrieve two cans from his rucksack. 'There you go, mate.' He threw one over to him.

'We're not supposed to have alcohol on the premises, it's the rules.' Callum reminded him.

'Who's to know, eh?' he said removing the ring-pull.

'They'll see the cans in the rubbish.'

'Whatever.'

Callum grabbed his belongings and went up the stairs at the end of the kitchen to find the bedrooms. They were cramped but at least he wouldn't have to share this time. He took the smallest room, threw his rucksack on the bed and pulled out the bag of plastic vials to take downstairs.

Hayes was in the sitting room fiddling with the television.

'Where have they put all the equipment?' Callum asked.

Hayes pointed to a pair of glass doors. 'They've left it all in the conservatory thing through there.'

Callum went through to put the bag of vials on top of the boxes. 'We'd better get set up,' he shouted to Hayes. 'They'll be here soon.'

Hayes was draining his can of beer. 'It's your turn.'

'No, I did it last week.'

'Yes, but you had Wilf to help you.'

There was no point in arguing so Callum began pulling the parcel tape off the boxes and unpacking the equipment.

Chapter 6

Sleet had turned to snow overnight in Osmotherley, leaving a thin coating of white on the fields behind the cottage. Mills was taking Harris out so Simon, who wanted a lie-in, offered to have the porridge ready for her when they returned. She took the dog down the lane for about half a mile and into a field that was almost totally enclosed. If she stood guard at the entrance she could let him free, knowing he couldn't escape. She smiled as he cavorted around in the snow, running back to her occasionally with his nose covered in white. On a normal Saturday morning, she would be walking him on the tops in Swaledale but Simon had persuaded her to stay put, to avoid a long drive back to Nina's for tea that afternoon. She'd agreed but only if they took Harris with them and continued straight to Mossy Bank afterwards.

Eventually she enticed Harris back with a treat, keeping him still long enough for her to put his lead on. He was keen to get back to the cottage for his breakfast and she had to tread carefully to avoid being pulled over on the slippery track. She gave him a quick rub down in the lobby before letting him loose in the main part of the cottage. The sound of him attacking his food bowl began before she had even removed her wellingtons. Simon was busy laying the table with a variety of toppings for the porridge.

'Sit down,' he instructed as he began filling the bowls. 'I thought we could go to your friend's the pretty way; there must be things you haven't seen round here yet.'

'Don't forget we'll have Harris with us and it's bitterly cold out there.'

He paused while he sprinkled seeds into his bowl. 'So, we'll take him for a long walk. We can wrap up warm. Why don't we go to Cod Beck Reservoir?'

'Where's that?'

'Just down the road from the village. If we walk right round it, Harris can have a good run about off the lead.'

Mills considered the options and agreed that the dog would enjoy another outing in the snow. So they cleared up after breakfast and Mills packed the few things she needed for the weekend. They were becoming practised in dividing their time between Osmotherly and Mossy Bank. The lurcher grew excitable when he saw the bags come downstairs and needed no encouragement to bounce into the back of the car. It was a tight squeeze for him in the Mini but much roomier than Simon's MG.

They left the car in the village and Simon pointed to a snow-covered lane that would take them to the reservoir. Harris was pulling so hard Mills had to give the lead to Simon, hanging onto his arm to prevent herself from slipping over. Despite the cold, the clouds were moving to reveal patches of blue sky and it was changing into a pleasant day. To begin with they were walking past cottages but soon the lane was bordered with trees and fields until they finally reached the reservoir. Mills agreed it was an ideal place to let Harris off. It took less than an hour to complete the circuit but there was a cold wind and Mills was glad to set off back into Osmotherley for a hot drink at the local tearoom.

Simon insisted on having a bacon roll, declaring it was pretty much lunch time. Mills ordered hot soup, warming her hands on the bowl when it arrived.

'Do you think we should take a bottle of something this afternoon?' Simon asked.

'Not for teatime,' Mills said, 'but perhaps some flowers? We can do our shopping at the same time.'

In the end there was only just sufficient time to stop off at the supermarket outside Darlington to pick up essentials, and there was a long queue, resulting in them arriving half an hour late. Mills carried a bunch of early tulips, and books for the children, while Simon extracted the lurcher from the car.

'D'you mind if we bring Harris in?' Mills asked, thrusting the flowers into Nina's hand and giving her a hug.

Simon was hesitating on the doorstep.

'Of course not,' said Nina. 'Come in, Simon.' She went towards him but Harris leapt up at her as they awkwardly tried to embrace. 'Nige is just upstairs. He'll be down in a minute.'

Mills gave the children their books, receiving a shy hug from Rosie. Then she introduced Simon to each of them in turn.

'This is Rosie, she's a great artist, aren't you? Rosie is ten,' she explained, adding that Simon had a son of a similar age. 'And these two scamps are Tomos and Owen. You can tell they have a Welsh heritage.'

'From Nige, is it?' Simon asked.

'How did you guess?' she replied sarcastically.

'And how old are you?' he asked them.

'Eight!' they shouted in unison.

Mills explained that it had been their birthday last month.

'Twins? That's nice,' he commented.

'Do you play Fortnite?' Tomos asked Simon.

'Of course I do,' he replied with a grin, looking at Mills.

'Not now,' Nina called from the kitchen. 'Maybe after tea, if there's time.'

'Can I play with Harris?' asked Rosie.

Simon had been hanging onto his collar but Mills nodded and, once freed, the dog started investigating the tiny room. As soon as Rosie made a fuss of him, he settled down beside the sofa, forcing Nina to edge past carefully with a tray. Mills helped by unloading the sandwiches, crisps and savoury pies while Nina disappeared to return with cakes and a fruit tart. Owen and Tomos gathered round to admire the contents of the table. Nina called Nige to come down for tea and instructed Rosie to wash her hands thoroughly.

There were just four dining chairs so the children settled on the floor with their loaded plates, declaring it was like having an indoor picnic.

'Well just make sure Harris doesn't eat yours,' Mills warned.

Although it was hardly necessary to introduce Simon to Nige when he came downstairs, Mills felt it was important that they were on first name terms. Nige dismissed her attempt, saying that of course they knew each other. Simon admitted that he and Nige had been together on the panel that decided the appointment of Mills to the joint lectureship between Archaeology and Forensics. She wondered whether that could have caused Nige's negative attitude to Simon.

'But aren't you in the Chemistry Department?' Nina asked, offering him a slice of quiche.

'Yes, my laboratory is in Chemistry but I'm really part of

Forensics. It's all the same Faculty.'

They were distracted by the children giggling loudly.

'Are you giving your food to the dog?' Nige asked sharply.

The boys looked at each other and then at the floor. Mills explained to them that although Harris liked sandwiches, they probably wouldn't do him much good. The atmosphere went quiet for a while as they ate, despite Nina's attempts to keep the conversation going.

'Oh my goodness,' she said, suddenly. 'I forgot the tea. Do you drink tea, Simon?' She rushed out without waiting for an answer, returning with four mugs. 'I've put milk in already, is that all right?'

Simon thanked her, saying it was perfect. The children came back to the table when their mother was cutting the chocolate cake, so Mills warned them that Harris definitely mustn't have any of it. Nige ate his cake quickly, drained the mug of tea and stood up.

'Wales are playing France in the Six Nations,' he announced then disappeared upstairs.

Mills could tell Nina was annoyed. 'Are you a rugby fan, Simon?' she asked.

He admitted he was but supported England. 'They're playing tomorrow.'

Mills helped clear the table, offering to help wash up. Nina said the dishes could wait but she'd make another pot of tea. Rosie was sitting next to Simon on the sofa, showing him her drawings so Mills joined them. The boys were on the floor beside Harris, who lay patiently as they tickled him behind his ears.

Nina brought in the tea, settling herself in the chair opposite. 'So, how's the new lab progressing?' she asked.

Mills described the current layout and how it was going to be refurbished. Her friend was impressed with the scale of it, asking when it would be ready.

'It will take months,' said Simon. 'It will probably be ready in the summer.'

'But we've started business already, thanks to you, Nina,' added Mills diplomatically.

'And how is that going?'

'He's started work on the samples, haven't you, Simon?'

He was half-listening but Rosie was wanting his attention, so Mills continued, 'He's got a postgrad helping him, in fact you may have met him. His name is Callum, he shared a flat with Wilf Marriott.'

'Did he?'

She could tell from her expression that Nina was digesting this information. Mills knew it wasn't appropriate for someone connected to the investigation to be involved in the analyses.

'I'm going to contact Donna to see if she's interested in an analyst's job,' she confided, checking that Simon wasn't listening. 'She would be brilliant.'

There was a shout from upstairs and the boys raced off, leaving the lurcher to stretch out undisturbed.

'Someone's scored,' Simon commented, as Rosie climbed off the sofa to sit beside Harris.

'Has Callum been given any details of what the samples are?' Nina asked, looking at Simon.

He seemed confused for a moment, pausing to think before shaking his head slowly. 'No, definitely not. Of course he knows they're blood and urine samples, and that we're analysing them for a range of non-prescription drugs, but that's all.'

'I suppose he could put two and two together?' Mills suggested.

'I don't see why.' He looked concerned.

'It's not a problem at this stage,' said Nina lightly. 'And if it becomes a criminal investigation, we'll need some corroborative measurements done in Wakefield anyway. We just want an indication from you in a timely manner.'

'Unfortunately Callum goes away at the weekends so he wasn't around for long yesterday, but we did manage to get the straightforward work done. I found a small amount of cocaine in the blood.'

'And in the urine sample?'

'No.'

'That's odd,' Mills commented.

'No, not at all,' he explained. 'If the drug has only recently been ingested, there may not have been time for it to appear in the urine.'

Nina sat up straight. 'Are you saying that he'd taken cocaine as well as ecstasy soon before he died?'

'That's what it looks like, although if that was the case, the amount of cocaine he took was very very small, which suggests it was probably in the ecstasy.'

There was more shouting above them, followed by the pounding of feet down the stairs. Owen reported that they'd scored a try, before they ran noisily back up again. Nina apologised but Mills just laughed, suggesting it was probably time they were going anyway. Harris had been very patient with the children but she wasn't sure how much more handling he could stand. Simon thanked her profusely for inviting him and told her what delightful kids she had. Nina asked about his own son.

'He's nearly the same age as Rosie actually. He lives with

59

his mother in the States so he has a strong American accent. He'll be here in the summer so you'll be able meet him.' He looked at Mills. 'Although I hope you'll come over sooner than that. We'd love to see you, and Nige and the kids of course.'

They were all standing by now, including Harris. Nina called up to Nige that they were leaving but he simply shouted his goodbye. Rosie gave Mills and Simon a hug. The boys waved from the top of the stairs. Nina looked embarrassed, apologising for her husband's behaviour before opening the front door. As they left, she asked Simon if he could get his preliminary results to her as soon as possible.

'Well, that went well,' muttered Mills once they were in the car.

'It was fine. The guy is obviously a devoted rugby fan that's all.'

She decided to ask him straight out. 'Did you have a disagreement when you were on the panel discussing my appointment?' She was driving so she couldn't see his expression. 'Well?'

'It was slightly difficult. He was incredibly supportive of the plan to fund you jointly but there were colleagues in my department who were wholly against the idea. I can't remember exactly who now but there was strong lobbying before the meeting. I have to admit that I may not have come over as fully behind the scheme.'

She didn't know what to say.

'I didn't know you then, Mills. I didn't appreciate that you were a dynamic, entrepreneurial, high-flying…'

'Stop being silly, it's not funny. Nina is my best friend and I've known Nige for just as long. It's important to me that you get on with him.'

'It's hardly my fault.'

'I know it isn't. Sorry. We need a way to sort it out though.'

They drove in silence while Mills went through the afternoon in her mind. 'I'm glad using that student to do the work won't affect Nina's investigation,' she commented. 'But it will be better to take on a professional analyst like Donna.' There was no answer. 'Especially if Callum disappears on a Friday. Did you say he goes every weekend?'

'Yes.'

'What does he do? Caving? Climbing?'

'I don't know, Mills.'

She stopped talking but carried on thinking about Callum, a student who shared accommodation with Wilf Marriott. Alison had said that Wilf went away every weekend too, so perhaps they went to Skipton together. If only she knew what they did there. Alison said she hadn't seen Wilf take ecstasy, but she wasn't there at weekends. Perhaps Skipton was where they bought drugs and used them down there.

'Have you ever been to Skipton?' she asked Simon.

'No, I don't think so. It's quite a way from Osmotherley.'

'We could go tomorrow. It's a nice drive through the dales.'

'Seriously?'

'Why not? You said yourself that you don't know the Yorkshire Dales well enough.'

'That's because I live on the edge of the North York Moors.'

'Well I've seen Cod Beck Reservoir now, so I'll show you Skipton. It's got a castle and a canal, so there's loads to do.'

'What about Harris?'

'I think he'd rather stay at home after all the excitement today.'

Soon they were crossing the border into North Yorkshire and travelling down into Arkengarthdale. She turned onto the road to Surrender Bridge, over the watersplash and up onto the tops. Mills could feel herself relaxing as she drove carefully down the narrow lanes into Low Row, joining the road through the dale to Ivelet and up to Mossy Bank. It was great to be home.

Simon had just extracted the lurcher from the back of the car when Muriel opened her front door, a silhouette against her hall light.

'Is that you, Harris?' she called, rushing out to greet him.

Simon disappeared into Laurel Cottage while Mills followed her neighbour and the dog next door.

'I've made you some shortbread,' she explained, looking through an assortment of tins. 'Give me a minute.'

'How's work?' Mills asked.

Muriel had started a new job after Christmas, deep cleaning holiday cottages for a company that worked right across the Dales.

'It's a lot of travelling, particularly in the snow. I was over in Sedbergh yesterday, and I've even been down as far as Ingleton. But the money's very good. I said I'd keep it up until the summer. You should see some of the properties – beautiful! I went to an old mill last week that was perfect. Mind you, the state it was left in! Disgusting it was.'

'I suppose not everyone is as house-proud as you, Muriel.'

'Oh some are though. I had one place up from Settle where it was immaculate before we started.'

'I bet that's unusual.'

'Yes, but not unheard of, apparently.' She put on her "confiding" voice. 'The lady I was working with that day cleans a number of holiday-lets in the area on a weekly basis, and she said that she'd had two recently that had been gone over thoroughly with bleach by the previous occupiers. How about that!'

Mills suggested it was people concerned about coronavirus. Although the country hadn't been seriously affected, people were beginning to worry that it would soon be spreading to the UK.

'Anyway, how's young Harris?' she asked.

She gave him a few tiny biscuits from the tin she kept specially for him. Mills was grateful that her neighbour was so devoted to her dog. Muriel had walked him every day while she was at work but now Mills was living in Osmotherley during the week, Muriel tended to pounce on Harris at the weekends and was soon offering to look after him if they wanted to go out. Mills told her that they were thinking of going to Skipton.

'That would be lovely!' she exclaimed. 'Won't that be nice Harris, darling?' she added giving him a cuddle.

Chapter 7

It rained all the way to Skipton, even turning to sleet on occasions. Simon had suggested they postpone the trip when he saw the forecast, but Mills argued that Muriel was expecting to look after Harris and the weather would probably improve. Simon was fiddling with the car radio even though reception was bound to be poor, as she had already told him twice. Each time he found a clear signal and leaned back in his seat, it would develop a crackling noise that quickly turned into an unbearable hiss. Finally she persuaded him to turn the damn thing off.

She drove in silence while Simon stared out of the side window. The windscreen wipers had developed an irritating squeak as well as failing to clear the glass on the passenger side. She had decided to go on the prettiest route down past Oughtershaw to Buckden, through Kettlewell and past Grassington. She'd decided to show Simon the ruins of Bolton Abbey but, if it carried on bucketing down with rain, they would have to give it a miss, which meant they'd be too early for the pub lunch she'd planned on the way down. She was beginning to wish she'd listened to Simon and they'd stayed at home in front of the fire. She half-heartedly pointed out landmarks on the way but eventually gave up, driving for what seemed like hours until finally they reached the outskirts of Skipton.

'Quiet for a Sunday,' Simon commented pointedly, as they turned into the car park. 'Must be the weather.'

Mills didn't answer. It had been a daft idea to drive all

the way here just because Wilf Marriott might, just might, have come here with his flatmate to buy drugs. It was Sunday lunchtime and there were a few people hurrying towards the shops. She watched Simon running to get a parking ticket and race back, pointing excitedly to a coffee shop just up the road. A coffee and something to eat would help lighten the atmosphere, she thought, as they sprinted the short distance to get out of the rain.

'So what is the plan?' asked Simon with a sigh, once they were settled in chairs near the window with large lattes, and paninis on order.

Mills had to think. 'There's the castle at the top of the town. The canal is in the other direction, although the boats may not be running at this time of year.'

'It would be a pretty miserable trip,' he said, pointing to the downpour outside.

Mills had to agree. 'In that case we'll visit the castle.'

'If that's what you want to do.'

She felt it was necessary to apologise. 'Look, I'm sorry, you were right, it was a stupid idea to come here in the rain.'

He just smiled with a shrug, so she went on to justify herself despite her misgivings. 'Don't you think it's a coincidence that your student comes to Skipton every Friday, when his flatmate also went away at weekends?'

'Who are you talking about?'

'Wilf Marriott. He was Callum's flatmate.'

'Yes, I suppose he was. But what's that got to do with anything?'

'I wondered if they went together and, if they did, why Skipton?'

'Why not?'

There was a pause as their food arrived.

'You're not seeing it are you?' She watched him calmly biting into his panini while staring at her. She looked round and lowered her voice. 'Wilf was taking drugs, wasn't he? So where was he getting them from? Obviously not in the university, so they came down here. There's been publicity about heroin dealers on estates round here for years. It's well known, so they probably thought it would be easy to get ecstasy and cocaine.'

Simon put his cup down carefully on its saucer and took her hand. He frowned. 'So is this why we're here? I think they could have found what they wanted in Darlington, don't you?' He waited. When she didn't respond he smiled. 'Well, it's quite possible what you say is true, Mills, but what exactly are you planning to do about it?'

She blushed. 'I know. It sounds silly when you put it like that. I thought maybe something would occur to me once I was here.'

'Well, bar searching out crack dens, I suggest we find the castle and enjoy the rest of the day.' Then he added with a laugh, 'To think I could've been watching the rugby!'

The rain had eased off a little when they ventured outside, so they walked up to the castle and spent a couple of hours looking round. Mills was surprised to find that Simon had a much better knowledge of English history than her, which made their visit a lot more interesting. He also knew a great deal about castles in the North-East, reminding her that he had a young son to entertain on his visits in the summer.

By the time they emerged from the castle tearoom the rain had stopped and they wandered to the bottom of the town just to look at the canal. Mills was right, it was too early in the season to take a boat ride anyway. They agreed that in the summer it would be nice to take a trip down to Gargrave and back. Mills had never had a canal holiday but in Simon's view it was fun.

'I went with Mum and Dad when I was a kid. I was really pleased because they let me open and close all the locks.'

They stopped at Cracoe for a meal on the way home. Mills, feeling that Simon had forgiven her for dragging him down on a wild goose chase, avoided any discussion of the reason for the visit and the conversation turned to the new lab.

'By the way,' she said casually when they'd finished eating, 'I rang Donna on Friday, to have a chat. She's coming to see me tomorrow.'

'Why?'

'I said I'd show her the new lab space. She may have some suggestions. She's been down in Wakefield for a while now, so she'll have seen how the police forensic facility is laid out.'

'If you remember, I go down to the Wakefield lab on a regular basis, Mills. I have a student working down there.'

'Yes, I know, but that's toxicology. Donna works in a different area of chemistry.'

'And is that the only reason she's coming to see you?'

'Of course.'

Mills suggested they drive back on the most direct route; it was dark and she wanted to get home for Harris. They passed the occasional set of headlights travelling in the opposite direction but the roads were quiet. Sensible people were at home in front of the fire after watching England play rugby on the telly.

*

Callum was looking out for the headlights of the taxi. 'What time did you tell him?' he asked Hayes.

'Around six. He said it might be a few minutes after.'

He went upstairs to collect the rucksack he'd packed ages ago, hoping they'd get away a bit earlier. It would be nine o'clock before they reached Darlington at this rate.

'Do we know where we are next weekend?' he asked Hayes when he went downstairs.

'No. We'll know when we get there.' He disappeared upstairs to get his things together.

The taxi arrived three minutes after six. Callum left the porch light on so they could see their way out of the cottage and for Hayes to put the key back under the mat.

'Good weekend, lads?' the driver asked once they were moving.

'Yeah, good thanks, mate,' Hayes replied, sinking back into his seat.

'We'll get the twelve minutes past seven easy,' Callum said.

'No problem,' replied the driver. 'We're only twenty minutes away.'

Hayes signed the chit when they arrived at the railway station. They struggled inside with their bags and bought coffees while they waited, agreeing that it was the first decent drink since Friday, although that wasn't saying much.

'I'm knackered,' announced Hayes once they were on the train. 'Wake me up at Leeds,' he said, folding his arms and resting his feet on the seat opposite.

It had been a busy weekend for them both, as usual. It would be better if they had a permanent base to leave their stuff at, but whoever made the bookings selected a different cottage each time. He wanted to ask Hayes about that but he was asleep with his mouth slightly open. He was an odd guy. He realised he didn't really know him despite seeing him every day and all weekend. He knew he'd been to Charterhouse, which was partly why they got on all right; they'd both been to private schools. But that was all they had in common because Hayes was studying sociology which was arts and his building was the other end of the campus. He supposed that was why Hayes was way cooler than him. He and Wilf had had much more in common. They were both doing chemistry, which was how he came to be sharing the flat. He'd quite liked Wilf, although he was very quiet, withdrawn almost, but he joined in with things when asked. What he couldn't understand was what happened to him. He had wondered if Hayes knew something but when he'd asked him, he said he didn't and Callum believed him. What he hadn't told Hayes was that he was analysing forensic samples for drugs and, although Prof hadn't said anything, he thought they were from Wilf. That was what was really worrying him.

Simon unlocked the lab door to let Callum in and gave him instructions to clean the equipment thoroughly before they began the next stage of analysis. Meanwhile he went up to his office to contact Nina Featherstone.

'You asked me to call with the results of the tests I did last week, Nina. But first, can I thank you again for tea on Saturday. It was great to meet your family.'

'It was nice to meet you too. I've been asking Mills to bring you over for a while.'

The niceties over, he described what measurements he'd made on the blood and urine and gave her the BZE level in the blood in micrograms per litre.

'Don't worry,' he said when she asked what that was. 'It's the metabolite of cocaine we use in the analysis. I'll explain it all in a report later, when Mills has typed it out. Basically the time the metabolite stays in the body depends on how the cocaine was administered.'

'But we don't know that,' said Nina.

'Exactly, so it makes it difficult to be precise but the fact that I didn't find BZE in the urine could mean that it was administered quite soon before death.'

'But you found it in the blood sample?'

'Yes. The plasma had a very low level of the metabolite. Now that could be because the cocaine was taken hours or even days before his death but, in that case, I would expect to have detected it in the urine because it's excreted over a longer period.'

'So, let me see if I've got this right. You think he somehow inhaled or smoked the cocaine quite soon before he was found?'

'Yes. But if that's the case, I'm surprised at the low level of BZE in the plasma because to get a sufficient hit from the drug you would need a lot more than he appears to have taken.'

Nina told him to ask Mills to hurry up with the written report and thanked him for doing the first stage so quickly. He immediately called Mills to pass the message on. She'd insisted that she knew the correct format that the police required, so she would prepare the full report, but he would have to give her the relevant data once she'd prepared the template. There was no answer from the landline or her mobile so he assumed she was already busy in the lab with her friend Donna. Well he needed to get back to the lab: the qualitative run on the samples that identified cocaine had found something else interesting and he wanted to get the separation stage completed to see if he was right.

Nina returned from her discussions with Mitch to report that they were to continue to investigate where Wilf had obtained his ecstasy, at least until they received the results of the forensic analysis from the police forensics service in Wakefield.

'That means talking to his associates again, I suppose,' said Hazel unenthusiastically.

'Don't worry,' said Nina, 'I'll go over, if you like. They're not on strike today according to Nige. I can pick up the interim forensic report at the same time if it's ready.'

She added that Alison was her husband's tutee and Callum Wallace was a student of Professor Pringle's, so they should be easy to find. Hazel commented that it all sounded rather cosy.

Ruby was left with the trickier task of ringing round the Sociology department to locate Oliver Hayes. She finally put the receiver down, declaring that students didn't seem to spend much time in lectures these days.

'He's studying politics and economics,' Hazel said. 'If that helps.'

'Apparently they have less "contact time" in the third year,' said Ruby, pulling a face.

Nina gave a confident smile and pulled on her coat. 'Not to worry, I'll sort it,' she said, making for the door.

On the way she called Nige, who wasn't a great deal of help but did give her Alison's mobile number. They arranged to meet in her flat that afternoon when she was free from lectures. The girl gave her a detailed description of how to find her hall of residence. There was no reply when she called Simon Pringle but she left a message. When she rang Mills it went to voicemail so she just explained her plans, hoping they could catch up later to collect the report on the cocaine in Wilf's blood.

Nina parked close to the cafeteria where she'd spoken to the lad who had found Wilf's body. There was no sign of him but she guessed he worked the early shift and, anyway, would be behind the scenes in the kitchen. She took her sandwich and a tea back to the car, where she sat quietly watching the last few students and staff wandering into the building for a late lunch. It was a long time since she had been a student but she looked back at her time fondly. It had given her an independence she hadn't envisaged possible after growing up in such a protected family environment. And in just nine years she would probably be waving her daughter off to university too.

Her reverie was interrupted by a call from Simon Pringle. Callum had been working with him in the lab and would be back from lunch in an hour, if she wanted to see him. Nina had been thinking about how she was going to talk to Oliver Hayes and had a plan.

'Can you tell Callum that I will come to his hall of residence to meet him and his flatmate? Can you ask him to contact Oliver Hayes to let him know?'

'Oliver Hayes? Righto, I'll tell him. What time?'

'Can you spare him for a meeting at four o'clock?'

'No problem, Nina. I'm working on the fentanyl this afternoon and I have to do that myself.'

'By the way, Simon, are you absolutely certain that

Callum doesn't know about the origin of the samples? He doesn't know they're Wilf's?'

'Definitely not. I've made sure everything is anonymous as instructed by Mills. It's normal practice anyway and he doesn't have sight of any paperwork.'

'That's good. Please make sure you keep it that way.'

Nina finished the call and checked the time. She would walk slowly over to the halls of residence, checking out the bench where Wilf's body was found on the way. The wind whipped round the tall building as she climbed out of the car. She buttoned up her coat, grabbed her bag and set off past the lake, pulling her collar tighter to keep the wind out.

Once she was on the path to the residences, she could see that the bench was covered in gifts. She stopped to look at the flowers, balloons, toys, scarves, and scribbled notes that were scattered on the bench, and stretching in front of it, covering the path. She read the cards slowly in case anything among them gave a hint of how or why he died but they were just simple messages expressing sadness. Of course, at this stage, his peers weren't aware of how he died. She wondered if they would be more forthcoming if it turned out drugs were the cause.

'Isn't it amazing?'

Nina turned to see Alison standing behind her.

'I realised you wouldn't be able to get in through the front door if someone let the catch go. It's supposed to be locked all the time but it's sometimes open during the day.'

Nina followed her to the nearest building, where the girl used a plastic card to access the door, then up two flights of stairs onto a spacious landing.

'There are four flats to each landing,' she explained.

'This is mine and that's where Wilf lived.'

She pointed across the corridor before letting her into Flat 4. Nina was surprised how spacious it was. They were standing in a large sitting room overlooking the lake in the distance. There was a kitchen area at one end with a dining table and four chairs.

'How many of you share this?' she asked.

'Three. Would you like something? Tea or coffee?'

'No I'm fine thank you, Alison. Shall we sit down?'

Nina took one end of the sofa and the student sat on a large cushion. There was a brief silence while Nina searched in her bag for a pen.

'Thank you for seeing me again,' she began. 'I just wanted to remind myself of what we decided about Wilf's relationship with drugs. I think you told me that you'd never seen him smoking cannabis?'

Alison nodded.

'And what about ecstasy?'

She shook her head.

'Cocaine?'

The girl looked startled. 'Cocaine?'

It was Nina's turn to nod.

'Definitely not!' she replied angrily. 'You think he was using cocaine? Seriously?' Now she looked less sure of herself and began to shake her head slowly. 'You think you know someone, don't you? I didn't really know him at all.'

'At present we're just trying to build up a picture. So anything you can tell me, anything that occurs to you, will be very helpful.'

Alison re-iterated that she didn't think Wilf was into hard drugs and Nina thanked her again.

'Oh, before I go,' said Nina, standing up, 'have you had

any more thoughts about what Wilf did at the weekends?'

'Not really.' She was looking at the floor, her hands clenched. 'Although I think he might have been going with Callum Wallace and the other one in his flat, I don't know his name.'

Nina waited until the door closed behind her before crossing the corridor to Flat 2.

Chapter 8

The flat had the same layout as the one Nina had just visited, but there were no cushions on the sofa or the floor, the dining table was bare and there was no sign of a rug or a lamp. The effect was quite stark. Clearly student accommodation was provided with the bare minimum requirements and the lads hadn't attempted to make it more homely. Despite that, it was very tidy and Nina wondered if they had made a special effort because of her visit.

Callum Wallace answered the door and waited for her to sit down before perching uncomfortably on the edge of his chair.

'I'm sure Hayes will be here soon,' he said, looking at his phone nervously.

Nina took time to retrieve her notebook and pen from her bag before placing it beside her on the sofa. There had been no offer of a hot drink, which usually broke the tension, so she plunged straight into the reason for her visit.

Callum was picking at his nails. 'But we spoke to DS Fuller last week.'

'I know, and I'm sorry to put you through it again, but I'm trying to get a better idea of what Wilf was like. You must know him better that anyone, seeing him every day. Did you eat together?' she asked, glancing towards the kitchen area.

'Not really. We didn't see much of each other.'

'So what did he do in his spare time? Did he bring friends back here?'

'No.'

'What about his girlfriend?'

He shrugged.

'Alison, from across the corridor in Flat 4.'

He shook his head. 'I don't really know her, sorry.'

Nina looked at her notes. 'So was he here in the evenings and at weekends?'

'Probably, Hayes and I aren't around much.'

'You go away at the weekends?'

He nodded.

'And Oliver?'

'Yes.'

When she asked him if anyone had taken over Wilf's room, he showed her into a neat single bedroom with a view over the car park. It had been left untouched, waiting for Wilf's parents to collect his things. Nina said she would have a quick look round and Callum left her to it. A few clothes in the wardrobe and the chest of drawers. A pair of boots under the bed. A laptop on the desk. Drawers containing a few sheets of official paperwork. No-one kept a diary these days, everything was on their phone and Wilf's mobile was in a plastic bag of his belongings awaiting collection. It would be available for examination if it was necessary. She looked over at the laptop. They'd have to decide very soon whether they were treating Wilf's death as suspicious or not.

She heard voices in the sitting room and went back to meet Oliver Hayes, or "Hayes" as he liked to be called. He was a couple of years older and more self-assured than Callum. He shook hands, offering her a coffee and taking a seat on the sofa. She decided to be honest about her enquiries.

'Do either of you know if Wilf was using drugs?'

They hesitated. Callum was looking at Hayes for a response.

Nina smiled at them, hoping to put them at their ease. 'I know he may have smoked a bit of cannabis but I'm asking about class A drugs: ecstasy or cocaine, for example.'

Callum was clearly expecting Hayes to answer for them.

He crossed his legs and folded his arms before replying. 'I don't think he would be into that. He was a quiet guy, quite immature. He was a bit of a loner really.'

This was the line that Hazel had come back with, but before she left, Nina wanted to clarify something.

'Callum told me that you both go away at weekends?'

They nodded.

She gave another smile before following up with a casual question. 'That's nice. Where do you go?'

Once again, the look between the two of them with Callum letting Hayes answer. 'Just walking, climbing, bit of caving over in the Dales.'

'It sounds like fun. And did Wilf ever go with you?'

They exchanged glances but this time Callum answered. 'Yes.'

Hayes looked startled.

Nina pondered for a moment. 'Sorry, I was under the impression you didn't see him at weekends,' she said.

Callum reddened. 'That's my fault,' he said. 'I was worried about the drug thing.'

'What do you mean exactly?'

'When you asked about drugs, I didn't want to get us into trouble.'

Hayes was looking increasingly uncomfortable and finally intervened. 'What he means is that we have been known to smoke the odd joint at the weekends. Just recreational cannabis, nothing heavy.'

'So was Wilf with you the weekend before last?'

'Yes.' Now Hayes was answering the questions while Callum nodded in agreement.

'Talk me through what happened on Sunday night then.'

Nina carefully noted down exactly what Hayes had to say, while keeping an eye on his friend's body-language. It seemed they had spent the weekend in a cottage near Skipton, doing a few walks, going to the pub and watching TV. It seemed to Nina to be a long way to go when they could have stayed on campus and done the same but perhaps the freedom to smoke cannabis without being caught out by the university authorities might have been the attraction. Anyway, it was what happened when they arrived back that she was interested in.

'We caught the train just after seven and got into Darlington around nine. We took a taxi back here and I went out with some mates until late.'

She looked across at Callum.

'I went straight to the bar and came in around eleven, eleven-thirty.'

'And Wilf?'

Callum shrugged. 'I assumed he was here. His door was shut when I came in so I guessed he was asleep.'

Hayes nodded in agreement. It wasn't a criminal investigation yet so she didn't ask for any more details but closed her notebook and put it away. Picking up her bag, she prepared to leave. She headed for the door and Callum followed her into the corridor. He told her quietly he was helping Professor Pringle with some forensic work. She didn't respond so he continued by asking her if it was related to Wilf's death. She said she really couldn't say, which was her wonderfully ambiguous way of not lying but not telling the truth.

She had reached the top of the stairs before realising she hadn't given them her contact details. She turned around, fishing a card from her coat pocket, but as she reached the door to Flat 2, there were raised voices inside, although it was impossible to hear what was being said. She stuck her card between the door and its frame and left.

Mills offered Donna lunch after she'd given her a tour of the new laboratory. She had been suitably impressed with the facilities they'd planned and Mills decided to talk to her about a possible position as an analyst. She had to introduce the topic carefully, which is why she'd suggested they grabbed a sandwich in the cafeteria before Donna left.

'It's a wonderful opportunity that Brenda's given you,' Donna said, once they were settled in a couple of comfortable chairs.

Mills agreed, adding that they wouldn't have been able to do it without the space provided by the Chemistry Department. When she told her about Simon's involvement in the venture, Donna said she'd heard of Professor Pringle because he sometimes visited the toxicology team at the police forensic lab where she worked.

'Not that I've met him,' she added, 'but my boss sometimes had meetings with him when I worked in the toxicology lab.'

Mills skirted round the topic of how they were going to

manage the work once the lab was up and running until Donna asked straight out whether there would be any job opportunities.

'Absolutely,' Mills replied. 'We can't use students if it's to be run as an accredited forensics laboratory, which is why I was thinking…' She looked up to see a figure heading towards them. 'And here's Simon now!' she said cheerily, jumping up.

She introduced them awkwardly and Simon gave Donna a charming smile, although Mills guessed he was probably irritated that he hadn't been involved in her visit. Donna said she needed to get off and Mills promised to keep in touch. As soon as she'd gone, Simon sat down, asking if she'd offered Donna anything.

'Of course not! We were just catching up. She was very impressed with the lab though.'

There was a difficult silence before Simon went off to fetch a coffee, without asking if she wanted one. When he returned, he still looked annoyed.

'I've been leaving messages all morning,' he said.

'Sorry, I was with Donna.'

'Well I've given the cocaine figures to Nina but the police need a proper report.'

'No problem,' said Mills, trying to lighten the mood. 'If you bring the results to my office, I'll do them straight away.'

'I can't. The fentanyl samples are running; I need to go back and check the figures.'

'Are they positive?'

He was frowning. 'Yes. They're high, far too high. I'm going to re-analyse them this afternoon.'

'Does that mean…'

'If they are correct, and it's a big if, it's what killed him, no doubt about that.'

'Wow.'

'Exactly. So if you've finished your lunch, can you come back to my office and I'll give you the cocaine results to type up.'

Nina had waited all morning for the typed copy of the forensic results from Mills. She was out of the office when it finally arrived, and she only found it in her inbox late in the afternoon. She skimmed through the figures quickly before forwarding them on to Ruby and Hazel. She was pleased with the presentation of the report, noting it was the same template that Yardley Forensics had used but with the header changed.

'So the cocaine wouldn't have been enough to kill him.' Ruby commented.

'No, the levels are too low apparently.'

'And it was definitely taken soon before his death?'

'Apparently.'

Hazel looked up. 'Probably just contamination – don't they say every five-pound note has traces of cocaine on it?'

'Well he's finishing the analyses today, so if nothing turns up we'll have to assume it wasn't drug related,' said Nina.

Hazel smiled. 'Good, it won't be our problem then. His parents can collect his body and get on with the funeral. And I can get home at a reasonable time for once.' She fetched her coat and picked up her bag. 'See you later!'

Nina ignored her as she answered her phone. It was Simon Pringle sounding rather breathless.

'I need to confirm them, Nina, but I can't find any

errors. I've run duplicates, and I've checked for errors but I believe there's fentanyl in the samples.'

'Are you're sure?'

'I am. There's so much there it was easy to see. That's why I'm fairly certain it's not contamination.'

'How confident are you?'

'Eighty, ninety percent, but before we can report the results to you, Mills wants me to do another run with my assistant present to witness it, first thing tomorrow.'

'Let me know as soon as you can because we'll have to have the results corroborated by the accredited lab as a matter of urgency.'

Ruby was giving her a quizzical look when she put the phone down.

'That was Professor Pringle,' Nina told her. 'He thinks he's found another drug in the samples.'

'Fake drugs aren't uncommon, are they? But the last cases we had up here was a death in Leeds at the festival.' She was looking it up on her computer. 'Was it something called n-ethylpentylone? It's quite commonly mis-sold as MDMA, it says here.'

'But what about fentanyl? Is that used to fake ecstasy?'

'No way. That's a hundred times more powerful than morphine. Apparently two milligrams can kill you.' She continued to read out snippets of information as she found them online. Finally she said, 'Surely you remember the fentanyl factory they discovered in Leeds a couple of years ago?'

Nina thanked Ruby and began typing up her notes from her visit to Wilf's flatmates. If the forensics was correct and there was a lethal dose of fentanyl in the ecstasy, they were now investigating a serious crime, possibly murder.

Although she hadn't made a note of it, she was reminded of Callum's question about the forensic work he was helping Simon with, and immediately picked up the phone.

'Simon, when you said your assistant would be helping you, did you mean Mills?'

Simon was laughing. 'No, my postgrad, Callum Wallace. He's well-trained to help me with the work.'

Just as she'd feared. 'Can someone else do the witnessing?' she asked. 'Could Mills, for example.'

There was a long pause before he replied. 'Yes, I guess so but Callum…'

'Sorry, but could you please use Mills instead? I'm not sure, but at this stage I would prefer that Mr Wallace is not involved any further.'

'OK,' he agreed, still sounding puzzled.

'One other thing, Simon. Can you tell from your measurements whether this fentanyl drug was taken with the ecstasy or on its own?'

'You mean was it in the ecstasy tablet? No, it's impossible to tell. Why?'

She said she couldn't say any more at this stage and rang off.

'Ruby, I'm going to catch Mitch if he's still here. I think we should be treating Wilf Marriott's death as suspicious.'

She went along the corridor to find Mitch at his desk, behind piles of paperwork. He was obviously unhappy to be interrupted and threw his pen down to listen to her concerns with a resigned expression. When she'd finished telling him about the discovery of fentanyl in the bodily fluids, he picked up his pen again and muttered that they could do nothing until they had confirmation from Wakefield.

'But they said it could be another week,' she complained.

Without looking up, he muttered that they'd just have to wait. The university wouldn't thank them for raising panic across the campus on the say-so of an amateur forensics outfit with no official status.

It would be pointless to argue. She knew from bitter experience that the harder she pushed Mitch, the more stubborn he would become.

Mills arranged to meet Simon in the carpark at five-thirty. He was ten minutes late when she finally caught sight of him in her rear-view mirror. The passenger door swung open and he dropped into his seat, clutching a briefcase on his knee.

'Sorry, I had to shut up the lab this evening, Callum didn't come back after his interview with Nina.'

Mills started the car without comment. Once they were on the road, Simon told her about Nina's request that she witness the analysis of the forensic samples.

'Why?'

'Because you're experienced in forensic procedures, I suppose.'

'You don't think it might be because your postgraduate student shared a flat with the victim and you've just informed her that he may have died from an overdose of fentanyl, by any chance?'

'I didn't tell her that,' he argued. 'I only told her I could detect fentanyl and wanted to check it.'

'So when are you repeating the work?' Mills asked with a loud sigh.

'Tomorrow morning if possible.'

'I'm teaching.'

85

'Afternoon?'

'Tutorials.'

'Damn.'

'Wednesday afternoon is free,' she offered. 'How long do you need?'

'It'll have to do. At this rate Wakefield will be reporting before we do.'

They drove in silence the rest of the way to Osmotherley, where Harris was waiting for his walk. Simon said he wanted to check the fentanyl levels again, in case he'd made a mistake in his calculations, so Mills grudgingly agreed to take the dog down the lane before making tea.

It was cold and very dark outside. The beam of her head torch bobbed about and the dog's collar flashed several yards ahead of her. New potholes had appeared since the storms in previous weeks, which made progress slow but Harris was happy to sniff carefully along the hedgerows until they reached the end of the lane, where it met the main road. She continued for a few more minutes until she could feel the first spots of rain then turned, making her way as fast as she dared. The downpour became heavier and she thought she saw a flash of lightening, which was soon followed by thunder in the distance. Harris was more anxious to get home than she was. There was a patch of light at the side of the cottage and Simon was standing by the open door with a towel in his hand.

'I'll dry him,' he offered. 'And I've put dinner in the oven. But then, can you help me with those figures?'

After they'd eaten, Mills cleared the dishes from the kitchen table so Simon could use his laptop to show her the spreadsheet. The figures didn't make much sense to her, but she agreed the calculations looked correct.

'Good,' he said at last. 'And I prepared these other samples myself, so I knew what the result should be, and they've come out right.'

Mills quizzed him on his methodology. Gas chromatography was a mystery to her but she was familiar with spectrometry and knew what precautions were needed when carrying out analysis of minute quantities of chemicals and their components, and these were tiny amounts, just tens of micrograms.

'It sounds as though you've covered it,' she agreed when he'd finished. 'And well done you for detecting it. Are you sure we need to measure it again?'

'Yes. It's a lot more challenging when the work involves possible criminality and the results could be used in court,' he admitted. 'I know our work won't be admissible until we become an approved lab but then it will be serious. It's quite stressful, isn't it?'

'It is, which is why I want us to have a professional staff, not a bunch of students.'

Simon pulled a face. 'So you think we should offer your friend a job?'

'When we're set up, yes. And she's not my friend, she's an excellent forensic analyst with all the necessary training and experience. In fact she's worked for a short time in the toxicology lab at Wakefield.'

That caught his attention. Mills guessed he would be making surreptitious enquiries next time he was down at the police forensic labs.

Now the results had been checked, Mills was still puzzling over the tiny amount of the drug in Wilf's blood. 'So is it possible that less than a hundred nanograms could have killed him?'

'Yes, I would say so. I'm not medically qualified but I did quite a lot of work in the States on its detection. There was a study relating to people wearing fentanyl patches for pain relief and accidental deaths. I could look it up but the average level in the blood was much lower than in Wilf's, only around ten nanograms.'

'So it was easily detected in his blood?'

'Yes but not in his urine, which suggests he died very soon after taking it.'

Chapter 9

Mills struggled to zip up the lab coat Simon had issued her. It was far too large but the only clean one he could find. She sighed as she followed him into the lab, ready to watch him set up the equipment. It was the first time she'd seen him working on anything practical, apart from the time he tried to fix his dishwasher, so she was surprised at how carefully he handled the delicate syringes and glassware. He explained what he was doing as he prepared standards to calibrate the instrument, before preparing the blood and urine. The work took all afternoon and, although Mills thought she would be bored witnessing Simon, she was fascinated to watch him in his natural environment. She knew he was at the cutting edge of research in his field but he explained how his particular technique was the best available, which was why the police labs at Wakefield used him as a consultant.

'Does that mean they'll be copying the methodology you're using now?' Mills asked, as they waited for the machine to print out a stream of numbers.

'Probably. I don't see the details of their protocols but I've advised them over the technique in the past. In fact I was in touch with them yesterday.'

'Did they tell you how they're getting on with their analyses of Wilf's samples?' asked Mills, wondering if he was also checking Donna's credentials at the same time.

'No, I didn't ask, but they're still having problems with their equipment.'

'Did you enquire about Donna?'

Mills studied his face. He looked uncomfortable.

'I did happen to mention her name.'

'And?'

'Apparently they thought very highly of her when she was in their section.'

He rushed off to start preparing the next sample, leaving Mills to watch and wait. Looking round, she noticed that the laboratory was much larger than she was used to at Yardley Forensics, due to the size of the mass spectrometer. Now she understood why Simon was claiming a significant proportion of the space they'd been allocated for his set-up.

The next hour was spent watching data coming out of the mass spectrometer on the computer screen. At intervals Simon would bring up spreadsheets, muttering to himself. Finally he swung round triumphantly.

'The test samples are correct and the blood sample reading is close enough to last week's set of measurements for me to be sure. The average value is just over fifty nanograms.'

They waited for the next set of data to be completed, then he repeated the entire process.

'There, that proves it. I've got less than a nanogram in the urine.'

'That's it then,' said Mills. 'Or do you have to look for any other drugs?'

'No, that's the lot. Our first forensic job is complete. I just need you to type up the report.'

'Will you ring Nina now?' she asked.

He looked at his watch. 'It's after six.'

'No problem. I'll call her this evening.'

Simon spent another half hour cleaning the equipment before removing his lab coat and gloves, to wash his hands. Mills followed his example. Finally he switched off the lights and shut the door behind them.

Outside it was dark, rain was falling steadily as they made a dash for the car. But once they were on the road home, Mills had a question.

'Is it possible Wilf was experimenting with the fentanyl and took an accidental overdose?'

'I find that difficult to believe. The research project he was working on was to design a simple test for students and clubbers to check that what they were taking was safe. He understood the dangers of class A drugs. In fact he gave a very professional presentation on the topic just before Christmas. His test was for MDMA, since ecstasy is the most commonly used drug on campus.'

'Then he was trying to kill himself by taking it deliberately.'

'Who knows? You've spoken to his girlfriend.'

'Alison? Yes. She thought they'd had a good time when they went on a date a few days before he was found, but she didn't know him very well. She said he probably only smoked cannabis. Certainly nothing stronger.'

'The tiny amount of cocaine he'd taken could have been mixed with the fentanyl. It makes more sense to find those two drugs together.'

'And you're certain he died soon after taking a mixture of them all because there was nothing in his urine?'

'Not one hundred percent. We know what he took but not necessarily exactly how and when.'

Mills drove through the downpour for a while before asking, 'Can you do hair analysis?'

He thought for a moment. 'I can but it would only show whether he was a regular user of the drugs.'

'It would prove if he'd used cocaine or fentanyl previously.'

'I suppose so.'

Simon spent the rest of the drive describing how he would analyse hair for fentanyl. Mills was keen for him to have a go. He protested that he didn't have any hair samples and it would be left to the police lab to pursue that if necessary, but Mills was sure the student had enough hair to go round.

As soon as they were home, she told Simon it was his turn to take Harris out in the rain and while he was gone, she rang her friend. Nina had just got in from work and was in the middle of getting the kids to bed.

'Listen just for a minute, Nina. Simon has repeated the analyses. The results are the same, so we're certain they're correct.'

'That's great. Send me the report and I'll pass it on to Wakefield.'

'But won't you be treating it as suspicious?'

'We can't do anything until we get accredited results, Mills.'

'But that could take ages, Simon's heard they've got a problem with their equipment.'

'Sorry, Mills. Was that all? Only I've got…'

'Wait! Simon told me that to prove Wilf wasn't a regular drug user we need to analyse some of his hair.'

'I'll bear it in mind but now I've got to go.'

As soon as Simon returned, she repeated what Nina had said. 'Don't you think we should do something?' she asked. 'If there are dangerous drugs out there someone should find out who's supplying them.'

'I know, but we'll just have to wait for the police investigation. We can't do anything ourselves.'

'I've been thinking about that and I believe your student Callum must know something. For example, what is he up to in Skipton every weekend?'

Simon shrugged.

'Well, that's what I want to find out.' She waited for his response but he wasn't listening. 'Shall I peel some potatoes?' he asked.

She decided there was no point in pursuing it, she wasn't going to persuade him to help. She simply commented that they should finish the final report for Nina that evening and include the suggestion that a sample of hair be analysed for toxicology, to establish if Wilf used drugs on a regular basis.

Nina received the report from Mills by email first thing the following morning. She printed it out to read through then passed it on to Ruby, while she dealt with urgent paperwork.

The researcher leaned back in her chair when she'd finished reading. 'My first question would be how did he get hold of the fentanyl? It's not something you come across unless it's mixed with heroin or cocaine and, in this case, he'd taken ecstasy.'

Nina agreed.

'The next question is how did he take it? There were no puncture marks on his body according the post-mortem, and he was in good shape health-wise, it says, which doesn't point to him being a junkie.'

'That's what his girlfriend said.'

'Combined with the fact he took the drugs in the early hours then lay down on a bench in the cold, it looks suspicious. At least we should try to find out where the fentanyl came from and warn the university.'

'I'll talk to Mitch again,' said Nina.

But it was no use. The coroner had asked for confirmation of the forensic results prior to deciding whether an inquest was necessary. The parents were asking for their son's body but, until that decision was made, everything was in limbo. It all hung on the Wakefield forensic report. Her DI certainly wasn't going to delay things further by asking for hair analysis.

When Nina told Ruby, she expressed surprise that Mitch didn't see the death as suspicious.

'I've been looking at Wilf Marriott's background,' she explained. 'His parents live in a very smart area outside Leeds and he attended the Grammar School, where the fees are over four thousand pounds a term. In the holidays he was a volunteer at a local care home for young adults. He chose to study chemistry at university. He just doesn't sound like someone with a drug habit.'

'People can change,' Nina replied, but she had to admit the profile didn't fit. 'No-one seems to have known him well at uni. Maybe he just got into the wrong crowd.'

'Are you going to warn the authorities about the possible contamination of drugs on campus?' Ruby asked. 'I've got the number of the Student Welfare Team. I kept it, I thought you'd need it eventually.'

She tore a sheet from her notepad and offered it to Nina, who took the paper and dialled the number. The girl who answered seemed bemused by the enquiry and disappeared to find her manager. Nina was kept on hold for a couple of minutes but, just as she was about to hang up, a female welfare officer asked rather brusquely what she wanted. When she explained that it related to a student's death, the woman became defensive, saying she couldn't discuss personal cases. It took several attempts to convince her that all Nina wanted to do was warn students of the possible danger of drugs on campus – that they might not be what they seem. Finally she was asked to send an official request through to the office.

'What are you going to say?' Ruby asked. 'We can't give them all the details, can we?'

Nina simply wrote that a chemistry student, Wilf Marriott, had died on campus after taking ecstasy which may have been contaminated with an opioid, and students should be cautious.

'Does the university have a drug-testing service like they had at Newcastle when I was there?' Ruby asked.

She explained that it had been the first campus in the country to introduce it for students to check the quality and, consequently, safety of common recreational drugs.

'I don't know. Simon… Professor Pringle, told me that Wilf was actually working on a simple drug test kit as his research project.'

'In that case you'd think he'd be fairly careful what he was taking himself,' Ruby observed

Callum was already in the lab when Simon arrived to sort out material for Monday's practical class.

'I didn't think you were available on Fridays,' he said to the student, pointedly.

'I'm out this afternoon but I thought I'd see if you needed any help this morning.'

Simon unlocked the refrigerator containing the solutions he needed and started the dilutions. He didn't answer.

'I wondered if you needed any more help with those forensic samples?' Callum asked again.

'No, they're all done, thanks.'

The lad hung around, fiddling with drawers and playing with the computer until Simon had finished topping up the glass flasks.

Finally he asked, 'Prof, did you see the message from the Welfare Centre?'

'No, what was that?' He was putting the flasks away before locking the cupboard.

'It was about Wilf.'

Simon stood up to listen.

'Apparently they think he took contaminated ecstasy.' He paused. 'Is that what those samples from the police were about?'

Simon considered for a moment. 'I can't say.'

Callum was quiet. 'I was just wondering what the contamination was, that's all.'

'I can't discuss the results with you, Callum.'

'I know, but you *were* looking at cocaine and opioids, weren't you?'

'Callum, I'm really busy this morning. I'm going back to my office now so please make sure you lock up when you leave the lab.'

He'd arranged to see Mills in the cafeteria for a coffee. It had been her idea to meet every Friday morning to discuss progress on the lab. She was already at a table in the corner with two cups in front of her.

'I got your coffee,' she said. 'It should still be warm.'

'Sorry I'm late,' he said, sitting opposite her. 'Callum held me up.'

'Did he? I thought he went off early on a Friday.'

Simon drained his cup in one go. 'He does but not until later.'

'With his flatmate?'

'I don't know, Mills. Can we get on? I've got tons to finish before the weekend, unless you want to get back to Swaledale after midnight.'

'Actually that's fine. I told you I was thinking of going down to Harrogate this afternoon to see Brenda, that's why I brought my own car in. I'll collect Harris and see you back at Mossy Bank later. Don't worry if I'm back late, you know what Brenda's like, she'll probably give me something to eat.'

Simon looked surprised but agreed. Mills had a plan which she wasn't going to share with him. So she proposed they adjourn their Friday progress report and get moving.

'We can always hold our meeting on Saturday or Sunday at home.'

She gave him a quick kiss on the cheek and left. She needed to collect Harris and drive down to Skipton in time to meet the train used by Callum. He'd told Simon he had to leave the lab by two o'clock, so she reckoned he was catching the three-seventeen which arrived in Skipton just after five. She planned to drive straight back to Osmotherley to give the dog a quick walk before she left.

The department was strangely quiet since most of the lecturers were on strike and had either stayed at home or were on the picket line. She sorted out a few last messages, packed her laptop and locked the office door before making for the car park. Nige would be out by the entrance gates wielding a placard, so she looked straight ahead as she manoeuvred the Mini between the lines of pickets. It was a short drive to Osmotherley on country roads that were rarely busy. She put her foot down and did the journey in twenty minutes, leaving plenty of time for a cheese sandwich and a cup of tea.

Harris had already been out with the dog walker for two hours that morning running across fields with five other dogs and his feet were caked with mud. Mills decided that a quick walk along the lane in the puddles might help clean his paws up a bit. He lay quietly under the table while she ate her lunch, but when she pulled on her waterproof jacket and wellington boots, he lifted his head lethargically and stretched as he made his way slowly into the hall.

'Don't worry Harris, this won't take long and then you can have a nice long snooze in the back of the car.'

The sky was turning grey, the sun had disappeared, and a very strong wind was blowing. The trees waved over them as they fought against it, following the lane as it became a rough track beside a stream. The water was running fast, almost overflowing onto the grass where they were walking. She let Harris amble ahead, sniffing at the base of trees and poking around by the rabbit burrows, until she finally called him and led him back to the cottage.

By two-thirty she was ready to leave. Harris followed her obediently, jumping into the back of the Mini and settling down across the seat on his old rug. Mills loaded her bag in the boot and locked up the cottage, after double-checking she'd turned down the heating and switched off all the lights. They wouldn't be back until Monday morning.

'All right, Harris? Good, then we'll be off.'

She was glad she'd left in plenty of time, before the roads became busy with Friday traffic, and made good progress until she reached the outskirts of Skipton. She found her way to the railway station, parked in the car park, and bought a pay and display ticket, which she discovered would allow her to park all day. Then she waited until suddenly a large group of commuters were emerging in a gaggle from the station. She relaxed. It was too early; it was another forty minutes before the train was due in. She watched the passengers dispersing to their vehicles across the car park. Sets of headlights were switched on before the cars joined the long line queueing at the exit. Then it went quiet again until ten past five when the train she'd been waiting for arrived, and this time she was ready for action. Callum wouldn't have a car in the car park so he would have to walk out or wait because she'd seen the last available taxi disappear ten minutes ago.

Mills hoped to recognise the student by his shock of curly ginger hair but hadn't reckoned on the woolly hat pulled down over his forehead. However, when the crowd had emerged and dispersed there were two figures left at the entrance to the station, heaving large rucksacks onto their shoulders. One must have been Callum but it was his companion she recognised first by his distinctive long black coat. It was the man she'd seen Callum in discussion with outside the Chemistry Department.

Chapter 10

'Hurry up, Harris, it's time for a stroll!'

Mills jumped out of the car, struggling to get the dog off the back seat in time to follow Callum and his companion. She kept an eye on their progress as she locked the car, with no idea what to expect as she followed at a distance along the road towards town. She was surprised to see them disappear into a large supermarket. Grateful that it was a clear night, she hung around outside, hoping they wouldn't be long. After about twenty minutes they emerged, each carrying a plastic bag. She quickly moved between parked cars and watched them continue along the road until they reached the canal bridge. Here they stopped at a fish and chip shop, climbing the steps into the restaurant.

Mills hesitated. It was going to be a long wait if they were eating their tea in there. She wandered past and up the road a little way but the smell of fish and chips drew her back. It was six o'clock. Soon Simon would be at the fish and chip van in the dale. She sent him a message to say she was eating and would be back late. Tying Harris to the stair rail, she went into the separate takeaway to order fish with chips and a hot tea. She sat on the low wall outside the shop with her meal, feeding the dog with bits of fish and the odd chip. If it wasn't so cold, she would have been enjoying herself. She knew Simon would think she was mad and Nina would have a few sharp words to say, but Mills couldn't help wanting to get to the bottom of things, could she?

She'd finished eating long before the boys emerged from the restaurant. She observed them from the other side of the road as they walked slowly back to the station, stopping beside a black people carrier in the taxi rank. They climbed in without speaking to the driver. She really hadn't thought this through, had she? All she could do was stare as they drove past her towards the exit. But at least she had the presence of mind to memorise the licence number on the back as it went past.

'You lads know where you're off to this week?' the taxi driver asked.

They admitted they didn't.

'It's good one of us knows then,' he responded, good-naturedly. 'We're headed for the canal at Gargrave first, it's not far.'

Callum peered out, trying to see where they were going but they were speeding down a country road in the dark. Vehicles flashed past in the opposite direction but otherwise there were no lights until they reached Gargrave. The driver carried on through the line of shops until they were out on the empty road again. Eventually they slowed down outside a pub.

'Here we are. The canal's down there. I'm going to park in here on the left.'

'You stay here,' ordered Hayes without explanation. 'I won't be long.'

'Is he like your boss?' the driver asked when Hayes had gone.

'Sort of,' replied Callum.

He watched to see where Hayes was going then climbed

out to follow. He'd crossed the canal and turned down a towpath. In the darkness Callum could just make out a boat tied up. A light came on and a figure emerged from it, greeting his friend with a raised hand. They seemed to be having a serious conversation that lasted for the time it took them to smoke a cigarette. When it began to rain, they shook hands and Hayes started back up the towpath, leaving Callum just enough time to nip back to the taxi.

'Have you got the address?' Hayes asked the driver when he climbed into the back.

He nodded and started the engine. 'It's near Settle this time. Lucky you don't have to foot the bill.'

'What did he say?' Callum asked in a whisper.

'Nothing. He just wanted to let us know there are a couple of new lads starting tonight. We'll need to show them the ropes.'

More unlit roads until they reached the town of Settle but they weren't there yet. Through the centre then out into the darkness again until they suddenly veered off the road down a narrow bumpy lane. The taxi driver was using a satnav that was telling him he'd reached his destination. He argued there was nothing there and drove on for another minute until his headlights revealed a cottage on the left-hand side.

Callum spotted a sign outside indicating it was a holiday let. 'This must be it.'

They thanked the driver, who said he'd see them on Sunday night. 'It would be a lot easier if you two stayed in one place,' he called through the open window.

'I guess they get booked up,' Callum suggested.

'They will do if you only want a short let. Why do you only do weekends?' he asked.

'We're studying, aren't we? And the others are still at school or college.'

As usual, the key was under the mat. The boxes had already been delivered and left stacked in the hall. When they discovered how small the cottage was, they understood why they'd been left there. Once they had unloaded their food, selected their rooms and warmed the place up, they settled down in front of the television with a bottle of beer each.

'Pain the TV signal's so poor,' Hayes commented. 'The lads will be complaining.'

'They'll be too tired to worry,' said Callum. 'Specially the new ones.'

Hayes agreed.

After watching the taxi disappear into the distance, Mills had marched back to the car telling Harris to keep up. She was angry for being stupid enough to think she could resolve the questions that had been bugging her for the last few days. Why did she think she was so clever that she could tell when a crime had been committed, when no-one else was bothered? She should grow up, that's what people would say, isn't it? Simon would just laugh at her; Nina would be cross. She shouted at Harris because he wouldn't climb into the car when it started to drizzle, so when she finally left the car park she was in tears of frustration and rage.

Her penance was to have to drive through the dark and rain, with headlights suddenly appearing and flashing past on the narrow road. It took over an hour to reach Hawes and during the drive over Buttertubs she was overcome with exhaustion. Once she reached Laurel Cottage, Harris climbed out stiffly, making for the door before she'd locked the car. The log fire was burning and Simon was lying on the sofa watching the television. He offered to make her a drink but she refused, she couldn't bear for him to be nice to her, she was feeling too weary.

'I'm going for a bath,' she called as she fled upstairs. 'I might have an early night.'

Simon looked at his watch and raised his eyebrows. 'Shall I feed Harris?' he called after her.

She didn't answer.

When she came out of the bathroom half an hour later, Simon was waiting for her. She wondered how long he'd been sitting on the edge of the bed.

'Your stepmother called,' he said.

'Fiona.' She would never accept that description of her.

'She said your father had had an accident. She was in quite a state. She was ringing from the hospital.'

'What happened?'

'I don't know. She said she would try your mobile. I called you straight away but you didn't answer.'

It was in her bag. She hadn't looked at it since she left Osmotherley.

'When was this?' she asked, sitting down beside him.

'I don't know. The message was on the answerphone when I arrived. The thing is, Mills, I rang Brenda when you didn't answer.'

Her mouth went dry.

'I was worried when she said you weren't there,' he continued calmly. 'I thought something had happened to you on the way.' He paused and when she didn't respond he said, 'You'd better find out what's happened to your dad hadn't you?'

104

Mills went downstairs to ring Fiona but was surprised when her father answered.

'Dad? Are you all right? I heard you'd been in an accident. Fiona rang and left a message. I'm sorry I've been out. I've only just received it.'

'Don't panic, I'm fine. I slipped over on some ice in the street and bashed my ribs. Fiona went over the top as usual and insisted I went to A&E. Anyway they did an X-ray after a long wait and said I was fine, just bruised. So I'm back home safe and sound.'

Mills exhaled loudly. 'Well that's a relief.'

'Here's Fi, she wants a word.'

As usual, her father was passing her on to his wife for a chat. Mills really wasn't in the mood to listen to the minutiae of Fiona's life and the delightfully cute things her daughter Flora had been up to. But this time she was wrong. Fiona wanted to know what Mills was doing.

'So how is the gorgeous Simon?' she asked.

'He's fine.'

'Have you met his son yet? Is he coming over again soon?'

'He only visits at Christmas and in the summer holidays. It's a long trip from Washington and Alfie is only nine years old.'

'What a cute name! We must arrange to meet him in the summer.' Mills didn't answer. 'Anyway,' she went on, 'you must be tired. I know I am after all the excitement of taking Hugh to A&E. Flora had to go home with one of her little friends and I've only just picked her up. Hugh's putting her to bed.'

Mills smiled to herself. It was typical of Fiona to leave her father to carry on, despite his injury, because she was exhausted by the experience.

'Everything all right?' Simon asked when she'd finished her call. He handed her a mug of hot chocolate. 'Please sit down and let's talk.'

She obediently curled up on the sofa pulling her dressing gown over her bare feet and sipped the comforting chocolate drink.

'Where you've been is your business,' Simon began, 'but it would have been good to have been able to contact you, wouldn't it?'

She nodded.

'Good.' His mouth was smiling but his eyes weren't. He looked hurt.

The fact he wasn't demanding to know where she'd been made it difficult to begin. 'I was in Skipton.'

'Oh?'

'I was following Callum.'

He looked confused. 'Callum? Callum Wallace, my student?'

'Yes. I wanted to see where he went, where they went, there were two of them. I'm sorry I lied but I thought you'd think I was insane.'

'I think I do,' he said beginning to look less perturbed. 'I know you wanted to get to the bottom of what happened to Wilf but what's Callum got to do with it?'

'I don't know. I just feel that I need to find out what they get up to at weekends. It must be related. Nina won't do anything yet and it bugs me when I can't get answers to puzzles. You know what I'm like with crosswords.'

Simon sighed. 'That's true. So what happened in Skipton?'

'Nothing, that's what's so embarrassing. That's why I

didn't want you to know.'

He studied her for a moment. 'You look shattered. Let's discuss it in the morning when you've had some sleep.'

She admitted she was tired and handed him her empty mug, leaving him to let the dog out before locking up.

Callum waited until they'd unpacked the equipment before mentioning something that had been worrying him all day. Hayes could be quite abrasive, so he'd delayed broaching the subject until he had a couple of beers inside him.

'You know they're saying that Wilf died of an overdose?'

He got up to put more logs on the fire. 'Are they? I thought it was hypothermia?'

'I've been doing some work for my supervisor. He's been given a job by the police, forensic work.'

'Oh yeah?'

He wasn't sure if Hayes was really listening. 'They're blood and urine samples from someone. He wouldn't say who, but I'm wondering if they might be Wilf's.'

'Really?' he took a swig from his beer can.

'Prof has been looking for various drugs including cocaine.'

Hayes raised an eyebrow.

'But he didn't find much,' Callum added.

Now his friend was back watching the television programme.

Callum took a deep breath. 'But he did find some. Now, we don't know the samples do belong to Wilf, but…'

Now he had his attention. 'Callum, you don't know, do you? They could be from anyone. Is it likely they'd ask someone from the university to do the work if they belonged to a student?'

'I just thought…'

'Look, even if Wilf was taking drugs, it's nothing to do with us. We hardly knew the guy, did we? He only joined us a couple of months ago, he was hardly a mate.'

Callum knew not to push him. They watched television in silence until they heard the minibus arrive. The lads were earlier than usual and they quickly finished off their beers. The driver was shouting instructions, doors banged and a line of boys aged between twelve and sixteen appeared. Callum showed them upstairs to the three bedrooms they would be sharing between the ten of them and left them to argue over who would have a bed and who'd be on the floor; they'd just have to manage. Meanwhile Hayes went out to talk to the driver. Callum had made mugs of tea and coffee for them all by the time he reappeared, shaking white flakes from his sweater.

'The snow's started,' he said.

When the lads were gathered downstairs again, Hayes took over, giving them the usual spiel about safety, reminding them they must stick closely to instructions and to ask if anything wasn't clear. He told Callum to put the two new lads through the training course, while he took the others into the room where they'd already set out the equipment.

The two newcomers, the youngsters in the group, listened attentively to Callum as he went through the book of instructions. They answered his test questions tentatively but they were bright and he knew they'd be reliable. They usually came from one of the big academies in Leeds. Once they'd been quizzed on what they'd learnt, he took them in to join the rest, giving Hayes the thumbs up.

They finished late that evening. Callum always slept badly the first night in a strange bed: the duvet felt wrong and the pillows were too soft. He lay in the pitch-black listening to the rain on the window, wondering whether to talk to his supervisor about his concerns. Wilf's sister had died from an overdose, it was all described on his website. That's why he was designing a test kit for his final year project. He wouldn't risk taking anything dangerous. He tossed and turned until he eventually fell asleep some time after two o'clock.

Mills must have fallen asleep quickly because she remembered nothing until early next morning. It was still dark but she couldn't get back to sleep, so she grabbed a thick sweater and crept downstairs. Harris lifted his head when she put the light on but didn't attempt to greet her; he knew it wasn't time to get up yet.

She sat at the kitchen table sipping tea, going over the events of the previous afternoon. It had seemed hopeless last night but she now remembered that she had the licence number of the taxi. She was sure it would be possible to locate the driver from that information. Creeping into the sitting room, she retrieved her laptop to begin searching. A list of all the hackney carriage drivers in the Craven District was easy to find: the licence number was registered to a Richard Davison. It even gave the make of the vehicle, a black Ford Tourneo Connect. Now all she needed to know was how to contact him. It was just beginning to get light when she finished compiling a list of all the taxi companies based in Skipton.

'What are you doing?'

Simon had come downstairs without her noticing.

'Just looking something up,' she replied, shutting her laptop and placing her notepad on top of it.

She followed him into the kitchen and let Harris into the back garden while Simon made fresh tea.

When they were seated, he asked her to tell him what she wanted to do. 'Callum Wallace is my student…'

'So was Wilf.'

'Exactly. So if you think he's in trouble, I need to know. What is it you think he's done wrong?'

'I'm not sure but I think he's going down to Skipton to buy drugs.'

'And that's where Wilf got the fentanyl?'

'Probably. I want to find out where they go. I'd like to know who the other guy is too. I'm sure I saw him talking to Callum outside the Chemistry building.'

'It might be his flatmate. When DS Fuller came to interview Callum, she asked to see a sociology student called Oliver Hayes. And Nina wanted them both in the flat when she came over to speak to them.'

'Oliver Hayes,' Mills repeated.

'So where did they go in Skipton?' Simon asked.

'They took a taxi at the station. I know the licence number so I've got the driver's name but I don't know which firm he works for yet. I've made a list so I can call them.'

'And you think the driver will talk to you?'

'No need. The firm will have a note of the journey, they have to keep records, it's a legal requirement.'

Simon looked impressed. 'How do you know all this?' he asked.

She shrugged. 'Just things I've been involved with before.'

As soon as Simon went out with the dog, Mills picked up the phone, working her way down the alphabetical list of Skipton taxi companies. She found the simplest way of approaching them was to say she was calling as part of an ongoing investigation and just needed to know if a Richard Davison drove for them. The first two companies gave terse replies, no-one of that name worked for them. The next one was too busy to talk so she made a note and continued down the list. Two more confirmed they didn't know him and, surprisingly, the people at the other end really weren't interested in why she was calling. But when she rang Speedy Cabs, the sixth on her list, the woman who answered was cagey.

'Who's calling?' she asked sharply. 'What's he done?'

'Nothing, he's not done anything. We're interested in a fare he had yesterday evening, that's all.'

The woman sounded relieved. 'What time, love?'

Mills had to think. 'Around seven?'

There was a pause. Mills crossed her fingers.

'Right. He had a pick-up booked for seven-fifteen on account.'

'All I need is the destination.'

'It says here the final destination is Horton-in Ribblesdale, a property called "The Cot". Is that all?'

Mills jotted down the name. 'That's brilliant, thank you!'

'Can you tell me…' the woman began.

Mills said goodbye, replacing the receiver to avoid any further questioning.

When Simon returned with Harris, she told him the exciting news. 'And I've got the name of the cottage where they stay,' she added.

'That's great, but what do you plan to do now?' he asked,

but went upstairs without waiting for a reply.

Once he was in the shower she searched for the cottage on the internet. She found it on the website of a holiday cottage company advertising locations nationwide. The picture looked idyllic, a stone cottage not far from the village of Horton-in-Ribblesdale boasting off-road parking, wifi, original beams and a wood burner. It could sleep seven but no pets or parties. Pen y Ghent was close by for walking the Three Peaks Challenge. She told Simon when he came down.

'Shouldn't we talk to Nina about this?' he asked.

'No, she won't mind. She's used to it.'

'Used to it?' he asked. 'Mills!' he called after her as she ran upstairs to get dressed.

'We can get something to eat out,' she called down. 'And we'll take Harris, he'd like a good long walk somewhere different.'

So an hour later they were sitting in a café in Askrigg enjoying a late breakfast.

'This was a good idea.' Simon was squeezing more ketchup onto his bacon sandwich.

'There you are then. It's a win-win.' Mills grinned. She hadn't yet revealed her plan for them to carry on to Horton-in-Ribblesdale after breakfast.

'I still don't understand how you could find out where Callum was going, just like that.'

She smiled, taking another sip of coffee. 'You forget, I'm a forensic scientist.' She put the cup back in its saucer. 'I found the cottage where they're staying on the internet.'

Simon was concentrating on his sandwich. 'So long as you're not doing anything illegal.'

Mills shook her head. She hadn't actually impersonated

a police officer. She'd simply told the taxi firm it was an investigation – her investigation. She took the folded description from her pocket and handed it to him.

'There you are,' he said, after reading it. 'It's right by the start of the Yorkshire Three Peaks. They're probably doing the challenge, all three peaks in less than twelve hours.'

'I know what it is,' she said irritably. 'I just thought it would be interesting to see where they stayed.'

Simon was staring over her shoulder. 'Have you looked outside?' he asked.

She was sitting with her back to the shop front. When she turned round, she saw large white flakes blowing down the street.

'It's snowing!'

'Yes, it's snowing hard. If we don't want to be caught in a blizzard, we need to get back soon.'

He was giving her a sympathetic smile but Mills could tell he was pleased with the turn in the weather.

Chapter 11

Snow fell throughout Saturday, the temperature dropped and Callum had to keep the log basket well stocked from the outhouse in the back garden. They worked until ten that evening, and by the time they'd finished they were ready for the pizzas that had been left in the freezer for them. Callum cooked them with a pile of oven chips and handed out cans of cola. As usual there were complaints but Hayes reminded the lads that they were lucky to get it. They ate in front of the small television, arguing over what to watch, and Callum left them to it, he'd had enough of their bickering.

Before he went to bed, he filled up the log basket for the last time. Outside, the snow was several centimetres thick with a bitter wind that went straight through him.

'I hope it thaws tomorrow,' he told Hayes, who was tidying the kitchen. 'Otherwise we might not get out.'

'It'll be fine,' he replied, taking a beer from the cupboard.

'Don't let them see you drinking that or they'll all want one,' Callum warned. 'The older ones have already asked why they can't go to the pub they passed in the village.'

'They know the rules. Break one and they're in trouble.'

'They won't be allowed to come again.'

'And the rest.' Hayes was loading the dishwasher.

'What d'you mean?'

'It won't end there, will it? There'll be consequences. You can't jeopardise the future of the business without consequences.'

Callum watched Hayes close the dishwasher and press the start button.

He felt his heart rate increase. 'Is that what happened to Wilf?'

Hayes stopped what he was doing but didn't turn round. 'Don't be ridiculous.' He picked up his beer can and walked out of the kitchen.

Callum went up to his room and lay on the candlewick bedspread that covered the small double bed. The curtains matched the pink flowers on the wallpaper and there was even a cushion in the same fabric on the wicker chair. Although he hadn't known Wilf long, and he was a difficult guy to converse with, they'd got on well in the flat. It was Hayes who was the moody one who didn't pull his weight. He shivered and climbed into bed with his clothes on. It was freezing outside and he could see the cold draught lifting the curtains every now and then.

He woke when the rest of them went to bed. He didn't need to check his watch, there was a midnight curfew. It was noisy for a while as they fought over the use of the single bathroom and who was sleeping where. Gradually it went quiet and the only sound was the wind rattling the old sash windows as the storm increased in intensity.

It was Callum's job to wake everyone in the morning. Nobody wanted to get up in the dark but the rule was that they start work at seven-thirty. Once he was sure someone in each room was awake, he went downstairs to put packets of cereal out with bowls and a jug of milk, then he began making the endless piles of toast.

Most of the lads were eating, distributed between the

kitchen and sitting room, by the time Hayes appeared looking as immaculate as always. Callum had climbed out of bed in his clothes but Hayes looked as if he'd showered, gelled his hair and put on a clean pair of jeans. The lads eyed him and said good morning in a reverent manner.

'Come on then, everyone, let's get moving. A bit of snow won't make any difference to us will it?' He laughed.

The day seemed to go slowly. Callum kept watching the weather, hoping there would be a thaw, but it snowed again in the morning and it was only after their lunch break that the sun appeared and began turning it to slush.

'If it freezes later, we won't get out,' he warned Hayes, who told him to stop worrying, it would be fine. The minibus would arrive on time and their taxi would be ready to get them to the station for the seven-twelve train.

When they started packing up ready for the minibus to collect the lads, Callum went out to the front to check the state of the road. There were wide tyre tracks suggesting a vehicle had driven down during the day and the snow was beginning to turn to slush. He returned to inform Hayes that they were probably going to be all right. And at five o'clock the minibus arrived. Callum watched the line of teenagers scrambling inside with their bags. The driver was talking to Hayes. He thought the man might have been the same one he'd seen at the canal but when he walked back to the vehicle, Callum could tell he was shorter and stockier.

As soon as the minibus had gone, Hayes began cleaning urgently. The taxi was due at six as usual but he thought it might arrive earlier because of the state of the roads. He was right. A horn sounded at ten to six, just as they'd finished carrying the black sacks out to the wheelie bin.

Callum took a quick look upstairs in case anything had been left, while Hayes checked downstairs.

'All clear?' he asked.

'Yes, it's clean.'

Together they pulled on their jackets and rucksacks. Hayes led the way, Callum followed, switching off the light in the hall, slamming the door behind him, and placing the key carefully under the mat.

'All right?' the driver asked as they climbed in the back. 'Were you able to do anything with all this snow?'

'Yes, it was no problem,' replied Hayes.

The main road was clear of snow and they were back in Skipton before seven, in plenty of time for a hot drink. The station was quiet as usual, apart from a young couple huddled together on the platform. When the train arrived, Callum let the girl climb aboard in front of them, leaving the lad alone on the platform as they pulled out of the station.

'How long have you been doing this?' Callum asked Hayes once they were seated in an empty compartment.

'This?'

'Coming down here.'

'About a year I reckon.'

'Every weekend?'

'Weeks at a time in the summer. Why?'

'Just wondered.'

'You're not thinking of giving up? They'll need both of us in the summer.'

Callum didn't have long holidays. He was doing practical work that meant he had to be on campus. 'I won't be able to do weekdays.'

'Then you'd better let them know, mate.' He put his

earplugs in and leaned back with his eyes closed for the rest of the journey.

Mossy Bank was often cut off when it snowed. The road beyond Ivelet was too steep for most vehicles and there were no farms requiring access from that direction, so it remained impassable until the thaw. This had caused Mills issues in the past but generally she could work from home for a day or two. And, as she told Simon, they were on strike until Thursday, so what was the problem? He pointed out that they would run out of food and beer quite quickly as they hadn't yet had time to shop, but they solved that particular problem by walking to the Farmer's Arms on Saturday evening and had Sunday lunch in Gunnerside. Harris thoroughly approved of the arrangements. The rest of the time they curled up by the fire, reading, playing scrabble and watching rubbish television. To Mills it seemed perfect.

Simon remained anxious to be back on campus at the start of the week. He'd been getting pressure from his Head of Department to break the strike, although Mills couldn't see the point, since most of the students were supporting the academics.

'You don't teach postgraduates, do you?' responded Simon. 'They're paying their own way, with loans from parents or banks. They don't like to see their fees being wasted by days of action preventing them from working.'

He was pleased to see the snow was beginning to turn to slush as they walked back from the King's Head late Sunday afternoon.

'With a bit of luck it will thaw overnight,' he said.

And he was right. 'Look, it's nearly all gone!' he shouted

when he got out of bed next morning.

Mills was disappointed. She wanted to have a few more days at home before going back to Osmotherley. Simon showered and dressed quickly before throwing a few things into a bag. He said he didn't have time for breakfast but went outside to scrape his windscreen clear of ice. Back inside, Mills announced she'd leave later after spending the morning in the cottage.

'I'm going to work at home to avoid the pickets,' she said, not wishing to be seen going in on a strike day. 'I can give Harris a run on the tops before I leave Swaledale.'

The sun came out mid-morning and by the time she left Mossy Bank the rest of the snow had disappeared.

Simon was surprised to find someone was already operating the mass spectrometer when he reached the lab.

'You're in early, Callum.'

The student looked up in surprise. 'I didn't think you'd be in today.'

'Because of the strike? I'm not doing any teaching this morning but I can get on with something.'

Simon had wandered over to where Callum was working on the instrument software. When he saw him coming, his student quickly closed the screen.

'What are you doing?' Simon asked.

'Nothing.' His cheeks were turning red.

'I can easily go back and see,' Simon warned.

Callum looked uncomfortable. 'I was reviewing the list of recent jobs.'

'Why?'

He was biting his lower lip. 'I was curious about the forensic samples.'

'Still wanting to know who they belong to?'

He nodded.

Simon considered for a moment. Callum had shared a flat with Wilf. They'd worked in the same lab. It was natural he wanted to know how he died. What harm could it do?

'Yes, they are Wilf's samples,' he admitted.

Callum looked crestfallen. 'But we found cocaine.'

'Very little, although the fentanyl was definitely detectable.'

'Fentanyl?'

Too late, it dawned on Simon that Callum hadn't known about the fentanyl. Damn. Now he was asking if that was how Wilf had died.

'We can't say that. This is all very confidential, Callum. Seriously, you mustn't tell anyone about it, do you understand?'

He nodded. 'Of course, Prof.'

Thinking Callum could shed some light on Wilf's drug use, Simon asked if he was surprised to hear that his friend had taken the opioid.

'Yes, he was ultra-careful around any drugs. He was working on the kit for the campus, wasn't he? I shouldn't really say this, but I know he wasn't just using the compounds you synthesised for him; he was bringing stuff in from outside to test.'

'Where did it come from?'

His cheeks were reddening again. 'I don't know,' he said and left the lab.

Callum called Hayes as soon as he was outside the building. He left a message saying he needed to speak to him urgently. The mention of fentanyl had shaken him, particularly as he knew Wilf would never take anything, not even ecstasy – he'd told him so. The snow had almost disappeared on the lawns going down to the lake but the path was still slippery and he nearly went over a couple of times as he ran back to the flat. Hayes had been in bed when he'd left so he might still find him there. But he was unlucky. His flatmate had gone, leaving a note saying he wouldn't be in until late and there was a sausage roll that needed eating up in the fridge, if he wanted it.

Callum decided to send a text, hoping it would result in a response. He said they needed to talk, that Wilf had died from a fentanyl overdose. His own knowledge of opioids and how they worked was not extensive; all he knew was that fentanyl patches were used in hospitals for pain relief, because it was much stronger than morphine. He'd read that it was the cause of rock star Prince's death, and in America it was commonly found in cocaine and heroin. He spent the morning on the internet, trying to find answers, although he didn't know enough about what had happened to Wilf to ask the right questions.

He ate the sausage roll, which had passed its sell by date, and checked his phone before setting off back across campus to the cafeteria. Hayes was sometimes in there at lunch time with a bunch of his sociology mates. The sun felt quite warm as he walked slowly along the side of the lake. He was sheltered from the cold wind by the evergreen shrubbery that had grown up by the path. Several people ran past him in a group; the circular route round the lake was very popular in the summer but not usually at this time of year. Apart from the joggers there were few people about, probably because of the "industrial action" as the

121

lecturers called it.

Despite the sunshine, it was a relief to get indoors again. The cafeteria was nearly empty and there was no sign of his flatmate, so he bought a can of cola and sat near the door to keep a look out for him. He checked his phone but there had been no response from Hayes. He decided to go over to his department but before he'd finished his drink, Prof appeared. He waved, came over to him and flung his coat over the spare chair.

'Back in a minute. Want anything?'

Callum shook his head, wishing he'd left before his supervisor had arrived. Now he'd have to sit and make conversation when he really didn't want too. His headache was getting worse, he was beginning to feel unwell with the stress of it all.

'I thought you'd given up for the day,' Prof said, placing his tray on the table.

He started eating his soup, buttering a roll and pulling pieces off between mouthfuls.

'I wanted to think – about Wilf, you know.'

'I can understand that. It must have been a shock for you and your flatmate, Oliver isn't it?'

'Hayes, he likes to be called Hayes, it's his surname.'

'I see. Actually, I used to be called by my surname at school.'

Callum found that amusing. 'Were you at a private school, Prof?'

'Yes. And you?'

'Leeds Grammar. So was Wilf, that's how I recognised him when he started the course. He was two years below me.'

He paused while Prof finished his soup.

'Can I ask you something?'

'What's that, Callum?' He was busy extracting a teabag from his mug.

'Does the fentanyl mean there will be an inquest?'

'I expect so. It's hard on his family, having to wait to find out the cause of death.'

'But it must be the fentanyl that killed him, mustn't it?'

'We can't say that for sure. Our results won't even be admissible in a Coroner's Court because the lab isn't accredited. They'll have to wait for the Yorkshire Police Forensic Service to report. It could take a while – they're having problems with their mass spec.' He finished his tea and stood up. 'Anyway I've got to get on. Look, are you OK?'

'It's just… I don't know… hard to take in.'

'I know.'

As he walked away, Simon realised he should have offered more help to the lad. By the time he was outside he was considering going back. He slowed down, turned and was heading for the door when his mobile rang.

Mills decided it had been a good morning when she sat down to her lunch. Simon's cottage had been cold when she arrived back so she turned the heating up and took Harris for a nice long walk in the sunshine. You could go for miles up the lane, well it was more of a track really, without meeting anyone. She'd never seen a vehicle use the route and the fields were stock fenced so Harris could run free. Mills was looking forward to the summer, when she imagined the route would be nicely shaded by the trees. She turned back reluctantly after an hour, telling Harris it was time they had something to eat.

The cottage felt warmer after their walk, at least the kitchen was comfortable and Mills shared her biscuit with Harris before he settled down beside the radiator. Mills sat at the table with her laptop open. She'd decided to contact the owner of the "The Cot" in Horton-in-Ribblesdale, or at least the agent that managed letting. However when she searched for the holiday cottage this time, she realised it was advertised on more than one site. It was on "Airbnb" for a single night at a time and her finger hovered over the dates. It was available on Tuesday or Wednesday night but not later in the week. That was to be expected if the students were back down at the weekend.

She rang Simon's mobile. 'Hi, just a quick call, I'm sure you're really busy.'

'I've just had a tutorial. How's it going? Everything all right at home?'

'Fine, it's warming up, finally.' She took a deep breath, thinking it best just to ask straight out. 'I just wanted to know when would be best for you – Tuesday or Wednesday night? I'm booking a cottage down in Ribblesdale, just for one night. Did you want to come?'

'What? What are you talking about? You mean this week? What for?'

She let him calm down a bit before continuing. 'It's just one night. We don't even have to stay I suppose, although it would be a waste of the fifty-eight pounds. They allow dogs too.'

He asked her to repeat it slowly. 'And why are we doing this, exactly?'

'It's the place that Callum and his friend use at the weekends. But it's free during the week.'

'Can we discuss it tonight?'

'OK.'

But she decided it would be better to just book it for Tuesday. 'If Simon doesn't want to come with us, he doesn't have to, does he, Harris?'

Chapter 12

Nina arrived at work to find Ruby chatting to a young uniformed officer called Isabel.

'Issy was talking to Mr and Mrs Marriott yesterday,' the researcher explained.

'Wilf's parents?'

Isabel nodded. 'They came to find out why they couldn't arrange the funeral yet. They're utterly devastated and you can understand why.'

'Issy says that they lost their daughter to a drug overdose. She thought we should know because it could be significant.'

Nina took off her coat and sat down at her desk. 'Have you got the details?' she asked Isabel.

'I've given Ruby the link to a report I found in their local paper. I didn't want to ask them to make a statement since it's not being treated as significant yet.'

'Thank you. It sounds as if Ruby should follow it up.'

As soon as Isabel left, the researcher began pulling out the information.

'So she died three years ago at a summer rock festival. She'd take a large dose of ecstasy causing heatstroke, dehydration and resulting in damage to brain, heart, kidney and muscle. It wasn't clear why she'd taken so much but they thought it was because she'd underestimated the strength of the ecstasy tablet.'

'So not due to contamination with something else?'

'Apparently not, although there's no indication they

looked for anything else.'

'And how old was Wilf when this happened?'

Ruby thought about it for a moment. 'Seventeen or eighteen. He'll have just finished his A levels.'

'I wonder if that's why he chose to study chemistry and work on drug testing kits for his research project. Poor guy, losing a younger sister like that.'

'It makes you think he would be wary of touching drugs himself though.'

They sat for a while before Nina broke the silence. 'You're right, Ruby. Why on earth would he take ecstasy after that?' She stood up and made for the door. 'I'm going to see if Mitch is in.'

Mills needed to leave for Horton-in-Ribblesdale by two-thirty on Tuesday. She wanted to arrive at "The Cot" before it was dark, planning to stop in Leyburn on the way to pick up some groceries. Harris had been for a good walk before lunch and she was just putting a change of clothes in a bag when her mobile rang. It was Simon. She was in half a mind not to answer after the way things had gone that morning.

'Yes?'

'Mills, have you left yet?'

'No, why?'

'I'm coming.'

'But you said…'

'I'm sorry. I shouldn't have said that. I can be there in twenty minutes.'

'Are you sure? Drive carefully, there's no rush, really.'

She fiddled about, putting things in the car, writing a shopping list, looking at the menus for the pubs in the village. Simon arrived looking flustered as he grabbed clothes, stuffing them into his rucksack.

'Are you going in tomorrow?' she called, thinking it would be a rush to get back. 'Or are you on strike?'

'Yes, probably. What time are you driving back here?'

'Depends.' She didn't know on what exactly. Perhaps there would be something to follow up, if they found anything of interest at the cottage.

It was three o'clock by the time they left Osmotherley. They stopped in Leyburn to pick up some essentials in the family grocers. Essentials like wine, chocolate, crisps, nuts and biscuits; they would be eating their main meal in the pub. When they left, the satnav informed them they would arrive at their destination at five-fifteen.

'At least it should still be light then,' commented Mills.

They set off toward Hawes, with Mills pointing out that there was still a little snow left on the top of Penhill.

Finally Simon asked her, pointedly. 'What do you anticipate doing at this cottage, when we get there?'

'I thought we could wander along to the pub. It's dog-friendly, I've checked.'

'Mills, you know what I mean. Why, exactly, are we going there?'

'I told you: the students spend every weekend there and I believe they buy drugs to take back to uni.'

He was suddenly serious. 'Do you think they have a supplier in the village?'

'I don't know. Maybe we'll find out. If we go to the pub we might hear or see something, who knows?'

They drove in silence for a while before she spoke again. 'Or we might find traces in the cottage.'

Simon snorted. 'You should've said. I could have

brought my kit and taken some swabs to analyse back at the lab.'

'Really?' Mills hadn't thought of that.

'No! Not really, Mills. I think you need to keep a sense of proportion.'

The subject was closed. Nothing was said until Ribblehead viaduct came into view. Simon began describing the railway layout his father had helped him build, still reminiscing when they reached the village of Horton-in-Ribblesdale. The satnav instructed Mills to turn down a narrow lane even narrower than the one to Simon's cottage.

'Are you sure it's down here?' he asked as the route became more overgrown.

'That's what the instructions said. We pass a barn just before we reach it.'

Sure enough the whitewashed cottage appeared in front of them from behind a stone barn. There was a gap in the hedge beside the building where they could pull in off the lane.

'Well, the description is accurate, it is very remote,' Mills said as she climbed out, releasing Harris from the back.

He pulled her to the door where she found the key under the mat, just as instructed, and unlocked the door. She released the dog and went back outside for the groceries. Simon was carrying their bags upstairs already and shouted down for her to choose their bedroom.

'Do you want pink flowery or blue flowery?'

'You choose,' she called back.

The kitchen was quite large, with a back door leading into the garden. She went out to check whether it was adequately fenced before letting Harris out to explore.

There were fruit trees, daffodils and a small swing. While she boiled the kettle to make tea, she packed the few items of groceries in a cupboard. Finally Simon appeared, leaning on the doorframe with his arms folded.

'Happy now? Want to start with a fingertip search?' he asked with a smile.

She ignored him.

'Oh dear, we've forgotten the magnifying glass.' He laughed and she couldn't help joining in.

They took their tea into the small sitting room, where the wood-burning stove was laid ready for them. Simon, who prided himself on his fire lighting abilities, soon had it burning well, keeping it stocked from the large basket of logs provided. Harris came in from the garden, ate his tea, and settled down on the rug in front of the stove. Daylight began to fade, leaving the glow of the flames as the main illumination. Simon's eyes were closing.

'Don't get too comfortable,' Mills warned. 'We're supposed to be going down to the pub for dinner.'

She shook off her lethargy, gathering their coats and gloves from the hall. Simon and Harris were eventually cajoled away from the warmth of the fire and out into the cold.

'I think we'd better drive,' said Simon. 'We'll never find our way back in the dark.'

Mills sighed, unlocking the car, settling Harris into the back and opening the passenger door for Simon. In a couple of minutes she'd parked and they were in the warmth of the pub. She was hoping it would be full of locals who could tell them all about what Callum and his friend were up to. Obviously, the students would be in the pub in the evenings, providing locals with a good source of gossip. So she was disappointed to find the bar empty except for a family sitting at a table in the window. Then she spotted two old men seated by the fire. Although it might be difficult to engage them in conversation, she thought, it would be worth a try.

Simon was chatting to the barman while Mills tied Harris to the leg of the large table nearest the bar. When he brought the drinks over, Simon handed her a menu, pointing to the specials board. He had already chosen the steak pie.

'Here's to our micro-break,' joked Simon, clinking glasses with her.

'I think it's nice here,' Mills said. 'If it stays fine, we could have a good walk before going back tomorrow.'

'The landlord says it's going to rain.'

An old man came in alone. He waved his walking stick in the direction of the table by the fire as he walked unsteadily to the bar. Removing his cap, he asked for "his usual". Mills couldn't catch the conversation between him and the landlord, but at one point they both looked in their direction. Soon afterwards the old man turned to make his way over to their table.

'I hear you're staying at "The Cot",' he said.

'Yes, it's an Airbnb.' said Mills.

'Ay, I know. It was my brother's. He's gone now.'

Mills wondered whether he meant his brother had died or simply moved out, but didn't like to ask.

'It's a lovely place,' she said.

'Damp. Needs a new roof but that costs money.'

'But it's in a beautiful location,' she offered.

'Ay. My niece looks after it now. Are you here all week? The forecast's not good.'

'No, sadly we're just here tonight.'

'Doing the Three Peaks, are you?'

'No.'

'For the best. She said the booking for last night called off on account of the weather. That's why most come here – to do the walk.' He was leaning heavily on his stick with both hands.

This was her opportunity. 'A couple of friends of ours stay there at weekends. They recommended it to us.'

'At the "The Cot"?' he asked sharply. 'Not last weekend. My niece heard it was a group of teenagers. Her neighbour saw a bus go down the lane full of lads on Friday night. Happen it'll be school kids, she said. They would've come to do the walk, but with the snow I'd be surprised if they tried.'

The landlord called over to tell him his pint was ready. Mills asked if he'd like to sit with them but he tottered off to join his cronies by the fire, carrying his pint in his free hand.

Simon had sat studying the menu throughout the conversation.

'Have you decided what you want to eat?' he asked, getting up.

She looked quickly at options, selecting the fish and chips. The father of the family by the window was settling his bill at the bar, while Simon waited to order. Mills considered what the old man had said: a group of school children had stayed at the cottage over the weekend. Did that mean the students were running adventure courses? Were they trained instructors or just assistants? It put a different light on things. When Simon sat down again, she expressed surprise at the discovery and asked him what he thought.

'I'm amazed he didn't know much about them if they're here every weekend,' he said, folding his arms, indicating that was the end of his contribution to the debate.

It was a relief when the food arrived so they could find something uncontroversial to talk about. They discussed where to walk on the following morning, asking the landlord's advice, and deciding that they might start up the track to Pen-y-Ghent, weather permitting. When they were leaving, Simon went to the bar to pay. Mills took the opportunity to pop over to the table by the fire.

'Just one question.' She addressed the old man with the stick but all three were watching her. 'Does the same group book "The Cot" every weekend?' she asked, adding that she might be thinking of coming one weekend later in the year.

'No, they were a new booking for my niece. She's quite relieved they're not coming back. She doesn't like the idea of big groups sharing.'

She wished them goodnight and turned to see Simon waiting by the door with Harris.

'I was just saying goodbye,' she told him as they left.

Next morning Mills was awake before it was properly light. The mattress had been hard and the unheated bedroom had left her feeling chilly all night, despite leaving her socks on in bed. She pulled on her jeans and a sweater, tiptoeing out quietly without waking Simon. Harris, who had been lying on the rag rug beside the bed, padded downstairs after her. There was an electric fire fixed to the kitchen wall but nothing seemed to happen when she pulled the cord, so she boiled the kettle and sat with her hands round her mug of coffee waiting for daylight. Harris was whining softly while staring at her expectantly until she finally succumbed; the wind nearly pulled the back door from her grasp as she let him into the garden. The dog was back inside after just a few minutes.

Her shower fluctuated in temperature but when it was hot it was very hot and Mills felt much better when she came downstairs again. A couple of slices of toast did the trick and so she shouted up to Simon that she'd take the dog out. She wanted to see the area in daylight before they had to leave. As she walked further up the lane it became more remote. Although she kept Harris on the lead, it seemed there would be few vehicles coming along. Apart from the occasional birdsong, there wasn't a sound until she heard a woodpecker in the distance. Eventually it was time to go back to explore the lane in the other direction.

But she didn't get past the cottage because, next to where she'd left the car, she noticed two wheelie bins, one clearly marked for landfill and the other for recycling. She let Harris into the garden through the side gate and went back to investigate, opening the lid of each bin in turn. The landfill bin was full of black sacks that smelt strongly of decaying food, although she couldn't see what was in them. Assuming the uppermost was the recent, she pulled it out and untied the knot. Without delving inside she could see tea bags, kitchen roll, aluminium foil and slices of white bread. It would be difficult to go through the contents without emptying it out, so she shoved it back in the bin and slammed the lid.

The recycling was easier to manage. She brought the bin down so it was lying flat then opened the lid, tipping the contents near the top onto the ground. There were endless tins of soft drinks, a few beer cans, packaging from fish fingers, baked beans, oven chips, burgers, pizzas, tea bags, crisps, and biscuits. She counted over twenty cans of drink and numerous examples of each type of the packaging, which she guessed must have been used by the group over the weekend. Who else would need four packets containing twenty fish fingers in each? She searched further down the bin but it was just more of the same, so she shovelled it all back in and stood the bin upright again. She was tempted to have another look in the other bin but just as she was about to lift the top bag out again, Simon appeared.

'I've made a pot of tea if you want some,' he called, before disappearing.

Back inside, Mills carried her mug of tea round the house with her. She hadn't explored the rest of the property on the previous night so wandered from bedroom to bedroom, checking in wardrobes and peering under beds. There was nothing to see upstairs. The only room she hadn't been into was at the back of the house. It was presumably the dining room since it held nothing but a large table and eight chairs. French doors led to the garden, where she could see Harris wandering aimlessly around the lawn. She went outside, back to the side gate.

Simon had taken his tea into the sitting room to get away from the clinical smell in the kitchen that took him back to his childhood. He sat watching the breakfast news programme, something he never usually did. Mills had let Harris back inside, so the dog was now seated at his feet, drooling. He was going to offer him a bit of biscuit but the stupid dog made a grab for it, knocking the mug, splashing tea over Simon and the sofa. He jumped up, cursing, and

135

used his handkerchief to mop the fabric. It was a jazzy pattern that hopefully wouldn't show the stain but Simon picked up the cushion to mop it, and stopped. Underneath was something familiar – a small plastic vial, just like the ones that had gone missing from his lab. Callum had managed to locate a few for him, so now Simon wondered whether it was his student who had taken them in the first place. But why?

He rinsed his mug then went out into the garden with Harris at his heels. The dog ran up to the side gate barking at something by the car. To Simon's surprise it was Mills. She was crouched beside a rubbish bin that had fallen over and spilled its contents onto the ground. She'd been peering into one of the bags and was hurriedly stuffing a piece of paper into her pocket. She'd obviously seen him watch her do it.

'What are you doing?' he called.

'Nothing,' she replied, righting the bin and stuffing the bag back hurriedly. It wouldn't fit and she struggled to squash it in before lowering the lid.

'Did you lose something?' he asked when she was back in the garden.

She smiled at him. 'Of course, yes, I was looking for a receipt. I wanted to keep it.'

She followed him inside and Simon immediately checked that the pedal bin hadn't been emptied. He'd been right, Mills had been going through the rubbish. He asked her outright what was on the paper. She pulled it out of her pocket, smoothing it flat on the kitchen table. There were tea stains at the edges but the words were legible, handwritten in black pen. It was a list composed of just three items: MC1000, ME125, and DK100.

Chapter 13

Mitch hadn't listened to Nina when she passed on the information about Wilf's sister. She'd complained to Hazel that she was unhappy but her friend simply shrugged.

Ruby, however, was more sympathetic. 'Shall I have a look at his social media pages?'

'Thanks. It won't harm to cover his public posts, will it?'

'Just the public ones? I can…'

'For now, just the public ones, please. We'd better not overstep the mark.'

Nina knew Ruby would do a thorough job, she enjoyed tracing people through their social media posts and students always had plenty of material out there. Meanwhile, she wanted to know whether she could send Professor Pringle's reports to the police forensics lab for them to audit, in case that was a way of gaining acceptance for the results. She'd been trying to obtain Simon's permission, but he wasn't contactable and nor was Mills. It seemed that the strike at the university was causing all kinds of disruption. Certainly picketing all day out in the cold was making Nige grumpy, although he vehemently denied it.

Later in the morning, over coffee, Ruby went through what she'd discovered so far.

'His sister's death clearly had a huge effect on Wilf,' she explained. 'He set up accounts on Facebook and Instagram discussing drug-related issues, mainly focussing on the poor quality of drugs available on the internet. He gives advice to festival goers, pointing them to new test kits as they become available, testing and reviewing them himself. His activity on these sites is high all the time he's at university until the end of last year, when it goes quiet. He had a website with a blog that was updated very regularly, again, until early this year.'

'I guess his studies caught up with him. You know he was working with Professor Pringle to produce a test kit himself.'

'Even more reason to keep everyone informed, surely?'

'Whatever the cause, it sounds as though he would be well-informed about drug quality, even if he did take something.'

She decided to try contacting Simon first, then Mills again, and this time her friend answered her mobile.

'Hello Nina, how are you?'

'You sound very cheerful. Being on strike must suit you.'

Her friend explained that she had been away and was just thinking about driving back.

'Is Simon with you? Can I speak to him?'

Mills sounded excited. 'Has something happened? Do they want us to do the hair analysis after all?'

'No, nothing like that. Just put him on, please.'

As soon as he answered, she cut to the chase, 'Simon, I have a question: would you be happy if I send your report to our forensic science service in Wakefield to be audited?' Before he could reply she added, 'The reason I'm asking is because it may speed things up. I understand they are having problems down there.'

'Yes, their instrument's not working. They've called the engineer but it could be a day or two before it's fixed.'

'So, can I send the report?'

'Hang on.' She could hear him consulting Mills. 'Yes, that's fine but will they need to come and see the lab?'

'I don't think so. I'll let you know when I've heard from them.'

Ruby was waiting for her to finish the call

'Nina, I've been checking Wilf's website. It looks as though he's got a friend that works on it with him. There's someone called Gerry who does some of the blogging.'

'Can you find out who he is?'

'I could, but if he's a mate it might be quicker to contact his family.'

'That could be tricky. Uniform are dealing with liaison.'

'Exactly, I can ask Issy.' Ruby grinned. 'Or, better still, you could go to visit them with her.'

She immediately picked up the phone to ring Isabel. Within two hours, she'd arranged for Nina to meet her at the Marriott's house in Leeds.

'It sounds as if the police might use your analyses,' said Mills, biting into a ham and pickle sandwich.

'I guess so.'

Simon had insisted on a pub lunch to make up for having to spend a night in "The Cot". As he wasn't driving, he was starting on his second glass of Merlot.

'That would be a really good advertisement for the new lab.'

'Provided they don't want to visit my existing one. I'm not sure it's up to their standards.'

'Don't worry, Simon, your standards of housekeeping are absolutely fine.' Then she added, with a grin, 'In the lab, anyway. I'm not sure the same applies elsewhere.'

She was referring to earlier when they were cleaning up

the cottage before leaving.

'Come on, Mills, admit the only reason you hoovered so thoroughly was because you thought you mind find something under the beds, and I saw you emptying the dust out so you could go through it afterwards.'

'Well, we did find that list. I'm sure it's relevant.'

'Relevant to what? A schedule of activities probably.'

'Really?' She pulled the paper from her pocket, passing it over to him.

He examined it for a while. 'OK, so it's the initials of the winners of the races: one hundred, one hundred and twenty-five and one thousand metres.'

'Who does a one hundred and twenty-five metre race?'

'I don't know, perhaps a relay of five hundred metres.'

'Seriously?'

He pushed the paper back across the table. 'Anyway, you said we wouldn't discuss it until we got back.'

'You started it.'

When they'd finished, it was raining hard so they drove in the direction of Hawes, hoping the weather would improve sufficiently to walk Harris in Wensleydale before returning via Leyburn. But the closer they got, the worse it became.

'Let's go to Laurel Cottage,' Mills suggested. 'I can check the mail and see if there are any messages.' She didn't admit that she was missing her home.

She realised it was a stupid idea as soon as they got there. The place was freezing cold and they had no milk, so she couldn't even make a cup of tea. She listened to a couple of missed calls and threw the junk mail in the bin. She was about to suggest they leave when there was a knock on the door.

'Didn't expect to see you until Friday,' Muriel said when Mills let her in.

'We just popped in on the way back from Ribblesdale,' Mills replied.

'By 'eck it's colder in here than outside,' she remarked, as the dog jumped up at her. 'Why don't you pop next door when you're done? I've just made some gingerbread. Bring Harris, won't you.'

Simon said they were just about to go anyway so he accompanied her out with the lurcher. Mills locked up and followed them. The heat of Muriel's kitchen was almost overpowering as they sat round the table waiting for mugs of tea. Muriel had produced a huge tin, distributing large pieces of cake to them both, breaking a piece off for Harris, who was sitting obediently by her feet.

'So what have you been up to in Ribblesdale?' she asked.

'Just visiting Horton-in-Ribblesdale,' Mills said, looking at Simon.

It had occurred to her that Muriel knew some of the cottages and people who looked after them down that way.

'You do some work in that direction don't you?'

'I did, love. Haven't done recently mind.'

'But you said your friend does.' Mills persisted, despite Simon giving her a disapproving look. 'The one you told us about.'

Muriel put her mug down. 'You mean the lady from Settle who has the regular jobs? Found the places cleaned with bleach? Yes, she works down that way.'

They finally left, loaded with bags of biscuits and lumps of cake wrapped in foil, promising to call again at the weekend. The rain had stopped and the rest of the journey back to Osmotherley was uneventful. Mills thought Simon was quiet until she realised that he'd fallen asleep.

That evening they both slumped in front of the television and Mills was careful not to mention the visit to Horton-in-Ribblesdale. To her surprise it was Simon who introduced the subject in a roundabout way.

'You know when we were at Muriel's, she mentioned bleach,' he began.

She was only half-listening. 'Bleach?'

'You said something about her friend who cleaned houses with bleach. What was that?'

Mills sat up. 'She met a woman who works for the company who said that sometimes visitors clean the place thoroughly with bleach.'

'Oh.'

He went back to watching the TV but now Mills was intrigued. 'Why did you ask me that?'

'Just the smell. I couldn't work out what that disgusting smell was at "The Cot", not just in the kitchen.

'It's not a disgusting smell.'

'But it was bleach. My mum used to use it in the toilet. I couldn't think what it was until now.'

'Blame the pandemic,' Mills commented, wondering why she hadn't noticed it. 'Apparently bleach destroys the virus.'

The Marriotts lived in a gated estate situated outside Leeds. Nina had arrived too early, as usual. She'd arranged to meet Isabel outside the gate, since she had the code to get them inside, but now it was five minutes past the time they had told the couple they would arrive. Finally a patrol car screeched to a halt beside Nina and the driver's window lowered.

'Follow me!' she called before driving towards the gate.

Once they'd parked in the only two remaining visitors' spaces, they caught up quickly.

'Their house is the one on the end,' Isabel said, pointing to a large detached property.

'Wow.' Nina could see it was newly built and must have cost a fortune.

'You need to go very gently with them. They're really broken up over their son's death. And you know they lost their daughter just three years ago. Tragic.'

Nina agreed. 'Don't worry. I won't stay long. I just want to ask about his friends.'

She followed Isabel to the house, waiting while she rang their bell. The door was opened almost immediately by a tall man in jeans and a black cable sweater. His hair and beard were jet black. She was surprised by how young he looked. He ushered them through a spacious hall into the lounge. The flooring everywhere was beautiful pale wood, even the stairs. The room was furnished like a show house and it occurred to Nina that the property might have been a show-house for the estate, especially since it was closest to the gated entrance.

'This is my wife, Erica,' he said. 'And I'm Richard.'

Erica looked even younger than her husband. She was dressed similarly but her pale blonde hair contrasted with his looks. Nina introduced herself, assuring them she wouldn't keep them long. She said how sorry she was about their son's death, explaining that she'd been involved from when Wilf had been found. Richard invited them to sit down opposite them on the white leather sofa.

Nina had thought about what she was going to say as she drove down that morning and began quite confidently.

'I would like to ask you about Wilf's website, would that be all right?' She watched their reactions to judge whether it was going to be a difficult topic for them.

Erica answered. 'I was proud of what he was doing, we both were. After we lost his sister, we were all in bad place.'

She looked at Richard, who reached out to hold her hand.

'My wife is a psychologist,' he explained. 'She felt it was good for him to have something that made him feel he was doing something positive.'

'It helped,' she added. 'In fact, I believe it helped us all.'

'Did he have help with the social media?' Nina asked. 'Friends, perhaps?'

They looked at each other. 'I guess so,' replied Richard. 'I didn't notice really.'

His wife nodded. 'Yes, he has… had some good friends from school.' She recited a series of male and female names, but no-one called Gerry.

Nina asked if they would mind making a list for her, with their phone numbers if she had them.

'May I ask why you want them?' Richard asked, looking worried. 'Is there something you're not telling us?' He was looking at Isabel.

It was time to be honest. Nina took a deep breath. 'I'm trying to build up a picture of your son's contacts, his friends and colleagues. He was clearly working hard to keep the students on campus safe but, if I can be frank, there is evidence he may have taken something himself. We're still waiting for confirmation.'

'What!' Erica was standing. 'That's impossible!' She turned to her husband. 'Richard, tell them, it's the last thing he possibly could have done.'

Nina watched his expression. She could imagine him reviewing the death of his daughter, trying to figure out if it could have happened again.

When he finally spoke, all he said was 'It seems very unlikely.'

To calm the situation, Nina asked the couple about Gerry. They both stiffened visibly. She waited. Looking more distraught than before, Erica sat down again. Richard put his arm round her.

'She was our daughter's friend,' he said. 'We haven't seen her for three years.'

As his wife became even more upset, Isabel caught her eye, indicating with a slight movement of her head that they should leave. She was right, of course, but Nina would have liked a little more time before Richard saw them out.

'Gerry provided the drugs that killed Louise.' He spoke softly, as he opened the front door. 'Her mother is a GP in the village.'

Outside, Isabel offered to get the doctor's contact details while Nina waited in the car. It wasn't long before she came over with the address of the surgery and a phone number. The girl asked if she wanted to find something to eat but Nina, who was keen to talk to the GP, thought lunchtime was her best chance of catching her, so they went their separate ways.

The surgery was in an old stone building that looked as if it had once been a school or village hall. The door was unlocked but there was no-one behind the reception desk and the waiting room was empty.

'Hello!' Nina called, as she looked for the consulting rooms. There was a corridor running to the left of the entrance so she began to explore.

145

'Can I help you?' There was a haughty woman's voice calling her back.

'Yes, please.'

Nina showed her ID to the self-important receptionist, asking if Dr Chapman was around.

'She's on her lunch break.'

'When will she be back?' Nina asked.

A gentle Scottish accent interrupted them. 'Are you looking for me?'

'Dr Chapman? I'm Detective Sergeant Nina Featherstone. May I have a word in private?'

The GP was a short woman with a comfortable plumpness about her that reminded Nina of her mother. Her tweed skirt and permed hair made it difficult to judge her age but Nina suspected she was younger than she looked. She was led into a consulting room and ushered into a hard chair. Dr Chapman sat at her desk, swinging her chair round to face her.

'How can I help?' she asked with a smile.

As Nina slowly introduced the reason why she was there, the smile disappeared, a frown replaced it and Dr Chapman began fiddling with her wedding ring.

'...so I would like to arrange to speak to your daughter as soon as possible,' Nina concluded.

The GP bit her lip. 'She's studying at York University now. We haven't seen Wilf since Christmas.'

'So he kept in touch?'

She looked wistful. 'Yes, he visited quite regularly, nearly every weekend until then.'

'Did his parents know?'

She shook her head. 'I don't think so. He didn't visit them when he stayed with us. I think he found it hard. I understand Erica hasn't recovered from Louise's death.'

'She's not a patient of yours?'

A sad smile crossed her face. 'No, not since then. She blamed Gerry for what happened to her daughter.'

'How come?'

Dr Chapman stood up and wandered to the window. Nina couldn't see her face as she replied with a sigh. 'Gerry and Louise were inseparable. My daughter went through a headstrong stage after her father left us. I must admit I wasn't coping well. I was too busy to notice, I suppose. Anyway the pair of them started partying a little too hard. They were staying out late and Louise would stay over so her parents had no idea what they were up to. I wasn't taking sufficient notice.' She turned to face Nina. 'They were at a festival when it happened. Gerry says it was Louise who suggested they try MDMA but it was my daughter who bought two tablets of ecstasy, one each. The post-mortem suggested that Louise had taken three times as much as was safe, which suggested the tablet should have been split.'

'What happened to Gerry?'

'She was lucky, very lucky. She was unwell but survived. I suspect the doses in the tablets were highly variable and Louise got the short straw. Anyway, Erica blamed Gerry for leading her daughter astray, for buying the drugs and killing her, basically.'

'Did your daughter blame herself? Is that why she was helping Wilf with the social media blogs?'

Dr Chapman came back to sit at the desk before replying. 'She was in a terrible state, physically initially but mentally for a long time. Erica encouraged Wilf when he started working on the blogs so I thought it might help

Gerry as well. That's why he came to stay with us most weekends. It was like a therapy for them both.' She paused. 'Can I ask you, did Wilf take his own life?'

'Do you think it's likely?' Nina asked.

'I'd be surprised, but who can tell what state of mind he might have been in. I thought he was quite driven to get the message out about the dangers of drugs. He told me he was developing some sort of test.'

Nina had one last question. 'Why did he stop coming to see you?'

She shook her head. 'I have no idea. You'll have to ask my daughter that.'

Chapter 14

Friday was the only day that week when there was no industrial action planned at the university. Mills was lecturing in the morning and Simon had to be in early to set up two rescheduled practical sessions with the second years. It seemed strange not to have to run the gauntlet of the pickets outside the main gate.

'I'll see you for lunch!' he called as he started off in the direction of the chemistry building. 'But it will have to be quick, I've got teaching all day.'

Mills wandered down the corridor to the office, where Nige was already hard at work.

'Hello stranger, you look busy,' she said.

He looked up briefly. 'I'm not catching up. I'm just working at my normal rate.'

'Of course, Nige,' she agreed, knowing full well he was doing exactly that.

'What about your Professor Pringle?' he asked. 'I heard Chemistry was rescheduling lectures against union policy. I hope he's not capitulating.'

Mills sighed. 'I have no idea. He's got practicals all today, that's all I know.'

She sat at her desk for a few minutes before messaging Simon to find out. He replied almost immediately to say that the Head had rearranged the timetable, so he was running two practicals that should have taken place on Tuesday and Wednesday. However, there was no sign of Callum and he couldn't manage it with only a technician to help. Mills was intrigued. Did this mean Callum was off for the weekend earlier than usual? Simon replied that nobody had seen him for several days and he'd also missed a couple of booked sessions on the instrumentation earlier in the week. He'd left messages on Callum's mobile but they just went to voicemail. Mills suggested he told his Head of Department that practicals affected by the strike cannot be held another time.

Her own teaching was timetabled for that morning so she had no excuse to avoid it. The lecture room was full, the students were unusually attentive and she finished feeling it had been a success until the questions began. The students wanted to know what was going to happen about the four days of lectures they'd missed that week, and was this the end of the strike?

'I'm sorry but next week there is industrial action every single day. That means there will be no teaching at all.'

There were groans, one or two cheers and a lot of muttering. Not unexpectedly, the main concern was over end of term exams.

'The official line is that we will take lectures that have been missed into account, either in the exam paper we set or when we consider your marks. It may mean there'll be a delay in your results if we're not able to complete all the marking in the usual way. Thank you.' She made for the door before she had to confront any further hostility.

At lunch she related her experience to Simon.

He grimaced. 'You think that was difficult. I had to turn away thirty students who had managed to drag themselves out of bed for a rescheduled lab session that was cancelled. They weren't happy, I can tell you.'

'Oh dear,' Mills laughed. 'Did Callum not turn up?'

Simon shook his head. After half an hour, he looked at his watch, preparing to leave. 'I'd better go and give the other group the news that their practical won't be running either.'

'Does that mean we might even get to Swaledale before it gets dark tonight?' Mills asked.

'Possibly, although I do need to catch up with some paperwork first.'

Mills went back to her office, where Nige was still typing furiously.

'You'll be pleased to hear Simon is not teaching the rescheduled practicals,' she told him.

He looked up and grinned. It was the first time she'd seen him smile for a while and she'd missed his usual cheeriness.

'Busy weekend?' she asked.

'We're playing England tomorrow. I suppose your professor will be supporting them?'

She shrugged. 'I don't think he's a particularly enthusiastic rugby fan,' she replied diplomatically.

He looked back at his computer screen in silence. Mills wanted to ring Nina but she waited for Nige to leave the office, meanwhile she began marking the coursework papers sitting on her desk. An hour later, when Nige began preparing to leave for the day, the pile had reduced a little.

'Don't forget,' he said at the door, 'no taking work home to catch up, we're working to contract.'

'OK, Nige, I promise.'

She waited for a minute before making the call. 'Nina, I'm sure you're busy so I won't take up your time…'

'What is it, Mills?' It was a bad line and her friend sounded distracted.

'Sorry, are you driving? I just wanted to let you know… It's about Callum…'

'Callum Wallace?'

'He's Simon's postgrad, the one who helped with the work you gave him.'

'Right, is there a problem?'

'He's not turned up today, although he's supposed to be helping Simon with his practicals and no-one's seen him for a few days.'

'So?'

'I just thought, as he was Wilf's flatmate…'

'I know, I have spoken to him about Wilf Marriott.' She sounded irritated. There was a pause. 'I'm afraid I can't do anything.'

'Sorry, I just wanted you to know, that's all,' Mills said before ringing off.

Nina was on her way to Dr Chapman's house. Her daughter was coming home from York for the interview. Nina guessed it was because the GP wanted to be present when she spoke to Gerry. The house was several miles outside the village in farmland down a quiet lane that petered out abruptly when she reached a large, old farmhouse. As soon as the car stopped, two black Labradors came hurtling out from behind the house, tails wagging furiously. Nina wasn't used to dogs but assumed their boisterous behaviour was fundamentally friendly and climbed out. The large front door was opened by Dr Chapman, who called them inside, disappearing for a minute before returning to invite her in.

'Gerry's in the lounge,' she said. 'She doesn't want me, so I hope you won't be hard on her.'

Nina instinctively patted her arm. 'Don't worry, I just want to know about Wilf, that's all.'

She reluctantly opened the lounge door and left Nina to it. When she walked into the room, she was immediately struck by the low oak beams, the window seat, the inglenook fireplace, rugs and throws on the battered old sofas and chairs. It was warm, cosy and comfortable. Through the window she could see sheep and a couple of ponies.

'Gerry?'

The girl was standing awkwardly by the fire. Nina had expected someone less conventional looking, after her mother had described her as being "out of control" in the past. She had blonde hair falling in soft curls round her shoulders. She was wearing jodhpurs and a roll neck sweater. Her slippers had rabbit faces on them. Nina suggested they sit on the sofa before bringing out her notebook.

'You've heard what happened to Wilf?' Nina began.

The girl nodded. 'Mum told me.'

'That's why I wanted to chat, because I understand you ran the website and social media platforms with him.' She nodded again. 'I don't want to go over the reason why it began. I'm more interested in how it finished. Why the blogs came to a halt after Christmas.'

Gerry watched her, as if she was expecting her to continue. Nina raised her eyebrows and tilted her head slightly.

'Oh, I see,' the girl said finally. She looked relieved, as if she was expecting a completely different question. 'That's easy. Wilf used to come down most weekends so we could update the website, write the blogs and decide what was next. It was fine when I was still at school but once I'd started uni I wasn't coming home so often.'

'Couldn't you have continued online?'

'Yes, that's what I suggested but at Christmas he said it would take up too much time. He didn't want to affect my studying.' She hesitated, as if deciding whether to elaborate. 'Actually he had something else going on.' She looked across at Nina, as if deciding whether to divulge any more.

'He's not going to worry, Gerry, if you tell me what he was doing, is he?' she suggested.

'I guess not,' she agreed reluctantly. 'Wilf was working on a cheap drug test kit for students. He was going to spend more time on that. He saw it as a practical thing he could do. And… well… he reckoned he'd met someone who might help him get some samples to test.' She was biting a nail.

'And this happened in the last few months?' Gerry nodded. 'So does that relate to what he has been doing at weekends since Christmas?' Nina asked.

'I don't know. I've been really busy at uni, we didn't catch up much after that.' She blushed. 'I'm with someone in my department now. I think Wilf might've been a bit disappointed.'

'Oh, I didn't realise that you and he were…'

'We weren't, not really. We were close, because of Louise, but we weren't like… together.'

Nina was thinking about the cause of death. 'Do you think he might have been depressed?'

The girl laughed. 'No way! He was devoted to the cause. He was determined to achieve his goal.'

'Which was?'

'To stop anyone else ever ending up like Louise.'

Mills was disappointed by Nina's lack of interest in Callum's disappearance and when Simon confirmed there was still no word from him, despite leaving several voicemails, she wanted to call her again.

'Why don't you wait until Monday?' he suggested over dinner that evening. 'You know Callum is away at the weekend, so he probably doesn't have a mobile signal.'

She agreed reluctantly but while he was watching television, she examined the piece of paper she'd retrieved from the bin at "The Cot". She searched the internet for the things on the list. There were several items that included the code MC1000, including a controller, an amplifier, a handheld computer with a barcode scanner, and something called a variable frequency drive; none of which made much sense to Mills. The only reference she found to ME125 was a dirt bike and DK100 appeared to be a cycle race in Kansas or a set of noise cancelling headphones. Possibly the dirt bike could form part of an activities course and the noise cancelling headphones might be handy but she couldn't understand what the other things might be used for.

When she exclaimed aloud that it was hopeless, Simon asked what she was doing She explained that she was trying to work out what the letters and numbers on the piece of paper meant.

'I told you, it's a list of races and winners: the numbers are the distances in metres, the letters are the winners' initials. It's obvious.'

Mills laughed, she wasn't convinced.

'You just want it to be something more sinister,' Simon

argued.

He made her promise not to mention the subject again for the rest of the weekend, suggesting they find something more interesting to occupy their time. He'd seen there was a steam train on the Wensleydale Railway line the following day so suggested they go over to the last station at Redmire to watch it arrive and leave.

'Why don't we combine it with a walk for Harris and find a teashop for you somewhere nearby afterwards?' he added to make his proposal more attractive to her.

She agreed reluctantly, appreciating he was rather keen on his trains.

'Did I tell you about my train set?' he asked later.

'Yes you did. Your dad created this amazing layout, apparently.'

He was watching a YouTube video of "Tornado", the train they would see at Redmire. 'One hundred miles an hour! That's as fast as the Flying Scotsman.'

Mills ignored him at first, then decided to change the subject. 'We should spend some time working on our plans for the new lab this weekend. Perhaps on Sunday? It looks as though it is going to be wet and windy all day.'

'Sure. By the way, I forgot to tell you, they finished putting the services in this week. My technician has been keeping an eye on it. He says it's looking good.'

'Why didn't you say? We could've gone in to have a look before we left.'

'It'll wait.' He went back to watching the video.

Food shopping in Leyburn was followed by a pub lunch and a quick walk for Harris. Time had somehow gone quickly, so the steam train was already at the station when

Mills and Simon arrived at Redmire. A group of enthusiasts were gathered round, photographers hogging the best spots. Mills waited in the background while Simon took some pictures on his phone.

'I'll send them to Alfie,' he said. 'He'll love them.'

He rarely mentioned his son but whether that was deliberate she didn't know. He obviously missed him so perhaps it was easier to push him to the back of his mind when he wasn't around. There was only one photograph of Alfie with Simon at home and none of his wife. Mills was pleased about that because she was certain that Mrs Pringle would be a slim, attractive blonde with a very high IQ.

After they'd watched the train disappearing back along the track, Mills suggested they found a warm tearoom but Simon had other plans, because England were playing Wales in a Six Nations Rugby fixture.

'I didn't think you were much of a rugby fan,' she commented as they drove back to Mossy Bank.

'I'm not a fanatic but when England's playing… particularly against Wales,' he said mischievously.

'Nige will be watching, that's for sure.'

'Then I'll be able to gloat if we win.'

So, while Simon was glued to the television, Mills looked at the coded list again. She wasn't convinced by the suggestion that the numbers referred to metres run but she played with the idea that it might be metres of something; rope, for example. The only appropriate match she identified was called "Mammut Eternity", a climbing rope sold in tens of metres. She couldn't find a length longer than seventy metres but perhaps it was possible to get it specially made, hence ME125. Encouraged by this, she searched several specialist websites until she found "Metolius Chalk", used to give grip to sweaty hands. Again, the biggest bag on the website contained under five hundred grams but maybe the author wanted two bags, approximately a kilogram, explaining the code MC1000. But she drew a blank for DK100 and, giving up, she was distracted by Simon who was cheering. At the end of the game, when he had recovered from the excitement of an England win, Mills gave him her explanation of the coded list.

He nodded. 'And DK might refer to dynamic rope or descenders,' he suggested.

'You know about these things?' Mills couldn't hide her surprise.

'I used to do indoor climbing at college,' he said. 'What you say sounds feasible if it was some sort of Outward Bound course.'

She tossed the piece of paper into the fire and admitted to herself that Simon was right, she was disappointed that the weekend trips to Skipton had proved to be so innocent.

The University of North Yorkshire campus was usually quiet at the weekends in the winter. A proportion of students lived locally and those staying in halls of residence rose late, hunkering down in the warm or disappearing into the cities. But there were a few hardened enthusiasts who turned out for a run round the grounds at ten o' clock every Sunday without fail. There were around twenty of them, men and women, dressed in anything from head-to-toe Lycra to jeans and a sweater. The route followed the perimeter of the campus, a total distance of just over eight kilometres. It was described as a five-mile fun run but some took it seriously, sprinting ahead, while most kept together, with a small group trailing behind. It was one of the four stragglers who noticed it first, as they were jogging slowly round the back of the lake.

All four stopped to stare at the bundle of clothes in the water. The girl in a pink tracksuit moved nearer the edge and tugged at it then jumped back with a shriek. The others gathered round.

'It's a body!' a man shouted. 'Don't touch it.'

'Is it dead?' the girl asked. 'Shouldn't we get it out?'

'Look at him,' he replied.

They could see the skin was puffy and wrinkled, the face distorted but recognisable as a male. One arm was resting on sandy soil, his face half-hidden, the lower part of his body disappearing under water. It was almost as if he'd been positioned that way. Someone phoned emergency services, another called the university security office. In less than fifteen minutes several uniformed men had joined them, including a police constable.

By the time Nina had driven over, the joggers had gone and a pathologist had arrived to examine the body prior to it being removed from the water. It was something she'd insisted on as soon as she heard that another dead body had been found on campus. She was just in time to see a mobile phone being retrieved from the dead man's jacket and handed to the uniformed officer. She watched him open the cover to remove a plastic card, turning it over to read out the name. It wasn't necessary. Nina had recognised the ginger curls sticking to his cheek. It was Callum Wallace, the missing chemistry postgraduate. Mills had been right to be concerned about his disappearance after all.

Chapter 15

The discovery of Callum Wallace's body resulted in all the stops being pulled out to get the post-mortem results as soon as possible, consequently Nina had received them by lunchtime.

She relayed the gist to Hazel and Ruby. 'The body was found in the water... detachment of the keratin... trauma to the skull...'

'Hang on,' called Hazel. 'Do they say how that happened?'

'Possibly caused when he fell into the water, it says.'

'Go on,' urged Ruby.

'Let's see. It suggests the actual cause of death was drowning but he was most probably unconscious when he entered the water.'

But Ruby was more interested in the toxicology report. Nina carried on reading silently, scrolling down the page before finding what she wanted.

'Here it is: 3.8 milligrams per litre of ketamine and 1.1 of cocaine in his blood. Apparently, that would have been enough to kill him if he hadn't drowned but explains why he was likely to have been unconscious when he went in.' She carried on scanning the page. 'The 21 milligrams of ketamine in his stomach suggest it was taken orally.'

'Another daft student who should've known better,' remarked Hazel.

Ruby spun round on her chair. 'I think you're wrong. He was Wilf Marriott's flatmate, so he had every reason to avoid dangerous drugs. It definitely should be treated as suspicious, shouldn't it, Nina?'

She nodded in agreement.

Hazel sniffed. 'If you think so, but Mitch will say we're wasting resources.'

Nina interrupted. 'It says here he died two to three days ago, probably on Thursday night.'

She asked Ruby to copy the report so she could take it with her to the university. 'I'm going to speak to the remaining flatmate and while I'm there, I'll catch up with Professor Pringle.'

It amused her that she would be going through Nige's picket line at the entrance to the university. There was a large crowd of staff and students milling around the gates as she approached, who became very vocal as she slowed, unable to get through the blockade. An aggressive-looking woman started forward as Nina wound the window down but Nige ran over to intervene. He was explaining something to her that Nina couldn't hear. He would know why she was there. The woman shouted to the crowd to let her through. She gave her husband a wave as she passed, smiling at his embarrassment.

She found the entrance to the halls of residence unlocked but no-one was answering the door to Flat 2. She went back downstairs and out into the cold. Was it always windy on campus, she wondered as she marched across to the chemistry building. She'd asked Simon for a meeting before leaving, so he at least would be expecting her. She suggested they went to his office, before telling him about Callum Wallace. He seemed unable to take in the news.

'Mills did ring me to tell me he was missing. He was

found in the lake yesterday. They think he drowned,' she explained slowly.

'He drowned, here, in the lake?' He seemed to be having difficulty registering what she was saying.

'Yes, on Thursday, we think. That's why it will be useful to know when you last saw him.'

He considered for a while. 'He didn't turn up on Friday… and he hadn't used the equipment on Wednesday or Thursday, although he'd booked it. I was away with Mills on Tuesday and Wednesday. It must've been Monday when I met him in the cafeteria. He was quizzing me about the fentanyl.'

'Fentanyl?'

Simon reddened. 'Yes. He'd already guessed the samples we were analysing belonged to Wilf, and when he heard that I'd identified fentanyl, he asked whether there would be an inquest.'

'Really?' She went on to ask the usual questions about Callum's state of mind. 'He must have been upset by his flatmate's death?'

'Yes. It didn't show at first, but he told me they'd attended the same school. Something he said made me think that Wilf had been testing drugs in the lab that he brought in from outside.'

'That makes sense – he had a younger sister that had died from taking MDMA. His friend told me he'd been testing drugs. Look, I have to ask you something rather difficult, please don't be upset.'

'OK.'

'Callum's post-mortem found high levels of ketamine and cocaine in his blood, enough to kill him if he hadn't drowned. Is there any way he could have got hold of that in your laboratory?'

He looked shaken. 'It's possible,' he admitted, 'but very unlikely. I can easily find out. Everything is locked away very securely. The students don't have access to any of the drugs. If you have time, we can go down and check now.'

He unlocked his desk and removed a key, dropping it into his pocket. She followed him down to the toxicology lab, where he unlocked the outer door and the door to the inner equipment room, then showed her the cupboard containing a small safe.

'Anyone wanting to take something from here would have to know where to find the key and have access to this room.' He pulled an A4 notebook from the drawer, turning to the last entries. 'As you can see, only my signature against any withdrawals.' He unlocked the safe and drew out the tray to show her the contents. 'These are our standard drugs,' he explained. 'We use them to quantify our measurements. The ketamine is in methanol. There's just one millilitre here. I don't work much with it to be honest. Cocaine is usually analysed by its metabolites but I do have one standard, again just a millilitre. Both bottles contain just one milligram of the drug. And here they are, unopened.' He indicated the two glass ampoules labelled as he'd described.

'They're tiny,' Nina remarked.

'Yes. I can't afford to purchase large quantities and, anyway, I prefer not to hold more than necessary. What you see here isn't going to give anyone much excitement. They contain about a hundredth of what a user might want to take at once.'

'Can I ask you about Callum's post-mortem results, in confidence?' she asked, opening the report.

'Of course.'

'It's the numbers. They don't mean anything to me. I'd appreciate your comments.'

She passed him the sheet containing the table of results. 'We're looking at blood, stomach and urine here,' she explained.

Simon gave a low whistle. 'I'm not medically qualified,' he said, 'but I am used to seeing figures like this in papers. They would be for deaths due to overdoses. The ketamine and the cocaine is very high in the blood. They are mixed sometimes, Calvin Klein they call it.'

'Can you comment on the high stomach figure for ketamine?'

'Yes, it confirms the drug was taken orally. That's quite possible. Did he have any needle marks?'

'The state of the skin made it difficult to say whether there were any.'

Simon shook his head. 'I can't understand any of it,' he admitted. 'He seemed a nice lad, sensible, private school, keen to do well in his research.'

'What was he studying?' Nina asked.

'The same thing that I'm doing, separating out mixtures of street drugs so they can be detected more easily. I focus on opioids but he was working on metabolites of cocaine that may be mixed with opioids in the blood.'

Satisfied, Nina waited while Simon locked everything away again. He pocketed the key, before they returned to his office. Once they were seated, she asked him about Oliver Hayes.

He shrugged. 'All I know is that he's in Sociology and he shared a flat with Callum and Wilf.'

'Yes, that's correct, I spoke to him and Callum in their

flat after Wilf's death. But I can't get hold of him now. He's not answering his phone so I thought I'd try the flat but no luck there.'

Simon suggested she try the Sociology department so she walked across, only to find the door locked with a note on it to say it was closed due to strike action. Clearly there was more solidarity in Sociology than the Chemistry Department. As she walked slowly back to the car park, Nina recalled what Simon had said about Callum Wallace. He could have been talking about Wilf Marriott: sensible, private school, a keen interest in his studies. Was that all they had in common or was there more? Callum had told her that he hardly knew Wilf but they'd attended the same school and shared a flat for a few months. She really needed to speak to Oliver Hayes, and the sooner the better.

Nina was back in the office early next morning with a job for Ruby.

'I need you to find out what you can about Oliver Hayes. He's keeping a low profile if he's on campus, although his department seems to be closed because of the strike. If that's the case it will be shut all week. Find his home address and see if we have anything on him.'

She spent the rest of the morning compiling everything she had relating to the dead students, and was therefore fully armed when she went to see Mitch that afternoon with Hazel. It was a tricky meeting but she was giving it her best shot.

'I believe that the two deaths on campus are related, not only because the students shared a flat, but because they came from the same backgrounds. Neither have the profile of a heavy drug user.'

She went on to explain that she didn't think they should believe in coincidences, there was every reason to be suspicious of the way they had both died. She'd carefully prepared her explanation of the drugs found in their bodies, to demonstrate how excessive the levels were. She highlighted the unusual way the drugs had been administered: ingested, rather than inhaled or injected. Finally she introduced two facts she thought most significant: that Wilf had lost his sister to a drug overdose so was unlikely to risk the same fate himself, and Callum had seen his flatmate apparently die of an overdose, so would also be very careful.

Hazel expressed the alternative explanation that they were both depressed, Wilf by his sister's death and Callum by Wilf's death.

Mitch sat with a fixed expression until their presentations were over. 'What about this third student, Oliver Hayes, the one you both spoke to.'

Hazel shrugged. Nina explained that she'd tried to contact him, unsuccessfully. The department was closed because of industrial action. Perhaps he'd gone home.

'Then you'd better find him, Nina,' he replied, dismissing them with a wave of his hand.

In the corridor, Hazel commented that it was no good, Mitch was too busy focussing on control measures for coronavirus now. She went off for a smoke, leaving Nina free to return to the office to give Ruby the gist of the meeting. The researcher was keen to relay the information she'd gained while they were out of the office.

'I managed to get hold of the administrator in Sociology. She's working at home but she can pick up calls via the internet. She says the department is on lockdown because of the strike and the rest of the campus will start following suit next week because of the virus.'

'Was she able to help us find the student?' Nina was impatient to move on with the investigation.

'She said most of the students have gone back home but she didn't know about him because he's a mature student.'

'What does that mean?'

'He was over twenty-one when he started his course, so he may not be living at home.'

'But she had a permanent address for him?'

'Yes but unfortunately when I contacted the address, they said he was no longer a tenant. It was a rental in Leeds.'

'Damn. In that case you'll need to delve a bit further.'

'The Administrator couldn't access his date of birth from home.' Ruby was looking at her watch. 'Is there anything else tonight? Only I wanted to get to the supermarket before the shelves empty again. Everyone's panic buying because of coronavirus.'

'Is it that bad?'

'You're lucky you've got Nige to do the shopping for you.'

'Only while he's on strike.'

'He'll be working at home when the campus closes next week,' the researcher warned. 'Which will be useful when they shut the schools down.'

'Doom monger!' called Nina as Ruby left.

Although Nige hadn't persuaded Mills to join the picket line, she remained at home in Osmotherley, withdrawing from any academic work, unlike Simon who thought doing his own research was acceptable. It was a particularly sore point with Nige, of course, who had made his opinion clear to Mills. She was going to tackle Simon when he came home but when he arrived, he was clearly very upset. He gave her the news of Callum's death, visibly shaken as he described Nina's visit.

'I had to go through the drugs cupboard in front of her, in case he'd stolen them from there,' he said. 'I told her we didn't carry anything like the amount he'd taken.'

He was quiet for the rest of the evening and left early in the morning to see if he could find anything on the lab computers that might point to where Callum had got the cocaine and ketamine from.

'I'm really worried in case he ordered it through the university,' he told her.

Mills was as surprised by Callum's post-mortem results as Simon had been when he was shown the report. After they'd debated the results at length, Mills wanted to ring Nina to find out whether they were treating the death as suspicious, but Simon dissuaded her, saying he probably shouldn't have been discussing the figures, since it was shown to him in confidence.

That left her at a loose end the following day. If she'd been in Laurel Cottage, she would have found something to do, even if it meant a bit of tidying up. But here in Simon's place there was little to occupy her. Besides, the cleaner would be arriving soon. She'd cancelled the dog-walker, planning to take Harris out for a hike but that wasn't going to happen until it stopped pouring with rain.

She opened her laptop and scrolled through the local news sites, studying the reports of Callum Wallace's death. Headlines read: "Second drug death on campus in three weeks", "UNY deaths due to drug overdoses", "Two young students dead in drug scandal". The general tone was one of outrage that the university allowed widespread abuse of drugs on their campus. The authorities weren't commenting but students were giving information about their use of recreational drugs that were frankly disturbing. It was obvious that the police hadn't released any details about the drugs found in Callum Wallace's body. The latest editions were dominated by the coronavirus. Soon there would be no time for anything else and Callum Wallace would be forgotten.

She made herself a coffee before finding the phone number for Speedy Cabs. A man answered with the name of the taxi firm. It was easier than last time, she simply said that she wanted to check that Richard Davison was picking the lads up on Friday evening as usual.

'What time?' he asked.

'About six fifteen I think we said.'

There was a pause. 'Six, for a drop off at the "Anchor Inn", Gargrave, then on after that.'

'Did we give you the address for the onward journey?' Mills asked, pleased by her quick thinking.

'Nothing on the books, miss.'

'Never mind.' The conversation was over.

The "Anchor Inn" was the name of a pub so perhaps it had rooms. She opened the laptop to view its website. She found it was part of a popular chain known for its food, situated next to the canal. It did not have accommodation. Maybe Callum's mate was meeting someone in the pub or was just stopping for a drink or a meal. She thought it odd for students to keep a taxi waiting while they had a beer when there were plenty of pubs in Skipton. So this Friday, would there be just one passenger for the taxi, she wondered, or will the guy in the dark coat have a replacement for Callum with him?

The cleaner was due to arrive at eleven, so Mills donned her waterproof jacket in preparation for an hour's walk in the rain. Harris didn't mind, he dragged her out of the door and down the lane enthusiastically. She pulled up her hood against the persistent drizzle. Once she'd let him off the lead, she followed him slowly, going through what she knew about Callum Wallace. He'd seemed quite a pleasant student from the brief interaction they'd had. Simon couldn't understand why he would be involved with such a dangerous concoction as "Calvin Klein", as he called it. It wasn't something she'd heard before. C and K, Calvin Klein. It rang a bell but she couldn't think what it was. It worried her all the way along their walk but she still hadn't resolved it by the time she got back, an hour later, to a spotless house, with a muddy dog.

Chapter 16

Ruby had spent the morning searching for information on Oliver Hayes. He had no driving licence, which was unusual, so there was no vehicle registration or insurance, her usual source of material. Without a date of birth or an up-to-date address, accessing his phone or a passport if he had one, would not be easy. The world was full of men called Oliver Hayes, many of them living in the UK. Nina had plenty of other work to do and left her to it until lunchtime.

'Any luck?' she finally asked.

'I'm waiting for a response from my passport enquiry,' Ruby said. 'It will take a while.' She carried on typing.

Nina was eating her sandwich. 'The supermarket was out of tins of tomatoes and pasta,' she said to no-one in particular.

Hazel muttered something unrepeatable about people who hoarded food.

'Have you heard any more about the measures we're supposed to be taking for coronavirus?' Ruby asked, looking up.

'I'm just hoping they don't close the schools,' said Nina.

'But Nige will be at home, won't he?' asked Hazel. 'Isn't he on strike anyway?' She finished her apple, aiming the core neatly into the wastepaper bin.

'It finishes on Friday, although they'll probably be doing lectures remotely from next week.'

'There you go,' said Hazel. 'He'll be at home to look

after the kids. If Liam's college closes, he'll be watching box sets all day and wondering who's going to make his tea.'

They were interrupted by Mitch arriving. It was unusual for their DI to come down to see them in the office but he had some news. 'There's been a missive come down from above emphasising that we're to consider our priorities carefully as the coronavirus outbreak escalates.'

'So what does that actually mean, Guv?' Hazel asked.

He sighed. 'What it says, Hazel. We need to be aware that if one of the team has to self-isolate, we'll be a man down.'

'Or a woman,' Nina added under her breath.

'How do we decide what takes priority?' Ruby asked.

'I'll decide,' he replied. 'And that means not working on anything apart from major incidents.' He was looking at Nina.

After he left, Hazel stretched and grinned. 'That's telling you,' she said before going off for her post-lunch cigarette.

Ruby looked at Nina. 'Do I stop looking for Hayes now?'

'Do you want to?'

'No.'

'OK, but don't spend too long on it. Until one of us develops a cough we can afford to, can't we?'

Later that afternoon, Ruby had drawn a blank with the passport. It still had his old address in Leeds on it, as did his mobile phone account. She told Nina that she would have to contact the financial investigators to do a search for her. Before Ruby left at the end of the day, she reported that they wouldn't hear back from the Economic Crime Unit until Monday.

Simon looked exhausted when he finally appeared. Mills had spent most of the afternoon cooking a pasta dish she'd found online, a recipe which had required her to open a bottle of red wine. She poured them both a glass, telling him to sit down.

'I spent this afternoon with Callum's parents,' he explained. 'It was terrible. They'd come to meet the Dean but he'd decided they should talk to me. I was called to his office without any warning; he just introduced me as Callum's supervisor and left us to it.'

'How awful.'

'I didn't know how much to say about the drugs. The police clearly hadn't given them much information, just that it was drug-related but too early to give details. They must have thought I was pathetic, I just kept saying how sorry I was and what a good student he'd been.'

She refilled his glass.

He took a couple of sips before continuing. 'They were such a nice couple, Mills. She's a nurse so she's been working long hours at the General Infirmary preparing for the virus. His father is a maths professor at Leeds University. He came over as very clued up about student recreational drug use but he wouldn't accept that Callum was involved in drug abuse.'

Mills gave him a hug before turning back to the stove to finish off the dinner. She was pleased with the result but the meal was eaten in a subdued atmosphere that didn't dispel once the second bottle was opened. While they were washing up the pans, Mills remembered to ask if Callum had stored anything on the lab computer.

'Nothing of interest. He definitely didn't order the drugs

through the department, which is a relief.'

She told him about her call to the taxi firm, how the driver was taking the other lad to the "Anchor Inn". She waited for Simon to tell her to stop acting the private eye but to her surprise, he nodded, his face flushed.

'You know, Mills, I don't think the police are taking it seriously enough. Maybe they're busy focussing on the virus, who knows. If we know something, we should tell Nina.'

'But…'

He held up a hand. '…or we do something ourselves.'

Mills hid her delight at finally having an ally. She offered to spend the following day researching the area around the pub, in case anything interesting turned up.

Simon said he wasn't going into work again until the strike was over. 'Your friend Nige stopped me this morning as I was driving in. I'm not kidding, I reckon he would've punched me through the window if someone hadn't stopped him. I was tempted to point out that we beat Wales at rugby but thought it best to drive on.'

'So you'll be at home tomorrow?'

'Yes but I've got to do some work despite the strike. The Dean said the campus closure will be announced next week, so all teaching will be transmitted online in future, or at least until this is over. That means I need to voiceover every lecture until the end of term.'

Mills thought about her own teaching but declared that she was remaining on strike until the end of the week. They slumped in front of the television, waiting for the news; the Prime Minister had announced new measures against the spread of the virus, which included isolating anyone with a cough for seven days.

Still thinking about the "Anchor Inn", situated by the canal at Gargrave, she said, 'You know what, Simon, I think we should cheer ourselves up. The weather forecast is actually quite good for tomorrow, let's take Harris and have a day out.'

He grunted. He was half asleep.

'I'll take that as a yes then. We never did do our canal trip, did we? I think you can hire a boat for the day. Wouldn't that be fun?'

One look at the websites of the boat companies showed her that, not only was it really expensive to hire a boat for the day, after all they could hold up to ten people, but also, they were fully booked for several weeks ahead.

'What about we drive down to Settle?' she asked. 'I can show you the Hoffmann lime kiln at Langcliffe, it's really interesting.'

'If you insist.'

She hesitated before delivering the key reason for going down there. 'If we drive back via Skipton, we could stop at the "Anchor Inn" to see what Callum's flatmate is doing there.'

Simon sat up, looked at her questioningly then, to her surprise said, 'Yes, we could do that. I'm fed up with no-one taking any interest in what's been happening to my students.'

As promised, the sun was shining for their day out. After much discussion the previous evening, Simon had agreed to try "working from home" at Mossy Bank, so Mills was loading their bags in the boot. She was delighted that they would spend more than a few nights in Laurel Cottage but was nervous that the broadband speed might prove a breaking point. They drove through Wensleydale, down to Ribblesdale and into Langcliffe, stopping only for Simon to take photographs of the Ribblehead viaduct to send to his son.

To Harris' delight they stopped for lunch at the "Craven Heifer" at Stainforth before leaving the car to walk to the famous Hoffmann kiln. Mills had studied it when working on lime kilns as a new postdoctoral researcher. She delighted in explaining how the kiln worked, with each of the twenty-two burning chambers being used in turn so the whole circuit took weeks to complete.

'Why didn't they fire them all up at once?' Simon asked.

Mills hadn't expected him to be interested in the archaeology but he was a chemist so actually knew more about the calcination of limestone than she did.

'Because each kiln had to be cooled once the lime was ready to be shipped off site. It was a way of keeping the process going because it takes a long time to heat the chambers up. This way, as one chamber burned, the waste heat warmed the next two or three along so they would reach temperature more quickly when required.'

They wandered around for about an hour before calling Harris and heading back to the car. Mills suggested they went into Settle to find a teashop after their energetic walk. She knew Simon would be amused by "Ye Olde Naked Man Café". They ordered cakes with their tea and were in no hurry so they were the only people left in the shop when Mills realised it would soon be shutting.

'We ought to be getting to Gargrave,' she told Simon. 'We don't want to miss this Hayes fellow. The taxi's booked for six.'

'How far is Gargrave from here?' Simon asked, after

paying the bill.

'About ten miles, I suppose.'

'Plenty of time then,' he called, as he followed Mills back to the car park.

The "Anchor Inn" was on their right just before they reached the village of Gargrave. It was a long building, with a large car park at the front. Simon suggested they stayed in the car but Mills got out to wander along the side of the pub, for a view of the canal. It took her through another smaller parking area which she assumed was for the staff. On the way back she spotted chairs near the pub entrance where they could sit to watch for the taxi. It would give them a good view of the road.

'What if he sees us?' Simon asked.

'He doesn't know us, does he? You've never met him and I've only seen him from a distance. I think you'd better get us some drinks though, or we might look a bit odd.'

'It'll seem more than a bit odd sitting out here in the dark and cold anyway.'

'I'll fetch Harris, then it'll look like we just have to be outside for the dog.'

Simon sighed. 'This feels faintly ridiculous,' he said before disappearing inside to fetch the drinks.

By six o'clock their glasses were empty and they'd taken turns to use the toilets. Mills sat shivering, looking at her watch every minute. Simon got up to stretch his legs, wandering in the direction of the canal but he came back expressing more interest in the car he'd spotted.

'It's a limited edition,' he said. 'They cost over a hundred thousand pounds.'

He wanted to go back for another look but Mills told

him to stay put because the taxi was due to arrive. At eleven minutes past six she saw it coming down the road. It parked in the area behind the pub, close to the canal. As they watched, the door opened and someone stepped out.

'That's the guy Hazel was going to interview. It must be him,' Simon whispered.

'So that's Oliver Hayes,' said Mills.

He was walking away from them towards the bridge over the canal.

'Quick!' Mills pulled Simon by the arm as she sprang from her seat. 'We can go and admire the canal from over there.'

She dragged Harris along the footpath until they reached a spot that provided them with a good view of the other side. They watched him walk along the towpath to one of the canal boats and was talking to someone. The two men were in conversation for a few minutes, then Hayes disappeared into the boat.

'What do we do now?' Simon asked.

'I'm just popping over there to get a better view. He hasn't ever seen me so it won't matter if he comes out.'

Despite Simon's protestations, Mills handed him the dog's lead and made her way down to the opposite side of the canal, until she was level with a boat called "Mary Rose". Light from the interior illuminated the path. From there she had a good view of the next boat along, including the nameplate: "Kingfisher". She slowly became conscious of someone watching her from "Mary Rose" and turned to meet the gaze of a white-haired woman dressed in cord trousers, a striped shirt and knitted waistcoat.

'Beautiful barge,' Mills remarked.

'Technically it's a narrow boat, love, but, yes, it is

beautiful. Well, it's my home.'

'And this one?' She indicated the boat called "Kingfisher"

'Hired,' she replied, disdainfully.

'Lots of different neighbours then?'

'Not so many this year. It's been the same people for a while now. They're no trouble.'

Mills could see a figure emerging from the next boat and she hurried away, joining Simon back on the other side of the canal. Together they watched Hayes saying goodbye to the man from "Kingfisher" before heading in their direction. Without discussion, Mills hurried Harris and Simon back into the Mini, drove to the car park entrance and waited. Soon the taxi sped past towards Settle and they followed. Neither spoke. Mills felt nervous but excited at the prospect of finally finding out where he was going and what went on there. She assumed it would be another rented cottage like "The Cot", somewhere remote, and was prepared to leave the main road without warning.

As it turned out, they drove past Settle, continuing on the main road until they reached a signpost for Clapham. The taxi turned right, they followed for miles without passing a building, until finally they reached a sign for the village. When they took another right turn, Simon, who had been following the route on his phone, said they must be close because the lane wasn't taking them anywhere.

Suddenly the taxi pulled up on the side of the road, leaving Mills no option but to overtake and carry on. As they crawled past, Mills could see Hayes disappearing into the cottage. There was no alternative but to carry on down the lane before pulling in on the side. The taxi went past a few minutes later, then back the other way, presumably returning to Skipton.

'So what now?' Simon asked, studying his phone.

'I suppose that's that,' she said.

'Unless you're going to knock on the door to ask him what he's doing here.' He looked up. 'Well, the good news is that we're only thirty miles away from your place. Shame we won't catch the fish and chip van, although we could stop at the chippie in Hawes.'

'Let's just wait a few minutes.'

They sat in silence. It was almost dark and somewhere in the distance a dog was barking.

'You know, Clapham is a good place for youngsters to do caving,' said Simon. 'There's Ingleborough cave and Gaping Gill. It figures. Last week they were at Horton-in-Ribblesdale, great for peak climbing, this week they're doing a bit of potholing. It does suggest that they're running outdoor activity courses.'

'Don't you think Callum would have told you if he was doing something like that. I'd be dead proud to be spending my weekends that way. Anyway, he didn't strike me as an outdoor type. What was Wilf like?'

'Quite puny actually.' He went quiet.

'We can check out what courses are available in the area on the internet,' Mills suggested. 'You must have their CVs, so you can check whether it's something either of them have mentioned before. You could've asked his parents,' she added as she started the engine.

'I really could not have asked them anything like that,' protested Simon. 'They were in no state. Why don't we leave the police to pursue any enquiries if they have to?'

He sounded tired so Mills didn't push it. He didn't understand that when things didn't feel right, she had to get to the bottom of them. She found a gateway into a field, where she could turn and drove slowly back down the lane then stopped suddenly. The road was almost blocked by a minibus with a stream of teenage lads climbing down and disappearing into the cottage.

'Don't say it,' ordered Mills. 'Just don't say I told you so.'

Chapter 17

Mills and Simon had reorganised Laurel Cottage so they could record their lectures for the start of remote teaching on Monday morning. The spare bedroom was converted into a study by setting up their laptops on the dressing table. Mills devised a timetable to ensure they weren't fighting over the space when they had online tutorials sessions with their students. There was space in the kitchen for one of them to work offline.

'We'd have much more room at my place,' Simon pointed out. 'And the broadband is faster.'

'But Harris likes it here. Muriel has missed him; he likes being fussed by her.'

She hadn't mentioned Oliver Hayes since Friday. In return, Simon had agreed they would give it a full week's trial in Swaledale.

'But if the internet cuts out just once when I'm lecturing, we're back in Osmotherley,' he threatened.

'They say we can pre-record our lectures, so you don't have to worry. Just upload them once you've done the soundtrack.'

'Soon they won't need us at all,' he muttered.

'It's the future,' replied Mills. 'Just think, once all the lectures are recorded, you'll have nothing to do.'

The idea didn't satisfy Simon though. Mills had come to realise that, as a dedicated toxicologist, he was frustrated by the fact he couldn't get into his laboratory. He was losing days of valuable research time. He had deadlines to meet on grants costing hundreds of thousands of pounds. Mills only dreamed of such commitments. While he had the spare room booked for the afternoon, she sat at the kitchen table scrolling through searches on the name Oliver Hayes, but found nothing relating to the mystery student. She also met a dead-end when she looked for the cottage they'd seen him enter. She was able to find it on the street view but couldn't read the nameplate. She thought she'd discovered the right one on a holiday cottage site but it was booked through the company so the owner's name wasn't available. She abandoned her search to take Harris for a quick walk instead.

Nina rang on Sunday morning for a chat. Apparently Nige was being a grump due to the coronavirus outbreak: the rugby match between Wales and Scotland was off because of the virus and his department was closing to students, so all his teaching had to be done remotely. She wondered if the closure also affected the Chemistry Department. When Mills said it did, she asked what would happen to her new forensic laboratory if something similar occurred in future when they were up and running properly.

'I don't know, but I guess even the police labs will have a problem if staff are off sick.'

'That's why I asked. I'm doing a risk assessment on the effect of losing our own forensic services. I thought you might be a lab to fall back on if necessary.'

'And what about your own work?' Mills asked.

'I'll be in work as usual but I'm unsure what I'll be assigned to now.'

'So the student deaths?'

'Low key enquiries only, not priority. I want to talk to

their flatmate though.'

'Oliver Hayes?'

'Yes, do you know him?'

'I've seen him around.'

'Recently?'

'I think it was last week at uni,' she lied.

'When exactly?'

'I don't remember.'

'Mills, his department has been closed all week because of the strike. He hasn't been on campus. He isn't in his accommodation. So where exactly did you see him?'

Time to fess up, Mills thought. 'It's a bit awkward… he went to a cottage in Clapham on Friday night. We happened to see him at a pub in Gargrave, then on our way back home we passed him again getting into this cottage…'

'Where?'

'He won't be there now, Nina. They only go for the weekend.'

'They?'

'The lads on the adventure course. At least that's what Simon thinks it is, although I still have some doubts about…'

'Stop, you really aren't making much sense.'

Mills went over it all in detail, confessing that she'd followed Hayes once before because she was suspicious of what he and Callum where doing each weekend. She admitted that at first it was her alone but that Simon had joined her on Friday.

'From what you're saying, we don't know where he'll be now?'

'No. Presumably he gets the train back again but if he's not on campus he could be anywhere.'

'Well, it's too late today. I'll have to hope Ruby comes up with an address for me tomorrow.'

Nina gave Mills the usual stern warning about meddling in police business, while thanking her for the intel.

'If you want to know where he'll be next Friday, I can give you the number of Speedy Cabs in Skipton. He uses the same taxi service every week,' Mills added.

Ruby received the information she'd been waiting for on Monday afternoon. The bank details she'd requested included a reference to an address in Middlesborough, belonging to a Mr and Mrs Frank Hayes. She soon confirmed they were Oliver's parents. Armed with that information, she discovered that the sociology student was known to the police.

'He was in trouble when he was fourteen,' she informed Nina. 'Arrested on suspicion of possession with intent to supply class A drugs, in Middlesborough.'

'Did it go to court?'

'Yes, he got a referral order for twelve months.'

'Interesting. See if you can find out anything about the dealers behind the offence. I'll get in touch with his parents to see if he's staying there. And, Ruby, keep trying his phone.'

She spoke to Oliver's mother, who sounded worried when Nina introduced herself. Yes, her son had been staying with them during the week because, she explained, the university had closed. She'd expected him last night but he hadn't turned up. No, he hadn't called her but he was a grown lad of twenty-six so she wasn't worried. Nina arranged to pop over to meet them, hoping that a face to face chat would give her the names of any friends he might be staying with.

It was a half hour drive through strong winds and rain to a rambling estate, down a road lined with cars. The neighbourhood was in stark contrast to where Wilf's parents lived. Nina found a parking space a few houses down the road and walked back to the middle of a terrace. The patch of garden was bare earth divided by a concrete path. The figure at the window quickly vanished, reappearing at the front door as it swung open. The man who was standing there looked dishevelled. Nina couldn't put her finger on exactly why, it was more a gradual deterioration of everything, his haggard face, his long greasy hair, his stained T-shirt, even his worn slippers.

'Mr Hayes?'

'That's right.' He was holding the door firmly, half-closed.

'I spoke to your wife earlier. I'm DS Featherstone.' She held up her ID.

He turned and shouted 'Irene!' then went inside, closing the door almost shut.

She waited for his wife to appear. When she finally arrived at the door, she was like a nervous little bird. Apologising for keeping her on the doorstep, she invited Nina inside. The interior was drab with a strong smell of tobacco smoke that made Nina cough involuntarily.

'I told him to take it outside,' Irene said, showing her into their sitting room. 'Would you like a cup of tea?'

Nina declined politely, taking a seat on the very edge of the grubby-looking sofa. 'Thank you for letting me come to see you, Mrs Hayes.'

'I hope Olly's not in trouble?' she asked anxiously, taking the chair opposite.

'No, not at all,' Nina reassured her. 'I just wanted to speak to him. Do you know when he'll be back?'

'I was expecting him yesterday evening after he came back from his friends, same as last week. It's so nice to have him here. We don't see much of him, it was a lovely surprise when he said he'd be staying. It's all because they've shut the university over this virus.'

'When did he first arrive?'

'It was on the fourth. I know because it was two days after my birthday. He brought me a card.'

'Did you know either of the lads he was sharing a flat with on campus?'

She shook her head. 'Oh no, we didn't meet any of his university friends. We've been a bit out of touch since he left home.' She lowered her voice. 'He doesn't get on with his father, you see.'

'I understand. I believe he rented a flat before he started his course.'

'Yes, for a year. He didn't go to university until he was twenty-two. Before that he went to college to do a special course to get the right qualifications. That's when he was in Leeds. Once he started at the university, he lived in student accommodation. It must be four years now.'

'So he didn't enjoy school?' Nina asked pointedly.

Mrs Hayes looked at her suspiciously. 'You must know about Olly's problems when he was a teenager.'

'I heard he'd had a referral order.'

'Well then, you know. He got in the wrong crowd.'

Nina nodded. 'He was very young. I expect they took advantage of him.'

She smiled for the first time. 'They did. And they kept doing it, right up to when we moved here. His father put him on the straight and narrow, got him working on his schooling again. I'm right proud of Olly, the way he's turned his life around. That's why I'm worrying about why you're here.'

'Sorry, I should have explained at the start. A student who shared a flat with Oliver has died and we want to speak to your son about this lad's movements before he was found.'

'But you don't think that Olly had anything to do…'

'No, please don't think that. We just need his help to fill in the gaps.'

The poor woman relaxed back. A door slammed and she jumped up. 'That's Frank.'

He was standing in the doorway. 'Is she still here?' he asked, glaring at Nina.

'It's all right, Frank,' said Irene. 'He's not in trouble. They need his help, that's all.'

'That's what they said before,' he muttered, disappearing upstairs.

'Don't mind him,' Irene said, as she showed Nina out. 'I'll let Olly know you need to talk to him and, as soon as he calls, I'll let you know.'

She read Nina's card before stuffing it in her apron pocket.

Next morning Nina was in early to brief Mitch and Hazel. Her DI showed little interest, changing the subject to update them on the coronavirus measures.

'Schools will be closing on Friday until further notice, except for key workers' kids. That means you will be able to send your brood in as usual, Nina. Uniform numbers are diminishing as people with coughs are on put on leave for a fortnight, so you'll probably be on other duties, and that includes Ruby too. I've heard there are plans to introduce controls on the public imminently, so the force is preparing to police that as necessary. You see, this is our priority now.'

'I'll just get the guys in Settle to check out the property in Clapham, in case Oliver Hayes is still there,' Nina said, as they prepared to leave Mitch's office.

He sighed but he didn't say no. Nina went back to tell Ruby what she'd learned from Mills about Hayes' movements. She contacted the force in Settle with a request to visit a remote cottage near Clapham, in case Hayes was still there. When they asked for the location, she gave the description that Mills had given her, hoping it was adequate. They had a PCSO in the area who was happy to deal with it immediately

Meanwhile Ruby was charged with contacting the taxi firm to find out where this driver, Richard Davison, was booked to take Hayes next Friday evening. Nina could hear that the researcher was having difficulty convincing the person at the other end that she was calling from the police.

'It's a cottage in Garsdale called "Garthview" on the booking,' she told Nina when she finally put the phone down. 'He's picking up at six-fifteen from Skipton and going to the "Anchor Inn" in Gargrave on the way.' She looked puzzled. 'Haven't the public been told to avoid pubs and bars because of the virus? He shouldn't be stopping there now.'

'He's going to Garsdale? But that's miles away, near Sedbergh. It must be in the East Cumbria region.'

Ruby typed for a minute then stared at her screen.

'Thirty-eight miles to be exact. It will take an hour to get there from Skipton station. Mind you it's just as far from Penrith or Darlington. Garsdale is in a very remote area.'

She had obviously located the rented cottage online because she turned her screen round to show Nina a series of photographs, saying, 'It looks really nice. I wouldn't mind staying there.'

Nina knew Mitch would disapprove of the amount of their time the investigation was eating up, but she was anxious to interview Hayes before drawing a line under the unfortunate deaths of the two young men he had shared a flat with. She wondered why he seemed to have disappeared, hoping that uniform weren't going to find a body at the cottage in Clapham.

Later that afternoon, Settle rang her back. Their PCSO had found the cottage. It was occupied by the owners, who had arrived from Lincoln having decided to isolate themselves from the virus by hunkering down in the middle of nowhere. The officer spent several minutes giving Nina his opinion of people coming into the area, possibly bringing the virus with them.

It was time to contact the Cumbria force to ensure they made contact with Hayes if he appeared in Garsdale on Friday. She took details of "Garthview" from Ruby before ringing Penrith. She asked for a sergeant who she knew by name but, in his absence, she spoke to someone who assured her the message would be passed on.

'Tell him we need to speak to Oliver Hayes urgently,' she said when she'd spelled out the name and address. 'Please make sure he'll be there all weekend and find out where he's going afterwards. We must ensure he's available for us to talk to him on Monday.'

She gave a few more details then put down the phone, hoping the message was transmitted correctly. Just to be sure, she sent a quick email.

Then she turned to Ruby. 'I hope Hayes is there on Friday. It was just something the PCSO told me about the cottage he used last week in Clapham. It was a comment he had made. He said at least the previous occupier had cleaned thoroughly with bleach throughout the property before leaving, so there are some considerate people around.'

The remark added to Nina's concerns about the student's whereabouts. Women like her mother used bleach to clean. In her experience, it was very unusual for young men to even tidy up after themselves, never mind apply bleach. Had someone reason to remove forensic evidence from the scene?

Chapter 18

PC Leslie Judd and PCSO Cathy Beck arrived at the property in Garsdale at six-thirty, and checked it was in darkness before parking their patrol car in a gateway further up the road, round several bends. It was Leslie's idea that they would see the headlights of any vehicle coming along the lane to alert them that the taxi had arrived, then they would drive down to confront Hayes outside the "Garthview".

'We'll be blocking the road,' Cathy pointed out.

'Exactly, so if he's not there, we can ask the driver where he is,' Leslie replied with a grin.

Cathy was impressed. He was definitely a smart copper. But as the time went on, she began to wonder if they would be able to see the headlights below them and round bends in the road. 'What if he's already arrived?' she asked.

Leslie was confident. 'Don't worry, he's not here yet. We'll give it another half hour.'

After twenty minutes they finally saw a set of headlights coming round the next bend. Leslie turned on the engine but before he could pull out, a vehicle drove past them in the opposite direction. It was a large black minibus. There were no marking on the side or back. Cathy took the registration, just in case, as Leslie drove them back down the lane, screeching to a halt outside the cottage. There were lights on inside now. They both looked back as they got out of the car but there was no sign of the vehicle.

'Did you see the driver?' Cathy asked.

Leslie shook his head. He knocked on the door and waited. Cathy saw a curtain move. Her colleague shouted for someone to open the door. When nothing happened, he announced that they were police and if they didn't open up, he would have to take extreme measures. Cathy knew this was to make them think he would break the door down, which she was certain he wouldn't, and couldn't, do in the circumstances. As far as they knew, no crime had been committed. After a few seconds the door opened a crack to reveal a lad, no more than fourteen or fifteen years old.

'Hello son. I'm looking for Mr Oliver Hayes.'

'He's not here.'

'May we come in?'

Someone, a figure that had appeared behind the lad, tried to shut the door but Leslie was ready with his boot to jam it open. A quick push and he was across the threshold.

'Make sure no-one comes out,' he called to Cathy.

She waited outside, ready to prevent anyone leaving the property. It was an unpredictable situation since she had no idea how many people were inside. She was wondering if it was the wrong cottage when Leslie banged on the window to attract her attention, indicating she should join him. She pushed the door open warily, stepping into a hall covered in rucksacks and boxes. She picked her way through into a small living room crowded with teenage lads. Leslie stood in the middle, giving them instructions. The group had the appearance of a school trip, with the younger boys dressed in uniform and the older ones in hoodies and jeans. It certainly wasn't what she'd been expecting. She looked questioningly at Leslie but he just shrugged.

'Since none of you will tell me where Oliver Hayes is or why you're here, my colleague is going to take your names and addresses,' he said. 'She'll need to see some form of photo-identification: a driving licence…' He looked round. 'Bus pass, student ID, whatever you have with you.' He selected the smallest lad and told him to follow him into the other room. Cathy reckoned he was no older than twelve, a rather sweet kid with a mop of curly blond hair. The rest of them remained still, silently watching her. Some looked nervous, the older ones less so. She stayed blocking the doorway in case of trouble.

'Just relax boys. This won't take long. Form an orderly queue,' she added, hoping to lighten the atmosphere.

The younger boys lined up as she prepared to make notes. They produced bus passes for the Leeds area, all for children under sixteen. She knew Leeds well and was surprised by the addresses they were giving her, which were in the smarter parts of the city.

'So what are you all doing here?' she asked in a friendly way. No-one spoke. She tried again. 'Do any of you know Oliver Hayes?' No answer.

Not one of them had said a word to her except to give their details but when they did, they spoke politely.

'Stay there,' she commanded when she'd processed them all.

She stepped back into the hall to call PC Judd, positioning herself in between the lads and the front door. Leslie came out with the small boy.

'This is Robert. He's twelve. We've had a little chat and it appears he's come here in a minibus from Leeds for the weekend – to work.'

'Work?'

'Aye. He's not sure exactly what they will be doing because it's the first time for him. He plans to be here for several weeks, now that his school has shut.'

Cathy knew too well about the school closures because of the virus. Her husband was going to try to work at home while looking after their son aged ten and his eight-year-old sister. He had grand ideas about home schooling but she knew better how it would turn out trying to confine her energetic children.

'Take him in with the others and get his details,' ordered Leslie, 'while I call this in.'

Cathy wanted to give little Robert a cuddle, he looked so lost. As she led him back into the living room, she could hear chattering that stopped the moment she appeared, and, although she tried asking the younger ones about themselves, they remained resolutely silent. She wondered whether someone had drilled them in how to behave in these circumstances. She was becoming concerned about why the boys had been brought to this isolated cottage to work for weeks and if they even knew the real reason.

She could hear Leslie on a call to their sergeant, telling him what they'd found and asking for instructions. He called to Cathy to ask the lads what was in the boxes. They shrugged as if to indicate they didn't know. Soon Leslie was ripping them open one by one and telling her what he'd found, while she made notes.

'This is a set of scales, and another… no three sets of scales.' He opened the next box. 'No, make that four… no, five sets of scales.' He straightened up. 'You know what this is, don't you?'

He made short work of the third box. 'Plastic bags, packs of them. Hundreds, probably thousands, of tiny plastic bags. Drug paraphernalia.'

Cathy glanced back into the living room. No-one looked particularly shocked by the discovery. Leslie went out to the car to find plastic gloves before unpacking heat-sealing equipment, spatulas, boxes of plastic gloves and tissues. There was even a supply of face masks.

'Here, Cath,' he called quietly.

He was holding up bags of powder one after the other, three in all. He shook his head and put them back in the box, closing the lid. The last box contained several industrial size bottles of bleach. He called Sarge again to give him the news, telling him it looked like at least a kilo of cocaine, and possibly ketamine. He ended the call by giving him the registration of the black minibus that had brought the boys.

'He's organising transport to take them back to Leeds tonight. We're to fetch this lot back with us.' He indicated the boxes.

He followed Cathy into the living room, where the older lads had taken up positions on the sofa and chairs, leaving the younger ones squatting on the floor.

'Right you lot,' Leslie began. 'You've been very naughty boys, haven't you?'

Cathy saw that the teenagers didn't like to be talked to in that manner but they kept quiet. Someone had trained them well. Little Robert, however, looked close to tears. He was sitting on the floor hugging his knees, next to another boy of a similar age, in the same school uniform. Four lads were pushing and shoving each other on the small sofa. She noticed their pristine white trainers, their clothes with designer logos, and it dawned on her where the money came from for them.

Leslie was talking. '…and because you're juveniles, we're not locking you in the cells tonight. You're going home, where you belong. But you'll be reporting to the police station in Leeds on Monday morning with your parents so you can be interviewed.'

This was mostly met with sullen looks but Cathy detected relief in the eyes of the youngsters on the floor. Leslie instructed them to stay put until the transport arrived, parking himself across the doorway, with Cathy waiting in the hall. He told her to leave the drug paraphernalia as it was, but to take some photographs. They would be removing them when they left the cottage.

It was two hours before the bus came to take the boys away. During that time several of the lads asked to go to the toilet. Cathy accompanied them upstairs one by one, confiscating their phones while they were shut in the bathroom unobserved. She doubted they would know who to call anyway, these insignificant workers wouldn't have direct contact with the organisation. However, there was still no sign of Mr Hayes.

She searched the kitchen for glasses to offer water in case they were thirsty and was surprised to find the fridge and freezer stuffed with food. It suggested someone had visited earlier to deliver supplies. At least it meant she could hand out biscuits and pop. Under her colleague's disapproving gaze, she handed out the cans and watched as the packets of biscuits were passed around politely. She even heard an occasional "thanks".

The police minibus had been driven up from Preston. It would be a two-hour journey to Leeds and then another hour back home for the driver. The two burly officers crammed into the hallway while they discussed what was to happen to their charges. They were going down to Leeds police station to have their details taken, before being collected by their parents or guardian. That way they could be sure to see them again on Monday morning, when someone from North Yorkshire CID wanted a word with them. They looked a sorry bunch as they were led out to collect their bags and climb into the marked police minibus.

'Make yourselves comfy, lads. It's a long way back cross country and we're not stopping for MacDonald's on the way. Right, we're off!'

Cathy waited for the police van to turn round, giving the driver a wave as it passed the cottage. She sighed and began helping Leslie load the boxes into the back of the patrol car.

'D'you think they had any idea they were going to be weighing out class A drugs and sealing them into plastic bags?' she asked.

'Of course they did. They'd be earning good money so that's how they chose to spend their weekends.'

'They were well-spoken young men from middle-class homes. I don't understand it. I can't imagine their parents know what they're up to.'

'They certainly will by midnight tonight.'

'Not a good weekend for their mums,' reflected Cathy, 'with it being Mothers' Day on Sunday.'

'My mother is really disappointed we can't visit her, she was so looking forward to meeting you. Anyway, the flowers arrived, so thanks for sorting that out,' Simon said.

He'd been on the phone to his parents for a long time, finishing the call by promising they'd be down as soon as the virus restrictions were lifted. Mills was secretly relieved. Plans for the visit had escalated over time from just Sunday lunch to driving down on Saturday for the weekend, maybe popping in to visit an aunt and uncle on the way. What if Simon's parents didn't like her? It was a long time to be under scrutiny. Simon didn't understand and turned it round, asking if they would have been visiting *her* mother if she was still alive.

'I hope you would have wanted us to meet' he said.

She had to think about that. It was difficult to imagine such a situation, it was such a long time since… well, anyway he couldn't meet her… ever.'

'Of course I would,' she said.

'Good, because I was thinking, perhaps we could visit your dad on Fathers' Day.'

Mills was appalled by the prospect of Fiona fussing round Simon but nodded, confident that she would be able to find an excuse for not visiting London by the time June came round. 'Yes, that will be nice.'

They planned to do a big shop at the supermarket to stock up for their week in Mossy Bank, so Mills went next door to see if Muriel needed anything.

'Are you going to Catterick?' she asked. 'It's pandemonium in there. There's nothing on the shelves, no pasta, no tins of tomatoes, no toilet rolls. I need flour, I've only got three bags of self-raising left.'

It sounded like hoarding but Mills knew that her neighbour would probably use it in a week.

'You're better off going into Reeth or Leyburn to get what you need,' Muriel suggested. 'I hear the local shops have most things and you won't have to queue for hours. They say you should keep away from crowds now, don't they?'

Mills thanked her for the advice as her neighbour handed her a list of baking essentials that she hadn't been able to get at the supermarket.

'What's this?' she asked, looking at the scribbled writing.

Muriel peered over her shoulder. 'Fancy cases. Don't worry if you can't get them but I thought I'd cheer everyone up by making cupcakes.'

She was right, their trip to Leyburn was a success. Simon insisted on buying bread flour, saying he used to make his own when he had time. They bought a bag of self-raising flour for Muriel and a pack of paper cases. Mills wanted to have lunch while they were out – some of the outlets had already shut their doors but a couple were still operating. However, Simon had become quite concerned about getting ill and insisted they went straight home.

Mills was surprised, when she answered the phone that evening, to hear her father's voice. He never contacted her except in an emergency, it was always Fiona that made the call.

'Millie? I just thought I'd see how you are.'

Mills laughed. 'Did Fiona ask you to call?'

'No, well not exactly. She's been chattering away for hours with her mother so I thought I should… we don't… do we? Are you all right up there? How are the shops? Can you get what you need?'

She explained they were fine, hunkering down in the dale. She asked what it was like in London.

'Not very good. Fi is having difficulty with her Ocado orders so we went down to Waitrose, which pretty bare. We don't have a lot of storage space in the fridge/freezer so we can't buy much. Flora's school has closed so she'll be home all week from tomorrow.'

'How will Fiona be able to cope with that? Although I suppose she won't be doing any of her classes and coffee mornings, lunches and therapies now. You'll save a fortune!'

'Not exactly. She does the classes online now. It will be very disruptive when I'm working at home from next week. I'm only going into the office tomorrow to get the things I need.'

'It's going to be quite cosy in the apartment then.'

'Yes, it will be.' He sounded resigned.

She told him about the university closure, how she and Simon were supposed to have been visiting his parents this weekend. They would be fine but she was worried about her father, stuck in the middle of Canary Wharf, telling him to stay indoors.

'I'm not quite in the old and vulnerable category yet, Millie,' he said.

'But you shouldn't be travelling on the tube,' she said. 'Do be careful.'

She hadn't realised how much she cared about her father's wellbeing. Although she rarely saw him, he was always there, the only real family she had. When he asked if she wanted to speak to Fiona she said not to worry and put the phone down.

'What's up?' Simon could obviously see she was close to tears.

She forced a smile. 'I've just realised, it would have been nice to be able to see Dad.'

'We can, in June when this is over.'

'Do you really think so?'

Chapter 19

Nina was driving while her colleague was stretched out with her eyes closed. It had been an early start on a Monday morning for both of them, but Hazel had protested the loudest. Nina, who fully expected Oliver Hayes to be found at the cottage in Garsdale, was surprised to hear they were to interview twelve juveniles from Leeds instead.

'So why exactly are we interested in these lads?' Hazel asked, sitting up and rolling her shoulders.

'Because they were shipped in a minibus to a remote cottage in the Yorkshire Dales to pack class A drugs for a County Lines gang from Leeds.'

'That's not supposed to be our problem.'

'It is, because the cottage where they were found with bags of cocaine, ecstasy and ketamine, is where we thought we would locate Oliver Hayes.'

'The guy I interviewed at the university?'

'Yes.'

'Sociologist studying economics and politics. Bought me a coffee. Very polite. Public school type. Quite good looking.'

'And also a dealer in Class A drugs.'

'We don't know that, do we?'

'I think we do, Hazel. He visits a different cottage every weekend along with his flatmates. There they are joined by a dozen school kids employed to pack drugs. Hopefully they will give us the evidence we need to prove it today. If the Leeds force can trace the minibus that transports the children, we can locate the owner. With any luck, we'll get a description of the driver today. It obviously isn't Hayes, someone else brings the equipment and drugs to the cottage ready for them when they arrive. Presumably Hayes is simply a middleman who supervises the work.'

'So why wasn't he with the kids?'

'I've been wondering about that. When their minibus arrived, uniform parked their patrol car outside the cottage. It would have been an obvious warning to Hayes if he arrived later.'

'You think the taxi just turned round and went back to Skipton with Hayes? In that case the driver will be able to tell us.'

'You're right. Meanwhile, we've got to finish deciding how we're going to handle the interviews.'

Eventually Hazel had to agree that they should split the juveniles into two groups. They argued about how to divide them up but Nina pointed out it was sensible for Hazel to take the older boys, since her son was closer to their age.

'We've no evidence that they've done anything wrong yet,' Nina warned. 'So the aim is to get as much information as possible about the adults involved in the packaging factory. So please go gently on them,' she begged. 'We need to make them feel comfortable talking to us. Apparently, they wouldn't tell uniform anything in Cumbria.'

'What about in Leeds? They must have processed them there.'

'We'll soon find out.'

They were pulling up outside a modern red brick building. Inside they were directed to a large room where the juveniles were seated. They each had an adult with them, except for two bigger lads who were sitting with their legs stretched out, a uniform officer on either side. One of the PCs came over to introduce himself, providing Nina with a list of names.

'They're all here, except two who haven't turned up yet. It was very late when they arrived here on Friday night so we didn't question them then, just a quick search and fingerprints when their parents arrived. Two of them weren't met by an adult, so they were taken straight home. We've kept them apart as best we can in here.'

'Thanks,' said Nina. 'I assume one of you will want to sit in on the interviews. We thought we'd take half of them each.'

'No need. We'll record them. We don't want to crowd them, do we?'

Nina was relieved. Some of the lads on the list were very young and she wanted to put them at their ease. She chose the six youngest, made a quick note of their names before handing the paper to Hazel. Will you take the older ones then?'

'Sure, they look more civilised than Liam.'

They were shown to the interview suite and were allocated a PC each to fetch the boys in, one by one. Nina wished Hazel luck, went into her allocated room and waited. She had ordered the boys by age, starting with the youngest, but was still surprised to see how immature the first lad appeared. Robert was twelve, hardly out of primary school, she thought. He was accompanied by his mother, a chubby woman dressed in a black trouser suit. Her son was equally smart, in grey trousers, a white shirt, striped tie and a black sweater. Nina suspected it was basically his school uniform without the blazer.

Nina introduced herself to Mrs Huyton, explaining that Robert had not been arrested but he was found at a property where drug paraphernalia had been seized. Her job was to understand why he was there, who had taken him and what he was proposing to do there.

Mrs Huyton was shaking visibly. She knew nothing about what had been going on. She thought he was on a school trip, that's what he'd told her. She thought he was safe – anything could have happened to him. She made Nina feel guilty for not keeping him out of harm's way. When asked if Robert was happy to answer some questions, his mother said he was.

'We talked it over with Dad, didn't we Rob, and it's best to be honest, isn't it? Whatever the consequences.'

He nodded in agreement.

'Robert,' Nina began gently. His large eyes were fixed on her. 'Can you tell me how you came to be in the cottage on Friday night?'

'We went in a minibus. We had to meet outside the station at five o'clock.'

'I took him there,' his mother explained, near to tears. 'I thought he was going on an adventure course.'

It wasn't quite what Nina had meant. 'But who told you about the work?'

'Neil French, he's in my class.'

Nina consulted her list. He was aged thirteen.

'And how did he know?'

'He'd been before – at the weekends.'

'Did *his* mother know?' Mrs Huyton demanded.

Nina ignored her. 'So he told you about the work he'd been doing?'

'Not exactly. Not in detail. He said it was easy and they paid a hundred pound, just for a day's work. He got two hundred pounds extra just for recruiting me.'

Nina made a note to ask Neil for his contacts.

'So, did Neil tell you what you would be doing?'

'Sort of.'

'Which was?'

'Weighing things out and putting them in bags.'

'What things?'

He looked at the floor.

'Things like drugs?' Nina asked gently.

His mother had hold of his arm. 'Tell her, Rob.'

'Mrs Huyton, please…' Nina insisted.

The boy nodded. 'Yes. But it was the first time. I didn't touch anything.'

'I know, Robert,' Nina said calmly. 'I just want to find out about the people organising this… work. Did you see any adults when you met the minibus, for example?'

'Just the driver.'

'Did you see his face?'

'I sat behind him so I only saw his head. He had a tattoo up the back of his neck.'

'A picture?'

'Might've been. It was dark in the bus. I fell asleep.'

Hazel decided to start with the oldest lad first. He didn't want an adult with him so she thought he would be easier to deal with. She also believed he would know most about the drug operation.

'Gavin, is it?' she asked.

He leaned back on his chair, hands in pockets, chewing gum. 'Yes.'

'This can be over very quickly if you just answer the questions for me. I'm investigating two suspicious deaths that may be linked to the men that pay for your designer trainers. I'm not interested in your petty drug dealing; I want to know where I can find your bosses. Understand?'

The lad looked like Liam after she's told him he'd have to make his own tea: he hid the shock well but the anger persisted.

'Have you met any of these people?' No answer. 'What about Oliver Hayes?' Did she see a hint of recognition?

'No comment.'

'No, don't do that, Gavin. Please don't do that.'

But he persisted and soon she was letting the sixteen-year-old out to be replaced by the boy who was a year younger but still refused to have an adult with him. She had less success with him. Hopefully her colleague was having more luck.

Nina was talking to Neil, who sat between his very pleasant parents, Mr and Mrs French. They wanted her to understand that they were horrified by his behaviour. They had sent him to one of the best schools in Leeds to avoid him getting into exactly this sort of trouble. He had assured them that he'd never touched any drugs and they believed him. He was drawn into it for the money because he was saving for a fancy mobile.

Nina let them talk then turned to their son. He was a nerdy-looking kid with black-rimmed glasses and braces on his teeth.

'So how did you come across this work?' she asked softly.

He sat up straight. 'Instagram.' He answered

confidently, like someone on Mastermind.

'It was advertised on Instagram?' She tried not to sound shocked.

'Yes.' He looked up to the ceiling, as if trying to recollect the wording. 'It said the pay was good, you could work weekends and transport was provided.' Perhaps he had a photographic memory. 'You just clicked to find out more then they rang you.'

'You knew that it wasn't legal?'

'I guessed quite soon. They said to tell Mum and Dad it was a school activity weekend.'

His parents were looking at each other across the top of his head.

Nina continued. 'Tell me about the driver of the minibus. What did he look like?'

He thought for a moment. 'He had dark hair.'

'Anything else?'

He shook his head.

'So tell me about how you spent the weekends once you got to the cottages.'

It turned out he'd only been away twice before but the procedure had been the same both times. They would be picked up at Leeds railway station on Friday evening and driven to the Yorkshire Dales, where everything was set up ready to go. On the first occasion he was shown how to weigh out the powder and pack it into plastic bags before heat sealing them. Once the guy called Callum had trained him, he was given his tasks by a man called Hayes. They worked until late into the evening and all day each day until it was time to tidy up. Everything had to be packed away before the minibus came to fetch them at five o' clock.

'So you would be there until Sunday evening?'

'School's closed because of the virus so we were supposed to be there for a week this time. Then we were moving somewhere for a second week.'

'We thought he was at a special school camp for bright lads,' his father said through tight lips.

Nina suppressed a smile. 'Tell me about Callum and Hayes. Were they in contact with anyone else?'

'I don't know. They didn't speak to us except to tell us what to do. But they were all right.'

It seemed the boys were well-treated, had food and drinks, beds to sleep in or found places that were comfortable enough. The work was hard but they had breaks, wore protective gloves and were well paid at the end. Very well paid in fact, at a hundred pounds a day.

Hazel saw just two more lads, both aged fifteen. The last two on the list still hadn't shown up. She tried a gentler approach with them but she didn't fare any better. They listened to her politely while she explained that she needed to know who the ringleaders were.

'This is a County Lines operation, isn't it?' she asked each in turn. 'The bosses are safely tucked up in Leeds and you're sent into the wilds of the Dales to do their dirty work, preparing the merchandise for distribution across North Yorkshire. I'm not interested in what you've been up to, I just need a name, the name of whoever it was down here who contacted you.'

Both lads gave her the same answer: it was on social media. One had answered a Facebook ad, the other saw it on Instagram. All they knew was to join the minibus outside the station on Friday evening at five.

'But what if there's a change of plan?'

It was all done on social media, they repeated. They were always picked up and dropped off at the same place, at the same time. They were paid in cash at the end of their shift, before leaving the cottage in the minibus. They couldn't describe the driver.

She escorted her last interviewee and his father to the main entrance, past one of the PCs who'd been responsible for shepherding the boys in and out. As soon as she returned, he passed on the message that the minibus had been identified.

At last, she thought, some useful information. 'Is there a name?'

'It's a legit taxi firm. They do regular runs to the Dales with the kids, paid in advance. They thought a school was doing the bookings. Apparently, the driver was given the money for the fare when he arrived to pick them up. They were told it was easier for the school because the lads each paid for the trip in cash.'

'No contact details, I suppose?'

'No, just a mobile and not always the same number.'

She suggested they should check if they were still getting bookings. The answer was no but the taxi company wasn't surprised as all their school runs had been cancelled because of the closures.

When Nina had finished her interviews, she joined Hazel for a quick sandwich to compare notes. She soon reckoned she'd had more success than her colleague.

'I've got a partial description of the minibus driver,' she began.

Hazel laughed. 'It belongs to a local taxi firm. They thought it was a school outing.' She explained what she'd been told.

Nina pulled a face. She told Hazel what Neil had described to her as the routine. 'It's very organised. They target private school kids so they don't raise suspicion – young well-spoken white males. My youngest was twelve, the oldest fourteen. They're contacted via social media or they get them to recruit their friends. They're told to say it's a school trip – outdoor pursuits or football training, something like that.'

'I bet the parents are peeved after paying exorbitant school fees to find their little darlings are involved in County Lines.'

'It could've been a lot worse. They seem to have been well treated while they were away.'

'And they come away with a hundred pounds a day. I bet they thought it was Christmas getting a gig for a whole two weeks!'

'How did you get on?' Nina asked.

Hazel snorted. 'Three of them refused an adult and effectively did a "no comment". The last one came in with his dad, who glared at me throughout the interview. His son was fifteen and a bit less mature than his mates so he was fidgeting in his seat the entire time. The only useful bit of information he gave me was how much he'd been paid.'

'Our best bet is to find Oliver Hayes,' Nina suggested. 'He should have been there on Friday night. If he saw the police were at the cottage, he's probably hiding now. I'll check he's not gone back to Middlesborough.'

She used her mobile to contact Mrs Hayes, who answered her call immediately but her son had not reappeared. 'Do you think something's happened to him?' she asked.

Nina tried to reassure her without even knowing

whether he was still alive.

'I think we should drop in at the university, just in case he's gone back there,' she told Hazel, as they drove out of the city. 'After that, I don't know where else we can look.'

The university campus appeared deserted. They had to ask a security guard to let them into the accommodation block. He accompanied them to the door of Flat 2 and when there was no answer, asked if they wanted to go inside. The place was even tidier than when Nina had visited it before. They checked the three bedrooms in turn. The first had been cleared of anything personal, so the drawers and wardrobe were empty, the bedding had been removed, the ensuite bathroom was bare.

'This room was Wilf's,' Nina explained.

In the next room the bed was unmade, there were clothes on the floor, and the bathroom full of personal items. There was a photograph on the wall of a girl and boy.

'Looks like Callum Wallace,' Nina told Hazel, who agreed.

The third room was immaculate: the bed was made, just a few clothes hung in the wardrobe, including a long black coat that Hazel recognised.

'This one belongs to Oliver Hayes,' Hazel said.

Nina agreed. 'It's the biggest and he was the most senior. But he seems to have taken most of his stuff with him.'

They thanked the security guard, who locked up the flat and accompanied them to the car.

On the way back, Hazel stated that it had been a wasted journey. 'The whole day was a dead loss,' she complained. 'If the aim was to locate the missing Hayes lad, we've got zilch, apart from knowing where he isn't.'

Nina turned on the radio; she wanted to hear the broadcast by the Prime Minister about measures to control coronavirus. It was shocking news. On top of the closure of pubs and schools, the public were asked to stay at home and only make essential journeys for food and medicine. Shops were to shut unless selling essential goods and there were to be no public gatherings. Everyone had to keep two metres apart. Nina and Hazel looked at each.

'I guess as key workers, we just keep going,' Nina said. 'Can't see us working at home any time soon.'

'You heard what he said, if the public don't follow the rules the police will have the powers to enforce them, including fines and dispersing gatherings.'

Hazel groaned. 'We'll be on crowd control duty before you know it.'

'Then we'd better find Oliver Hayes quickly. You said he seemed like a nice young man. It shouldn't be difficult to persuade him to give us the important people in the County Lines operation.'

'You think? He's probably terrified of them if he suspects they were responsible for his flatmates' demise. No wonder he's gone into hiding.'

Chapter 20

It was chaos in the Featherstone household when Nina eventually arrived home. Nige was on his knees, scrubbing at the sitting room carpet while Rosie watched from a safe distance in tears. The boys, who were playing superheroes, were running up and down stairs dressed only in their underpants. Nige looked up, wiping his forehead with the back of his hand while the sponge dripped water on his jeans.

'If I'm stuck indoors with these three all day, every day, we need a bigger house. How do I get this carpet clean?'

'I was doing you a picture,' Rosie explained between sobs.

Nina gave her a hug. 'Best put newspaper down next time, love.'

She went into the kitchen to see what was cooking.

'I've ordered pizzas,' Nige called.

Nina counted to ten before joining them. 'Good. I suggest we have baths now, before it arrives.'

Everything calmed down once the children were in their pyjamas. Nige had worn them out with activities during the day. He admitted that he'd probably been over enthusiastic. 'Rosie did a bit of schoolwork but Owen and Tomos just messed about all day,' he complained.

Nina found a stain remover under the kitchen sink, which took most of the redness out, then laid the table.

'Did you hear the latest measures?' he asked. 'It's total lockdown. I need to get to the supermarket to stock up on beer. If "The Crown" wasn't shut, I'd be down there right now to recover with a pint or two. And we need more snacks now we're home all day.'

'You're not going shopping now? What about the pizzas?'

'Save me some. I won't be long.'

The delivery arrived soon after he'd gone. The children cleaned their teeth when they'd eaten and went straight to bed without a fuss. Nina cleared the plates, poured herself a large glass of wine and sat looking into space. Hazel had been right, it had been a shit day – like Nige, she would have enjoyed a night out at "The Crown" too. Perhaps it was thinking about pub closures that triggered a recollection of an inn Ruby had mentioned. It had been on the taxi booking taken by Hayes but, because the pub wasn't operating, they assumed he wouldn't be stopping there. Mills had also mentioned a pub but she couldn't remember why.

She picked up the phone, trying her friend's mobile and her Osmotherley number before she finally got a response on her Swaledale landline.

'Hi Mills, I thought I'd see how, and where, you were,' she began lightly.

'We're at my place. I managed to persuade Simon it's the best spot, especially after the latest announcements.'

'You heard?'

'Yes. But what about you? It's easy for us to self-isolate but will you be carrying on regardless?'

'Afraid so. Nige is doing a grand job keeping the kids occupied, although the house might be wrecked by the end of it.'

They talked for a long time before Nina felt ready to

introduce the topic.

'Mills, can I check what you told me about seeing Oliver Hayes in the Dales?'

'Sure.' She sounded hesitant.

'Did you say you saw him at a pub?'

'Yes, "The Anchor" at Gargrave.'

'So it was open then?'

'Yes, although… well, he didn't go inside.'

'So why was he there?'

'It's right next to the canal. He was visiting someone on a boat.'

'That's interesting.' Nina was deciding how much information to divulge. 'I should explain, we're still trying to find him to ask a few questions. Did you see which boat it was?'

'It was called "Kingfisher".' She paused, then added, 'It was a very pretty narrow boat.'

Nina used her stern voice. 'I'm sure it was, Mills. We may need to see if he's still there.' She ended the call by telling her friend to stay safe.

It occurred to Nina that if Hayes visited the boat before travelling to Garsdale, he may have returned there when he saw the police presence at the cottage, or had simply never left the boat that evening. A boat that might be owned by one of the County Lines gang.

She was disturbed by Nige slamming the front door. He'd returned with some of the items they needed but the list of things unavailable was even longer. It had been mayhem, he announced, as he put things away in the kitchen. When she told him she'd spoken to Mills, he remarked that he wished he was living in the middle of nowhere like her, preferably somewhere like Snowdonia.

Nina travelled to work early next morning to catch Ruby before Hazel and Mitch arrived. She described her interviews with the boys in Leeds and how they were driven to the Dales by taxi.

'They don't know where Hayes is, and he's not at the university or his parents place. The only lead is a boat called "Kingfisher" on the canal at Gargrave.'

'How did you…'

Nina held up her hand. 'Don't ask.'

Her phone rang. It was Mitch, telling her there would be an update for everyone in ten minutes. Hazel appeared just in time and they went along to the meeting room together. The atmosphere was buzzing as they waited to hear from their Chief Inspector. Everyone stopped talking suddenly when he appeared and they remained silent throughout his announcements. He confirmed that major investigations would take priority but warned that staff shortages would occur if members of staff went off sick. Already Nina knew of two people who had been sent home because they had a cough.

When he left there were questions that Mitch tried to answer but Nina could see he knew no more than they did. Their DI finished the meeting by emphasising that they should only work on major investigations. 'The clue is in our name,' he added.

There was a sombre silence as they filed out into the corridor. Hazel went off with a couple of smoking buddies, while Nina and Ruby made for the kitchen. They hung about drinking coffee while they discussed their domestic arrangement. Ruby shared a house with two nurses, who were working flat-out, and a barber who had his own shop, which had already closed. She was happy to come to work if required because it was better than the prospect of working at home.

'Right now there's something I want to tie up before Mitch puts a stop to it,' Nina said. 'I'm going to contact uniform at Settle to check out that canal boat.'

'Have you ever been on a boating holiday?' Jim asked his colleague. 'I spent a week on this canal with my family when I was about sixteen. I was bored out of my mind. We started at Skipton and came up past here. My old man wanted to get to Wigan but we didn't have time. It's so tedious and after a day or two you go slowly mad.'

PC Trevor Allen ignored the young PCSO as he led the way across to the towpath on the other side of the canal. It didn't take long to identify "Kingfisher". He thumped on the door and marched up and down the length of the boat while they waited. He tried again.

'No-one in,' said Jim after a while.

A woman wandered along the path towards them. 'They've been gone a couple of days. I saw them leaving with their bags. I think you've missed them.'

'Thanks, love. We'll just have a quick look round.'

Jim followed his partner onto the boat. He tried the door but it was locked. He walked back onto the towpath.

Trev was peering through a window, rubbing it with his jacket sleeve. 'Come here,' he called. 'There's someone asleep in there.'

They banged on the window, requesting whoever it was to come out. Jim could see the figure struggling to stand. After a moment, Trev kicked the door with his foot and it flew open.

'Magic,' said Jim, following Trev inside.

A young man was standing unsteadily in the gangway between two unmade beds. He had a black eye and dried blood on his nose and cheek.

'Name?' the PC asked.

'Oliver Hayes.' His voice was slurred.

'In that case, young man, we need to speak to you urgently.'

To their surprise he didn't argue or complain but nodded wearily, limping towards the bed, where he picked up a rucksack, looked round and allowed them to lead him off the boat. He nearly fell as he tripped on the steps.

'What about this door?' asked Jim, inspecting the damage. 'Do you want me to secure it?'

Hayes shook his head. 'It's not my problem.'

The woman who'd spoken earlier was sitting on her boat when they helped Hayes walk slowly along the towpath. She was watching them all the way to the pub car park. He was no trouble on the journey to Settle police station. He appeared to sleep on the back seat but it became obvious he was near collapse when he tried to climb out of the car. Trev rang the doctor, who said Hayes was probably dehydrated if he'd been left alone on the boat for any length of time. He would be over to check on him but meanwhile they were to give him small amounts of water. When the doctor arrived an hour later, Hayes was eating a sandwich and drinking tea. When asked what had happened, he would only say that he'd been locked on the boat after being given a beating. He was thoroughly examined but had no broken bones.

'Nothing that some rest, plenty of fluids and a decent meal won't cure,' the doctor said.

'I can't guarantee a decent meal but we can get you another sandwich,' offered Trev.

When Hayes was told that a DS was coming down from Northallerton to question him, he shrugged and continued eating ravenously.

Nina was introduced to DS Dave Mulligan from the Leeds Serious Organised Crime Unit when she arrived in Settle. He was a burly guy who looked almost ready for retirement. He was wearing a black leather jacket but the bulging midriff spoilt his attempt to look cool. He was going to sit in on the interview as part of their investigation of the County Lines gangs operating out of his city. Nina explained that she wanted to discover whether the deaths of two students was the result of their involvement in County Lines and, if so, who was the perpetrator. Dave basically wanted anyone Hayes could name associated with the drug ring. He already had plenty of intel on various County Lines gangs operating in Leeds and he was hoping Hayes would provide some links.

They assembled in a large room that had been set up especially for them. It allowed them to sit either side of a large table with a place for Hayes at the end. They'd been warned that he'd suffered a beating, had been starved for two days and was dehydrated, but when he came in, he assured them he felt fine. He was the same polite young man that Nina remembered from their meeting in Flat 2, Pease Hall.

As it was her case, Nina began by explaining who they were, telling Hayes that he was here under caution for a voluntary interview. He was entitled to a solicitor if he so wished. He shook his head. She was interrupted by the DS from Leeds.

'Right, son. You probably know how this works because you've been in trouble with the police before, haven't you? But you're not a juvenile now, so this time you're responsible for your actions. I'm just pointing that out so you're not under any misapprehension.' He leaned back with his arms folded, indicating to Nina that she could continue.

'Should we call you Oliver or Hayes?' she asked, recalling that he preferred to be called by his surname.

'People call me Hayes,' he said, wearily.

'And, for the record, are you sure you feel well enough to continue?'

'I'm OK.' He was leaning his arms on the table, his hands clasped.

'Well then, just tell us if you want to stop.' She cleared her throat. 'Last Friday twelve boys were driven to the Yorkshire Dales. They were employed by a County Lines gang to package Class A drugs. Is that something you knew about?'

'Yes.'

Nina was taken aback. She'd expected a denial or at least a "no comment".

'Were you planning to join them on Friday? We know you'd made a similar trip on previous weekends.'

Hayes sat up, looked her straight in the eye and said, 'I was going to Garsdale on Friday. I should've been there before the kids arrived but the train was late. I had to stop at the boat to get the address, and the orders for the next two weeks.'

'Orders?' Nina asked.

Dave had been fidgeting while Nina was talking. 'He

221

means orders for the drugs.'

She suspected he wanted to get onto his questioning but she had a feeling his heavy-handed approach might not get the result she needed.

'So you got your orders from the boat,' she continued, 'then what?'

'The police were already at the cottage when I arrived so I told the taxi to keep going and take me back to Gargrave.'

'Is that when they gave you a beating?' asked Dave unsympathetically.

Hayes scowled at him. 'When I rang to say there'd been a problem, they told me to go back to the boat. There wasn't anything I could do about it but they blamed me for arriving late.'

'Who were "they", Hayes?' Nina asked. 'The people on the boat that beat you. Did you know them?'

He was taking a long time to reply, she could only assume he was frightened of these people.

Dave was impatient. 'Come on, mate. You must know who's giving you the orders, paying you, keeping the operation running.'

'I knew one them from before. He's called Gee. I think he's Albanian. I didn't see the other one properly – he was too busy throwing punches. He did have a Geordie accent.'

'This character Gee,' Dave asked. 'Did you work for him in Middlesborough?'

Hayes hung his head. 'Yes, that's how they found me again.'

'How did they know where you were living?' Nina asked.

He shrugged. 'I don't know. They have their ways.'

Nina looked at Dave but he was busy making notes, so she continued, 'Did you go to the boat every week? Were the same people there each time?'

He sighed. 'Gee was always there. I never saw anyone else but they might have been on the boat. I only went inside once before.'

'How did he give you the orders?' Dave asked.

'Just a piece of paper with the numbers for each and the weights in grams.'

Dave consulted his file. 'Cocaine, ketamine and MDMA?'

Nina assumed he'd been interviewing the boys thoroughly again down in Leeds.

'Yes.'

'Was there ever anything else? Crack, heroin?'

'No, never. It was always just E, C and K on the list.'

'The party drugs, eh? Did you take them straight back to the university with you?' Dave asked.

'No, I wasn't dealing. We left them in the cottage with the equipment.'

Dave snorted. 'So, you'll be claiming that your part in all this was only to supervise the kiddies employed to do the work, is that it?'

'Pretty much.' He was fidgeting in his chair. 'And it was only ever dealing with recreational drugs. I wouldn't have done it if it was crack cocaine or heroin.'

'A man of principle, eh?' Dave sounded disgusted.

'Anyway,' he continued, 'I didn't have a choice, did I, once Gee had found me again.'

'If you want to have a break, just say.' Nina told him but he shook his head.

'I want to give a full statement, so just ask me whatever you want.' His hands were shaking.

Nina looked across at Dave, who was yawning. 'Hayes,

my interest is solely in your two flatmates, Wilf and Callum. They both had drug-related deaths and we believe that is suspicious.' She watched him as his demeanour changed, first to sorrow then anger. 'Can you tell me about either of them? We know they accompanied you to the cottages at the weekends.'

He leaned forward, more animated than he'd been before. 'Callum began working with me soon after I started. We were a team. He was a good mate, never touched the goods. That was the rules. It was him that recruited Wilf. Well he was trouble because he started taking samples and testing them. He said it was part of his research but then he was getting agitated because he said the ecstasy wasn't consistent quality. I should've kept quiet but I thought the bosses would want to know if their supplier was fiddling them. It was stupid. Next thing I know, Wilf's lying dead on a bench outside our halls.'

He was becoming very emotional, so Nina offered him a break.

But, no, he wanted to get it all out. 'Next thing, Callum suspects that Wilf was killed. It was something to do with fentanyl. I didn't follow it to be honest but he said he was scared.' He brushed his hand across his eyes. 'How could I have been so stupid? I told Gee on the Thursday that Callum wasn't coming again, that he wanted out.' His voice was quivering. 'Callum goes out really late Thursday night, saying he was meeting someone and then he's found dead.'

Ignoring the outburst of emotion, Dave wanted to know how he contacted Gee.

Hayes swallowed. 'He gives me a number to text. It changes every couple of weeks.'

Suddenly Nina and Dave were asking the same

questions because Gee, or someone working for him, was at the university when Callum died. But Hayes was adamant that he'd never seen Gee on campus.

Nina, who wanted a break, suggested she went to find them something to drink, leaving Dave with Hayes. The PC outside the door offered to fetch the tea and two coffees while she found the "Ladies". She took the opportunity to check her messages, so by the time she returned the drinks had been delivered. But Dave wanted a word out in the corridor.

'I've had a quick chat with the guys back at base and they know of this chap Gee. He used to be operating out of Middlesborough, probably still does but recruits from Leeds. I don't know what you're thinking, but we'd prefer to see if we can keep surveillance for a while, until he leads us to his boss and the suppliers. Right?' He turned to go back inside.

'No, it isn't,' Nina said sharply. 'If we can find him, he should be charged with two murders.'

He looked disgruntled. 'OK. In my view he's probably not the one who carried out the deeds, it's more likely his mate that taught Hayes a lesson. Someone local to the university. The drugs are obviously for distribution to youngsters and the campus is fertile ground. My guess is they've got someone based up there.'

Nina thought about what he was saying. 'How were you planning to locate Gee and his colleague?'

Dave grinned. 'Through Hayes. He's being very co-operative. If he helps us, we can help him. He's as keen to get these low-lifes behind bars as we are, for his own safety.'

Dave had already put his proposal to Hayes when she

was out of the room. Assuming the phone number he was given on Friday was still active, Hayes had agreed to text Gee that evening, to say he'd been questioned by the police but had told them nothing, that he was going back to his studies. He wanted out.

Chapter 21

Nina drove Hayes back to his flat. The campus was deserted now the university had "transitioned to remote running", as Nige described it. Her husband was getting increasingly stressed as he tried to work while keeping the family entertained. It was his own fault because, as a key worker, Nina was entitled to send the children into school, but he wasn't keen on letting them attend in case of infection.

'Looks like everyone's gone home,' she commented, as they got out of the car.

'Term ended last Friday,' Hayes informed her, hauling his rucksack out from the back seat.

'Are you sure about this?' she asked. She was leaving him just when he seemed to be most vulnerable.

'I'll be fine. I'm not scared, honestly. I just want them to get the punishment they deserve.'

As she drove away, Nina wondered whether he realised the danger he was putting himself in. She rang Ruby to see if Mitch was around. There was just time to drop into the office before heading home.

'Tell him I need to see him. I'll be there in less than half an hour.'

There was none of the usual rush hour traffic and she reached the office in good time. She went straight to give her DI an update on her visit to Settle. He was pleased she'd found Oliver Hayes because, to him, it meant she had finished with the case.

'You've questioned him about the students?'

She described how all three flatmates had been working for a County Lines gang and that she suspected the other two had been killed by the Albanian boss or someone working for him. When she explained that Leeds Serious Organised Crime Unit had arranged a trap for him, he agreed it was a good outcome.

'…so we can wait for Leeds to tell us when they have him in custody,' he concluded.

Nina had agreed with Dave that she'd also be there when Hayes met the Albanian. 'Don't you think I should be the one to make the arrest?' she asked.

'Not necessary, Nina. Let the boys from Leeds do the dirty work, eh?'

There was to be no further discussion. Everything from now on was to be focussed on controlling coronavirus. Ruby was compiling figures for traffic in the region, reflecting the level to which people were staying at home. The rules said to only travel for work if it was essential, to go shopping for food, or to collect medicines. Uniform were out stopping people coming into the area for recreation, advising them to stay at home.

'Was Mitch serious when he said you may have to go back into uniform?' asked Ruby.

Nina nodded. 'If many more people are sent home with a cough.' It wasn't something she looked forward to.

Later that evening she received a call from Dave Mulligan. Hayes had confirmed that the Albanian had accepted his request to meet. He would be outside the halls of residence at ten o' clock the following evening.

'We need to get access to the halls without being seen.

Do you have any thoughts?'

'Have you tried the security staff?' she asked.

'We don't want to alert them to this operation in case there's any involvement with the gang on site.'

Nina considered for a moment. 'I can ask someone who teaches there,' she suggested.

'Fine. We're meeting in the car park of the pub down the road. I'm bringing my guys and we'll be in two vehicles, one patrol car and one unmarked. We'll see you there.'

He rang off before Nina could tell him she couldn't be involved. When Nige asked who'd called so late, she told him it was work but didn't go into details, not that he was really interested. She knew he wouldn't want her to be mixed up in what Dave Mulligan was proposing. He said she had to consider her family and not ever put herself at risk again. Tomorrow she would let Dave know that she wouldn't be coming.

However, next morning she dressed in her black jeans with a black polo-necked sweater instead of her usual smart trousers and shirt, causing Nige to ask if it was dress-down Wednesday. She laughed it off, saying it was cold in the office.

She rang Mills as soon as she was at her desk. It took a while for her friend to answer and she sounded as if she'd just woken up. After exchanging greetings, Nina got straight to the point.

'A slightly odd question, Mills, but is there a way to get onto your campus without being seen by security?'

'I don't think it's possible by car. They have cameras on the gates.'

'What about on foot?'

'There's a pedestrian entrance on the corner of the site.

They don't monitor that one. It's used by the students to get in and out from the residences.'

'So it's close to the halls?'

'Yes. It's a short-cut to the local shops.'

'That's great, thanks.'

'By the way, did you find Oliver Hayes?'

'We did.'

'Good. Was he able to help you with what happened to Callum?'

Nina hesitated. 'Yes, but…' She stopped.

'I know, you can't discuss it,' her friend recited

'I'll tell you all about it when it's over,' she promised.

Hazel, who'd been listening to the conversation, insisted on knowing what was happening at the university, so Nina explained how Hayes was helping them catch the man suspected of killing the students. Her colleague was impressed.

'Wow, that's the most exciting thing that's happened here for a long time. I wondered why you were dressed like the "Milk-Tray man". I'd love to be in on that.'

'Really? I wasn't going to… I mean, I was going to tell him…'

'You aren't going?' Hazel looked astonished. 'But you'll miss the arrest!'

Nina looked at Ruby, who was nodding.

'Besides,' continued Hazel, 'you need to hang onto that man in case Leeds decide to use him to catch a bigger fish.'

Nina considered for a moment. 'Mitch didn't want me to get involved.'

'Then don't tell him.'

That was typical of Hazel, but Nina followed the rules, and Nige didn't like her putting herself on the front line.

What reason could she give for being out all evening? In the end she sent him a text telling him she was on surveillance and wouldn't be back until very late. She wondered if he'd believe her because it wasn't something she was required to do normally. He came back saying he thought she was up to something when she went out looking like a naval officer. She decided to ditch her sweater when she got back.

Nina avoided going home at the end of the day, in case Nige discovered her plans, so Ruby said they should order a takeaway and have a good gossip. Normally Nina would have enjoyed the prospect but her nerves were beginning to set in and she knew she wasn't good company. Ruby asked her about the family and, as she talked about the children, Nina felt increasingly anxious about how the evening would pan out. When the food finally arrived, she nibbled at her pizza, leaving the rest in the box. The researcher was doing a gallant job, trying to make her laugh by telling her about her latest dating disaster. She'd been using a dating app for several years now and she'd had some successes but nothing long-term. Now she was beginning to think she should get out more.

Nina looked at the time again and offered to make coffee. She put two heaped spoons of granules into her mug, hoping it would keep her awake. She would need it because it would be past her bedtime when she got home.

'Don't you think it's exciting?' Ruby asked, when Nina returned with a mug in each hand.

'What?' She passed Ruby the weaker of the two coffees.

'Being involved in a sting operation.'

Nina considered before answering. It *was* exciting but

also rather scary. 'Yes, it is. I am looking forward to arresting the man.' She just hoped that Dave and his mates would render him harmless before she did so.

Soon it was time to leave. Ruby told her to take the rest of the pizza with her, she might need it later. They left the office together and Ruby watched her go, wishing her luck while she waved her off, as if she was leaving on an expedition. Nina switched the car radio to a music channel, thinking it might help relax her as she drove through the empty streets. The shops were in darkness, everyone was safely indoors. She drove slowly, knowing she was going to be far too early but even so she arrived with half an hour to spare. Of course the pub was closed, the car park deserted. She turned off the engine and was suddenly plunged into darkness. More than ever she wished she'd done as her DI ordered and left the arrest to Dave.

A police patrol car arrived ten minutes later. She watched two plain clothes officers emerge and walk over with torches. She climbed out and introduced herself. The air was cold, their breath formed small clouds as they spoke.

'I'm Patrick and this is Melanie, Mel for short.' He sounded as though he came from Northern Ireland.

'Hi,' said Mel. She was petit, with dark hair tied back in a ponytail.

'Nina,' she replied, since they were using first names. 'DS.' She added her rank, hoping they would do the same.

There was a pause. 'Dave told us he'd be here,' Patrick said to fill the silence.

Mel was stamping her feet to keep warm. 'He'd better not be late.'

They all looked round at the sound of a car approaching

but it drove past and they turned back into the circle they'd formed. Nina wondered if it would seem rude to sit back in her warm car.

'This guy we're hoping to collar tonight, so why are you interested in him?' Patrick asked.

Nina explained the connection between him and the two students found dead on campus. 'They were all working for the County Lines gang.'

'So is that why Hayes is helping us?' Mel asked.

'Yes, I think he feels responsible for their deaths.'

They were suddenly caught in the beam of two headlights as a powerful car swept into the car park. A figure jumped out, slamming the car door, and walked over to them.

'Keeping a low profile I see,' he remarked.

Mel and Patrick spoke in unison, 'Sorry, Sarge.'

Now Nina understood the hierarchy.

'Are we ready then?' he asked. 'Nina's going to show us the way onto site. Hayes is meeting this guy outside his accommodation, so we'll remain hidden somewhere close by. We think he's the Albanian that goes by the name by Gee, we don't believe he's violent, he leaves that to his foot soldiers. Wait until I give the signal and turn off that torch, Mel, only use it if it's absolutely necessary. Nina, I suggest you stay at the back.'

She went over to collect her phone and lock the car. They were already off at a fast walking pace down to the shops and across the road to a metal gate in the fence. The pedestrian way onto campus was confirmed by a notice saying it was private property and only authorised people should enter by order of the university. They followed Dave in single file along the narrow path bordered with shrubs and trees. It became quite dark in places as Nina tried to keep up with Mel, who had broken into a trot. Finally she made out the illuminated accommodation blocks ahead of them.

They stopped before reaching the end of the path, where the opening would lead them out into the square of lawn formed by the halls of residence. Nina could see the bench where Wilf had been discovered. She pointed to the building behind it, indicating to Dave that it was where Hayes lived. Patrick and Mel were dispatched through the woodland to find a position on the opposite side of the square. Nina wished she'd worn thicker socks because her feet were frozen, but she daren't move. Dave looked relaxed but she was stiff with cold and anxiety.

It seemed they stood there for ages but it was actually only twelve minutes before Hayes appeared from inside the accommodation block wearing his long black overcoat. She heard the door slam behind him. He stood in the lamplight with his hands in his pockets, peering round as if searching for them in the shadows. Dave produced his phone. Nina guessed he was sending Hayes a text because the young man took his mobile from his pocket, looked at it and nodded.

As they waited, Nina was imagining what Nige would say if he knew where she was. She recalled the moment when she'd been chasing across a series of back gardens, scrambling over fences and through bushes. She'd fallen on a cold frame and damaged her back badly. It had put her in a wheelchair for many months, which was why Nige was so nervous of her getting involved in anything risky. She didn't believe that tonight would be like that though – and if the Albanian got away, she was sure Dave and his

234

team would be well ahead of her.

Finally the prolonged silence was broken by the sound of a vehicle approaching. Headlights swung across the lawn and she drew back instinctively. Footsteps announced the arrival of a man, at least she assumed it was a man. He was tall, dressed in jeans and a leather jacket, his head was covered in a woolly hat and he had a scarf over the lower half of his face. She expected Hayes to greet him as an acquaintance, if not exactly a friend, but he seemed to be edging away as the man drew close. When he spoke, she was surprised how the sound travelled.

'Where's Gee?' Hayes asked. Was he shouting so they could hear?

The man's voice was muffled, it was a lengthy speech. Then he moved towards Hayes again. She couldn't see clearly, but she thought she saw a flash of light.

'He's got a knife,' Dave whispered.

Hayes had turned and was opening the door to the halls with a card. The man pushed him inside.

Dave gave the signal for the others to move in, running forward with Nina following close behind. Patrick and Mel arrived first but they stopped at the door which was now locked. Despite pushing and kicking, it remained shut. Dave was instructing his team to look for other ways in while he searched for a weighty object to smash the security glass. Nina was left standing alone helplessly at the door when there was shouting and two security men came charging across the lawn.

'Stay where you are,' one called, while the other ran off in the direction Dave had taken.

'Police!' she shouted. 'Can you open this door?'

The guard reacted immediately, waving a card across the

lock. Nina pushed past him and into the building. 'Flat 2!' she called as she raced upstairs.

She stopped when they reached the landing, putting her finger to her lips. She tiptoed to the door and listened. Nothing. There was no handle on the outside, just a card reader. She pushed gently but it was firmly shut. She beckoned to the guard, indicating for him to use his card, as they had done on her previous visit. Pausing for a few seconds to catch her breath, she nodded and they barged in.

Nina hadn't known what to expect but she was surprised to find Hayes seated at the table with a pen in his hand. The other man was leaning over him holding a knife. He swung round when they burst in.

'Police! Drop the knife!' she shouted as the guard threw himself on the man.

They were struggling on the floor but the guard was superior in strength and soon he had the man's wrist pinned down, enabling Nina to prise the knife from his grasp.

Suddenly there was a commotion below them, shouting, a door slamming, feet pounding up the stairs.

'In here!' Nina called as Dave appeared with the other security guard, swiftly followed by Patrick and Mel.

They were all out of breath. 'You should've waited for back-up,' panted Dave.

'It could have been too late,' she replied, hurt by his reprimand.

The man was lying on his front held to the floor by the security guard, who was clearly enjoying his part in the action. He hauled him upright for Patrick to begin a body search.

'Who is this?' Dave asked Hayes, who shook his head.

'I don't know but I think it was him who knocked me about on the boat.'

Nina asked him to tell them quickly what had just happened.

'I thought Gee was coming to meet me but when this guy turned up, he said Gee had sent him to shut me up. I had two choices, he said. He produced the knife and told me he was going to kill me slowly and painfully, or he could give me something that would be more pleasant, I would just drift away, he said.' Hayes hesitated. 'He said... he said, "your friends both made sensible choices." Then he told me to come back to my room to write a suicide note.' His voice wavered and he covered his face with his hands.

Patrick had finished patting the man down. He showed them a small bottle. 'This was in his pocket.' He held it up to the light to read the label. 'Fentanyl Citrate.'

Mel had handcuffed the man and turned him round to face Dave. Now Nina could see he was an ugly young man, with a bulbous nose and pock-marked complexion.

'Name?' Dave demanded.

For a moment it looked as though he wasn't going to answer. Dave took one step towards him. That did the trick.

'Roscoe.'

'Roscoe who?' Another step towards him.

'Samuel Roscoe.'

'OK, Samuel. DS Featherstone here is going to read you your rights.' He looked at Nina.

Everyone fell silent to watch.

She cleared her throat. 'Samuel Roscoe, I am arresting you on suspicion of the murder of Wilf Marriott and

Callum Wallace, and the attempted murder of Oliver Hayes. You do not have to say anything, but it may harm your defence if you do not mention when questioned something you later rely on in court. Anything you do say may be given in evidence.'

While Mel went off to fetch the patrol car, Dave and Patrick held onto Roscoe. Nina informed him that he would be taken into custody in Harrogate for interview the following day. She turned to Hayes. He was still seated at the table with his half-written note in front of him. As she approached, he snatched it up and screwed it into a ball. His hands were shaking.

'Would you like me to drive you over to your parents' house?' she asked, guessing he wouldn't want to stay in the flat alone after the ordeal.

He thought for a moment. 'No, it would only worry them,' he said without looking up.

Nina spoke to the security guards, concerned about leaving Hayes alone without support. They offered to move him into one of the empty flats for academic visitors that were directly above the Security Office, and Hayes agreed gratefully.

Once Mel and Patrick had taken Roscoe away, it was time to leave. Hayes went with the security guards and Nina followed Dave back down the path to the main road and the pub.

'That was pretty cool what you did there,' he said as he unlocked his car.

She didn't know how to respond so she asked what was going to happen to Hayes. He was, after all, still part of the drug dealers' gang.

'He might get away with a caution if he continues to cooperate. Technically he wasn't dealing and he'll be your key witness in Roscoe's trial.'

Nina agreed, Hayes had heard him admit that he'd killed his flatmates.

'We'll want his continued assistance because we need to locate this Albanian chap. He's the one behind the County Lines operation and probably the one giving Roscoe his orders. He sent him to Hayes when he asked for a meeting.'

Before Nina climbed into her car, they arranged to meet the next day at Harrogate to interview Roscoe together. She was thankful the roads were empty because she was exhausted and glad to be home. The row of houses on her side of the street were in darkness, cars lining the road. She found a tight parking spot a few doors down and did her best to lock the car quietly. She opened and closed the front door carefully before tiptoeing upstairs. To her relief Nige was asleep.

Lying awake thinking about the events of the evening, she was pleased she'd played a key role but decided the security guys would have coped if she hadn't been there. But she had known which flat Hayes was in... but she wouldn't have been able to get in without a cardkey... what if she'd had to tackle Roscoe with a knife alone... perhaps it was best not to tell Nige about what had happened.

Chapter 22

Nina woke early after a restless night, resolving to get away quickly to avoid discussing the previous evening with Nige. She told him she had a busy day, stuck her head round the bedroom doors to say goodbye to the children and left without breakfast. Unfortunately there was no longer the option of popping into a café, since even the last outlet on the high street had now closed for business. She grabbed a coffee and doughnut from the canteen and made her way upstairs, excited at the prospect of telling her colleagues the good news.

To her surprise Ruby began clapping when she arrived. 'Congratulations, I hear it was a success,' she said with a broad grin.

She'd been keeping an eye on the grapevine overnight and seen that a dealer had been taken into their local custody suite in Harrogate. She wanted all the details and while Nina was giving her a step by step account, Hazel arrived, wanting her to start again from the beginning. Ruby immediately began trawling for intel on Samuel Roscoe while Hazel urged Nina to continue looking for the Albanian, who obviously had given the orders to get rid of the students. Soon it was time to leave for Harrogate.

Dave was waiting for her at the police station and he was anxious to give her an update before they went into the interview room.

'He's got a solicitor with him who I've come across a couple of times before in County Lines cases. He's a Mr

Shehu, no doubt he'll be advising him to go "no comment" from the outset. I'm not optimistic we'll get much from him. My lads are arranging for Roscoe's car to be searched and Patrick is getting his phone examined.'

Nina told him that Ruby was doing a search on Roscoe's previous record, address, bank details, background, and contacts, adding that her researcher was very thorough. She thought Dave looked a little irritated. 'She's also going to try again to identify Gee because he's behind the murders even if he didn't commit them.'

'He's our target too,' Dave replied. 'I hope she won't do anything to interfere with our investigation. I imagine Gee is well aware of what happened last night, even if he doesn't know the details yet.' He nodded in the direction of the interview room.

'The solicitor? Are you sure?' She moved towards the door. 'Let's see if he'll talk to us.'

The room had been arranged so they could keep two metres apart. The solicitor was a smartly dressed middle-aged man, quite good-looking compared to Roscoe's ugly face. He formally introduced himself as Mr Shehu, representing his client, Mr Samuel Roscoe. As soon as the preliminaries were over Nina knew they were going to get nowhere. They spent nearly an hour questioning him but all Roscoe said was "no comment". Nina asked him about the canal boat, the beating he gave Hayes, the fact they had a witness willing to swear on oath that he'd admitted killing Wilf Marriott and Callum Wallace. "No comment". She had seen him holding a knife over Hayes while forcing him to write a suicide note. He'd threatened to administer fentanyl, the drug that killed Callum Wallace. "No comment". The only information Nina had at the end of her interview was that he had a strong Geordie accent.

After a break, Dave tackled the County Lines angle. He asked who he was working for, how the dealers operated, was he supplying the university students, how did they recruit the children who worked for them? Most importantly, where was Gee? Was his boss going to let Roscoe take the blame for it all? He was looking at a very long sentence, did he want Gee free to carry on making stacks of money while he finished his days in HM Prison Wakefield? Dave persisted while Roscoe sat picking at his nails with his head lowered, refusing to make eye contact. They adjourned at lunchtime.

Nina and Dave compared notes over a sandwich in the canteen. Ruby had messaged her with some intel on Roscoe so she was able to tell him that he was born in Sunderland, and was known to the police for small-time dealing. He moved to Leeds five years ago and has been renting a flat in Darlington for the past three years. Then she saw something that made her laugh.

'Apparently he's registered part-time at the University of North Yorkshire to study, would you believe, "Crime and Investigation"! His attendance is poor and he's been registered for several years.'

Ruby had discovered that Roscoe had a brother, five years younger, who was also at the university, studying mechanical engineering. Nina forwarded the message on to Dave so he had the details.

'Convenient for recruiting students like Hayes and his mates, and for distributing the goods once their packaged,' Dave commented, looking at his phone. 'No joy with Roscoe's mobile so far but they've found Class A drugs in his car, more than for his own use, which is something.'

He made a call and wandered off to another part of the canteen. When he came back, he announced that the drugs found in Roscoe's car had a street value of fifty grand. He read from his phone.

'One thousand small polythene packs of MDMA, five hundred of ketamine, and cocaine: one gram packed in a thousand tiny plastic tubes.'

Nina was shocked. 'You don't think that was all heading for sale on campus?'

'Not now, most of the students have gone home to Mum and Dad. They won't be partying again until the lockdown is over.'

'So I wonder where he was taking it all?'

'Could be delivering to homes in the area or to somewhere to be stashed,' Dave suggested. 'Now we've got his address, I'll get it searched.'

Armed with the intel provided by Ruby, and Dave's team, it was time to have another conversation with Roscoe. As they approached the interview room, they could hear the solicitor's raised voice. He stopped talking as soon as Dave opened the door and Nina noticed Roscoe's flushed face.

She let Dave start with the kilo of cocaine found in Roscoe's car, in addition to a large amount of MDMA and ketamine. Was he planning to offload it at the university? "No comment". It was the same when he questioned him about his boss. Dave continued to ask about the County Lines operation: where the drugs came from, how they were transported into the country, where were they stored and how the money was transferred. Question after question, they all remained unanswered.

When it was Nina's turn again, she reiterated the

importance of finding Gee. 'We know he was giving you the orders. Did he tell you to deal with the students that way? Did he have the idea of making it look like a drug overdose, or a suicide?'

Roscoe gave the same answer. She put it to him that he had lured Wilf Marriott out of his accommodation late at night and persuaded him to take a lethal cocktail of drugs. 'Is that how you killed Callum Wallace,' she asked, 'before throwing him in the lake?' She got no response apart from the usual one.

It was Dave who suggested a break, offering to find mugs of tea. The solicitor went to find the "Gents" and Nina was left alone with Roscoe. He was staring at the floor.

'You should admit you were only carrying out orders,' she said. 'It will help your case if you co-operate.'

He shook his head slowly. Nina interpreted his response not so much as a refusal but more to indicate it wasn't possible. He had too much to lose. He was scared.

'Is it your solicitor?' she asked, thinking of the raised voice.

He looked up. She could see the fear in his eyes. He shook his head again then looked down, muttering something.

'What did you say?'

'The barbie,' he mumbled.

Nina was about to ask what he meant, when the door swung open and Mr Shehu walked back in. He laid his hand heavily on Roscoe's shoulder before taking the seat beside him.

'Let's get this over,' he said to Nina. 'My client is tired and he doesn't wish to communicate anything to you.'

When Dave returned, the solicitor demanded they charge Roscoe now or let him go. A young man in uniform came in and deposited four paper cups of tea on the table. Nina looked at Dave who nodded and they went into the corridor to confer.

'Do you want to contact the decision maker now?' Dave asked. 'It's your ground.'

It was true they were on her home territory so she went off to make the call, once they'd decided on the charges. These included the attempted murder of Hayes, and possession of class A drugs with intent to supply. The evidence for the murder of Marriott and Wallace, relied on Hayes as a witness so they needed confirmation that they didn't require further evidence, which would take a while. Satisfied that Roscoe was safely in custody and not going to be interviewed further, Shehu scurried off without further communication.

'Reporting back to Gee that his man behaved himself and didn't spill the beans,' said Dave, with contempt. His phone pinged and he read a message out loud. 'Roscoe's flat has been cleaned out. Someone came last night and took stuff away, a neighbour says. Great.'

'That suggests he was storing drugs. He must've been distributing up here for the gang in Leeds,' said Nina.

'It makes sense. Generally the drugs come in from the Netherlands via Immingham Docks, straight into Leeds. Gee will be managing that end and Roscoe is the connection in the North-East. If only he'd talked.'

'He did say something, when we were alone. I tried to persuade him it was best if he gave us Gee. He was obviously scared of his solicitor but he did say something. It sounded like "the barbie", if I heard correctly. Then he clammed up because Mr Shehu came back in.'

Dave grimaced. 'Does it mean anything to you?'

'Not immediately. I'll get Ruby to see if there are any clubs or bars with that name. Even if we find one, I'm not sure what we're looking for.'

'Gee, perhaps?'

Nina contacted Ruby, who told her that Roscoe had worked for an Albanian drug dealing gang in Middlesborough. She suggested it could be the same set up that Hayes had been involved with as a kid. Possibly that was how they'd located him again, if Roscoe recognised him on campus.

'There's nothing useful in his phone calls, the contacts are all on pay-as-you-go,' Ruby added.

'Well, concentrate on the "Barbie" lead, it must have been important for him to tell me. See what you can find in the Darlington area to start with, although it means nothing to me.'

They were still waiting for permission to charge Roscoe an hour later, when Ruby rang back. Nina answered quickly, hoping for news, but her researcher was only calling to say that she'd found nothing connected to a "barbie".

'OK, let's try to find Gee another way,' Nina said. 'Go back to the taxi firm, the boat hire company and cottage rental people. He can't have paid cash to all of them, and there must be some information they needed like an address or bank details. Ask Settle if they can talk to the boat hire company again.'

Finally they had the go-ahead to charge Roscoe with the two murders and one attempted murder, as well as the drug dealing activities. He stood motionless as they showed him the charge sheet while the custody officer explained what was happening. He seemed resigned to his fate as he was led back to the cells to await his court appearance in the morning. That would be the start of a long wait because no cases were currently being heard in the magistrates' court, apart from overnight custody cases and custody time limit extensions.

It had been a long day. Dave said he was looking forward to having a beer to celebrate a successful conclusion. Nina just wanted to get home to see the family. They stood outside the police station in the cold discussing the ongoing search for Gee but neither had any new suggestions.

'We'll know if Ruby has had any success tomorrow. All we need is an address,' Nina remarked as she left.

Despite having taken every care to avoid contact with anyone at the police station, Nina went straight up to wash and change her clothes when she arrived home. The children were watching a video while Nige cooked tea and finally she felt she could relax. She went into the kitchen to give Nige a hug, thanking him for being such a good househusband.

'Really?' he asked, still attending to the frying pan. 'Because I was thinking it must be your turn next week.'

'Sorry, darling, but I'm the key worker here, aren't I?'

He nodded and carried on cooking, expressing surprise when she opened a bottle of wine. Nina didn't often drink during the week.

'I think I deserve this,' she said, pouring two large glasses. 'It's a celebration.'

'What? For me surviving nearly a week of lockdown

with three children?'

'Yes, that, and I've just charged a man with two murders, one attempted murder and drug-dealing.'

'Well done you,' Nige said without turning round. 'Is that why you were out late last night?'

'Yes, that was the surveillance I was talking about.'

Nothing more was said.

After their tea, Nina offered to do the boys' bath but Nige insisted she'd had a more stressful time than him, just. So while she finished her wine, she wondered about how to find Gee. It seemed inevitable that she would end up consulting Mills because her friend had seen Hayes talking to him by the canal.

She began her call by asking how she and Simon were managing out in Swaledale.

'We're doing fine, thanks. We haven't driven each other mad yet. I went shopping in Leyburn and got most things. We'll manage.'

'It's great that you're getting on so well. Nige is finding it quite a strain entertaining the kids all day but Rosie is very good with the boys.'

'I bet he's enjoying it really.'

Nina took a deep breath. 'Mills tell me about the time you saw Hayes visit the canal boat at the "Anchor Inn". Can you describe the man he was visiting?'

'Not really. I only saw him from the back. Normal height and build, I suppose. The woman in the other boat could probably give you a description, she seemed an inquisitive sort.'

'What boat?'

'The "Mary Rose". She didn't know him but said he'd been renting a long time.'

Nina thanked Mills and made a note to ask Settle to visit the owner of the "Mary Rose", in case she could give them any further information. It was all they had to go on.

Chapter 23

The owner of the "Mary Rose" had spotted Jim and Trev on the towpath before they reached the boat.

'Back again?' she called.

'Just a few questions, love,' said Trev, showing her his warrant card.

'What me?' The woman looked surprised but pleased by the attention. 'Come on in then.'

They offered to stay on the towpath but she said it was too cold for her and insisted they came inside, promising she would keep two metres away from them. Trev looked at Jim, who nodded. They followed her onto the narrowboat and down into a tiny sitting area. Jim gave a low whistle. The interior was as gaily painted as the exterior. Every piece of panelling and furniture was painted with flowers and country scenes, varnished and maintained. The curtains were lace. They sat on benching by the door while the owner moved down the boat to the next section, where Jim could see a black stove with pots and pans hanging on hooks, all covered in painted flowers. A smell of bacon pervaded the air.

'I'm Sylvia, by the way,' she called from her position in the kitchen. 'Coffee?'

Trev never refused refreshments. While they sat waiting for the kettle to boil, a tabby cat appeared from the other end of the boat and sprang up to sit beside Jim.

'Is it about those men on "Kingfisher"?' Sylvia called, tipping heaped spoons of instant into three mugs.

'It is,' Trev replied. 'Anything you can remember about them?'

She came back in with the coffee, then returned to the kitchen area. Jim stirred two spoons of sugar into his mug.

'They would arrive on a Friday and leave on a Monday morning, regular as clockwork,' she said, leaning on the doorway between them. 'They never spoke to me. Kept themselves to themselves. One of them wasn't from here, if you know what I mean.'

'Albanian?' Trev asked.

'Could be, I don't know about that.'

'What about visitors?'

She shook her head. 'That lad you went off with on Tuesday is the only one I've seen.'

Trev took a sip of coffee. 'So how did they get here each weekend? Did they come by car?'

She shrugged. 'I suppose so. If they did, I never saw it. They'd have left it over there.'

'Where d'you mean?' asked Jim, stroking the cat absent-mindedly.

'In the pub car park, that's the only place to leave it round here.' She waved in the direction of the water.

'Across the bridge.'

Trev looked up from his notes. 'So you don't know what sort of car they drove?'

'No, sorry.'

They thanked her for her help, finished their coffee and crossed back over the canal to where they'd left the patrol car. It wasn't an official car park for the pub but even if they'd wanted to check for cameras, the place was closed for business and no-one appeared to be around to ask.

Back at the station Trev relayed the information to the

researcher in Northallerton. The lass, called Ruby, sounded disappointed but thanked them for letting her know that Gee probably had left a car on the other side of the canal.

'All they said was that they think Gee had a car,' Ruby told Nina. 'It's pretty obvious really. Then I thought Mills might have seen it, if she was at the canal when Hayes visited him.'

Ruby had already spoken to Hayes, who said he hadn't noticed a car. He explained it was almost dark when he arrived at the boat. Nina thought it unlikely that Mills would have seen something that Hayes had missed, but Ruby offered to ask her.

'Mills, this is an official call,' Ruby warned when she got through.

'Ooh, is it? Does that mean no gossiping?'

Ruby laughed. 'Yes, definitely. Seriously, it's about the boat on the canal at Gargrave. Tell me where you were parked when you saw Hayes meet the man from the boat.'

'In the pub car park.'

'Were there any other cars?'

'A few in the main car park. But it was early, half-six. And there was one parked in the other spot nearer the canal.'

'Close to the canal?' Ruby picked up a pen. 'Can you remember anything about it?'

'What? Well actually, Simon got quite excited when he saw it.'

'Why?'

'Oh it was some limited-edition thing.'

'Tell me about it.'

'What?'

'Give me the details, everything you can remember.'

'Look, you'd better speak to Simon.'

There was a brief silence, then Ruby could hear Mills telling Simon to speak to her.

'Hello, Ruby is it?'

'Hello Simon. Can you give me any details of the car you saw by the canal, please? Anything you can remember.'

He sounded puzzled. 'So, it was an Audi R8 coupé in grey… oh yes, it had black wheels… I couldn't see inside; it was getting dark.'

'Did it have a personalised registration plate, something memorable perhaps?'

'Sorry, I've no idea.' He asked Mills but she hadn't noticed either.

'Shame, never mind, that's been a great help. Did Mills say it was a limited-edition?'

'Yes, only a thousand ever made.'

'Thanks, I owe you a drink when the pubs are open again.'

She told Nina about the car. It was expensive and the only one in that parking area so it could have belonged to Gee. She had enough information to start a check on Audi R8 owners. At that price, she couldn't believe it could be purchased without giving full details to the supplier. It couldn't be that hard, she had the colour of the car and she would be looking for an Albanian name to go with it. If she could get the registration information, she'd have the full name and address. Once she had that there was all sorts of intel available to her.

'I assume you've squared this with the boss?' Hazel asked, when Nina updated her.

Her colleague must have guessed by her expression that

she hadn't.

Nina explained. 'As far as Mitch is concerned, we've charged Roscoe for the murders and that's the end of it. I want to see this Albanian caught because he's behind the killings. Leeds are after him anyway and we wouldn't have caught Roscoe without their help.'

'If it takes much longer, you'll have to fess up. He's stopped all investigations now because of the virus. They're already talking about deploying staff down to Harrogate to help patrol the streets, breaking up gatherings. We'll be back in uniform before you know it.'

Mills had been concerned that spending all day, every day on her own with Simon would prove too much of a good thing and feared for their relationship. However, she discovered that he was very organised and methodical and within a few days they had a routine that seemed to work pretty well. So after breakfast, Mills took Harris up on the moors for a good long walk. Fortunately the weather had remained dry, although there was a cold wind. Curlews and lapwings were making their presence felt with loud calls as they circled and swooped across the tops. From her position high on the fell she could see that some early lambs had already appeared in the fields below. She took her time, knowing Simon would appreciate the peace and quiet to get on with his work. He was reading a thesis from another university that he was due to examine remotely the following week and he had a quarterly report to complete for his grant-giving body.

Back in Laurel Cottage a couple of hours later, she made sandwiches for an early lunch. Simon would be taking Harris down to the river in the afternoon, while Mills got on with the paper that she'd planned to present at a conference in July, despite the fact it would probably be postponed.

The final part of their daily schedule was to have a cup of tea followed by a "business meeting". They called it that because there were quite a few administrative issues that had to be resolved before they could offer a truly professional forensic science service. In the excitement of setting up the lab, Mills had ignored what she referred to as "the boring bits". Simon had lectured her on how they needed to set up a finance system, including a business plan, accounts, VAT, cash-flow forecasts and more. Fortunately he would be in control of that side of things, with his experience of managing large grants. Her responsibility would be staffing and quality assurance, which meant handling the accreditation that was essential for any work that was going to be used in court.

They gave up at five o'clock when they couldn't agree on a logo for the company. Mills started preparing their evening meal while Simon had his nightly FaceTime with his son. He'd been anxious about the situation over in the States, although his ex-wife assured him they were keeping safe. The schools had closed in Washington, so Alfie was being home-schooled by his Mum. His only complaint was that he was bored.

Meanwhile Mills made a shopping list. They'd managed well so far and she reckoned if they visited the shop in Leyburn each week, they would be fine. In fact it sounded as if they were better provided for than Nina and Nige, who relied on a large supermarket where the shelves had been quite bare. Of course Muriel was still complaining about not being able to get enough flour so she hadn't been baking as much as normal. She had apologised to Mills from her back garden for not bringing her any goodies. She would call to Harris over the wall between them while he wagged his tail furiously at her. On reflection, Mills missed not being able to pop next door for a chat and a scone or a brownie.

When Ruby's endeavours were successful, everyone knew it. She would at least let out a "Yes!" but had been known to do a victory dance round the office. This time she stood up, gave a loud cry of satisfaction and went over to hug Nina but stopped abruptly, suddenly remembering the "two metre rule".

'I think I've found him! He's Mr Getoar Kadare, or "Gee" to his friends, I guess.'

'Well done,' said Nina.

'It wasn't difficult once we had a description of the car. Thank goodness he ran to form and bought a flashy vehicle with his ill-gotten gains. He has an address in Leeds and there's a phone number but it's all legitimate stuff. He obviously keeps a respectable persona. I'll be getting info on his bank account but I suspect he'll have a legitimate business to launder his money.'

'I was wondering how Gee's going to keep his drug dealing business going now we have Roscoe and his little helpers,' Nina said.

'He'll move areas, take on more children and start again. Although I admit it will be more difficult now with the travel restrictions in place, and he'll have lost his sales on campus.'

'That can only be a good thing.'

'Apparently some dealers are doing home deliveries

now. Party drugs may not be so popular but people are using cocaine to relieve the boredom and addicts won't go without their heroin. I see that the supply from abroad is dwindling and fentanyl could be substituting for heroin. That's dangerous stuff to administer in the correct dosage.'

Nina was always impressed by how Ruby kept up to date with information on a wide range of policing matters but, of course, that was her job.

'Can you send Leeds all the info you have on Gee?' asked Nina. 'Hopefully they'll find him at the address. We can't do any more at this stage. Just ask Dave to let us know when they've got him, I'm looking forward to asking him about Wilf and Callum's deaths.'

Before she left for the weekend, Ruby told Nina that she wasn't any closer to finding out what Roscoe's words meant. She'd searched for pubs and bars called "The Barbie", or something that sounded similar, in Leeds but drawn a blank. She'd tried the Darlington area, where Roscoe was living, but found nothing. She had discovered there was a Barbie doll shop in Liverpool until last Christmas but that was all she had. She'd concluded that Roscoe must have been referring to a barbecue, and that could be anywhere. The only other possibility was the university, since he was registered as a student, but she'd drawn a blank. Nina asked her to double check with Dave that she hadn't missed something significant in Leeds, when she was back in on Monday.

Nina had a free weekend and she was looking forward to some time with the children. Nige had obviously been finding it stressful at home so she planned to let him have some time to himself, if that was possible in their tiny house. She had offered to do the family shop and planned to take the kids for their walk in the park so he could sit in front of the television. But then she heard there would be no football or rugby taking place, unless they ran old matches.

When she arrived home, it was unusually quiet. Rosie was at the table doing a jigsaw and Tomos was building something out of Lego. Nige was sitting in front of the fire with Owen, reading a book.

'Something smells good,' she commented before going upstairs to change.

By the time she came down again, the table was cleared and Rosie was putting out knives and forks. Nina asked her what was cooking.

'I made the Yorkshire pudding batter,' she announced proudly, 'and Dad cooked the sausages.'

'Toad-in-the-hole?' Nina asked. 'Yum, my favourite.'

They discussed their day seated round the dinner table, or at least the children did. They'd gone to the park but it was boring because they couldn't go on the playground. The boys had wanted to take a football until Nige explained they weren't allowed to play games.

'But some boys did,' complained Tomos.

Nige agreed. There were three older lads having a kick around.

'Dad told them off,' said Owen, 'but they just said rude words.'

'They should have police patrolling the park,' complained Nige.

'I'll pass the message on,' said Nina, laughing. 'I'm sure they'll send a patrol car down to arrest them immediately.'

'You may joke, Nina, but that's exactly what should

happen.'

'Anyway, this meal is excellent, don't you agree boys?' Having successfully changed the subject, she asked what everyone wanted to do tomorrow.

Rosie said she was going to get on with her jigsaw, Tomos and Owen had a Lego boat to build and Nige planned to paint the boys' bedroom, something she'd been asking him to do for ages. It sounded as if it was going to be a peaceful weekend.

Certainly it began well. The children settled in bed without a fuss, the kitchen was tidy and the shopping list was ready in preparation for Nina's trip to the supermarket on the following day. Nige poured two glasses of red wine from the bottle they'd opened earlier in the week but Nina was still thinking about work as she sat watching the flames rising from the logs.

'Here's a puzzle for you, Nige,' she said when he sat down next to her. 'Do the words "the barbie" mean anything to you?'

'As in the doll or the barbecue?'

'I don't know – anything.'

There was a long pause before he answered, 'No.'

'Are you sure? Only it might be something to do with the university.'

'Our university?'

'Yes. Maybe something like a bar on campus, but it could be anything.'

He thought again, staring into the fire. He sipped his wine and pondered with his eyes shut.

'Well?'

'No, sorry, nothing.'

She had a coping mechanism for shutting out work

while she was at home, so now she told herself there was nothing to be done until Monday and she put the puzzle away in its box, mentally.

The following morning she headed off early with the shopping list. Parking was difficult, the queue to get in was long, the wait at the till even longer. Certain shelves were still empty and some items were limited to one per customer. It was nearly mid-day by the time Nina was home again. To her surprise everyone was huddled in the back-yard eating hotdogs, made on their rusty old barbecue. Clearly her questioning had prompted Nige to bring it out from the shed. She had to admit that it was fun to be eating outside, despite the freezing cold.

The barbecue also prompted Nina to ring Mills. Her friend was far more observant than Nige and might have an answer to the barbie riddle, if it was to be found on campus. Mills was always keen to help an investigation. Sometimes too keen.

She rang when she was alone in the kitchen. 'Question for you Mills and don't laugh. Does "the barbie" mean anything to you in the context of the university?'

Silence. 'No' Another pause. 'Hang on, do you mean the summer bar?'

'Summer bar?'

'It's the shed on the far side of the lake. The students use it in the summer for barbecues, that's why it has the nickname "The Barbie". It's a dump really but they set up a makeshift bar in there.'

'Is it only used in the summer?' Nina asked.

'I guess so, there's power for lights and they can have a DJ but there's probably no heating. Anyway there wouldn't be enough room inside, it's just a summerhouse really. I went to a few events when I was a student. The problem is the midges, being by the lake, and it's muddy if you do go into the water. It's a health and safety nightmare; the Safety Unit is always trying to have the parties stopped.'

'So why didn't Nige know about it when I asked him?'

'Probably not somewhere he ever went. The summer parties were more a thing for undergraduates. I expect postgrads would think it too juvenile for them.'

'You think? We are talking about Nige, remember.'

Mills then asked why she was interested in "The Barbie".

Nina had to admit it was part of an investigation, just something they were looking into.

But her friend wasn't giving up that easily. 'Is it about Oliver Hayes?'

'Look, thanks for your help, Mills. So how are you both? How's Simon?' asked Nina, quickly changing the subject.

'He's fine, we're both fine.'

Her friend knew when to stop probing and they chatted for a while until Nige came in to indicate it was time to go to the park.

'Thanks again,' said Nina before putting the phone down.

Sounds as if we might have found our barbie, she told herself. On Monday she would go up to the campus to have a look at this summerhouse, to see if it's what Roscoe was trying to tell her about.

Chapter 24

The wind had dropped so Mills spent Sunday afternoon tidying the garden. A few daffodils had appeared and she'd spotted some primroses pushing through the dead leaves that formed a layer on the flower beds. She stood up to watch a curlew as it circled across the dale with its piercing cry. But it was turning quite chilly now the sun had disappeared, so she called Harris to come inside. She put the kettle on for a mug of tea and peered into the sitting room. Simon, who was on his regular face to face chat with Alfie, was getting the lurcher to wave a paw at his son. She wondered whether she should do a video chat with her father. It wasn't something he was very comfortable with but Fiona would love it, especially if she could see Simon for the first time. She'd think about it, maybe.

Nige had followed Nina's suggestion and linked up with his family in the morning. They'd been delighted to see their grandchildren and chatted to Nige in Welsh much to the boys' amusement. Afterwards, Rosie, who knew a few words that Nige had taught her, declared she wanted to speak Welsh fluently so she could talk her grandparents like Dad.

After their walk in the afternoon, Nina began cooking their Sunday dinner. They planned to eat around six so the children had an hour or so before bed, when they could chill out with a Disney film, although they were still arguing over which one to choose. The meat was almost done, the potatoes were roasting and needed another fifteen minutes when her mobile rang with a ringtone that meant work. Puzzled, she picked it up to see it was Dave calling.

'Nina, Patrick has just had a ping on the ANPR. Gee is on the move.'

'OK.' Nina wondered what was coming next.

'He was clocked on the A58 at Hollin Park. It means he's heading for the A1M. I thought you'd want to be in on the chance to finally collar him.'

'Right.'

'I'm picking Patrick up and following, but he's in a powerful Audi so I've got a patrol car waiting at junction 50 to follow discreetly, in case we lose him.' He sounded excited.

Nina decided she had to go. 'I can join you at the junction before the A66M turn off,' she said.

Nige was standing in the doorway.

'You heard that?' Nina asked, on her way through to grab her coat. 'They've spotted a suspect we're after.'

Nige followed her into the hall. 'You're not going on your own?' he asked.

'Well… I was…' She thought quickly. 'I can get a patrol car to pick me up at Northallerton.'

He gave her a hug. 'Please do, and be careful.'

'Look after the potatoes,' she called as she left.

She rang HQ as she drove to Northallerton. The uniform patrols were all busy but there was an unmarked car with two officers who were coming back in for a break. They were free. Nina could feel her apprehension give way to excitement, knowing she would be in company.

She was still waiting for the unmarked car to arrive when she got another call from Dave. 'As we expected, he's just joined the A1M at junction 46. The road is almost empty so he's taking a risk. We'll follow well behind.'

Nina was explaining that she had to wait for the unmarked car, when it appeared. 'It's here.' She rang off.

Once she was in the back of the car, she recognised the driver. 'Hi Graeme.'

He introduced his colleague, Jen. When Nina explained they were following a drug dealer heading for Darlington, Graeme said he would join the A1M at Leeming Bar. They moved off quickly through the empty streets while Nina calculated when Gee would be passing. They were in plenty of time before he was due to arrive, and they were a few minutes from the junction when Dave called again.

'We've only bloody lost him. He must've speeded up and turned off to Thirsk because there's no sign of him and he hasn't gone past the patrol car at the next junction. We're assuming he's avoiding the main roads. We'll carry on to Darlington and cover the incoming routes. Will you take the A19 in case he's heading for Middlesborough?'

Nina told the driver to stop. 'He's taken the Thirsk road.'

Jen sighed. 'Back to Northallerton then?'

Nina hesitated. 'Yes, over to the A19. He might be going to Middlesborough.'

She supposed Gee would still have contacts over there, maybe he was moving his operation back to the area. She was pleased Oliver Hayes was safe on campus and not at his parents' house. But what if Gee wasn't heading there but going to the university? Would Hayes be safe? And she hadn't had the opportunity to tell Dave about the other university connection: "The Barbie". Was that where Gee was going?

Jen contacted the patrol car to inform them of their new route and was told there were traffic officers at Thirsk that would look out for the vehicle. They were just travelling through Northallerton when Jen heard that Gee had left the A19 and was travelling in their direction. She told Nina that he would be there in about ten minutes if he stayed on course.

'So where does he think he's going?' asked Graeme, pulling the car to the side so they had a good view of the road.

'He could still be going to Darlington or Middlesborough, avoiding the main roads,' replied Nina. 'There's very little traffic about and he won't want to draw attention to himself – the Audi is distinctive enough.'

They sat in silence. Nina looked at her watch – it was six-fifty. Another few minutes before he was due, if he was still on route. A single car had passed while they sat there. Finally, a pair of headlights appeared, travelling well within the speed limit. Graeme was the first to catch the registration.

'That's him.'

He waited far too long before moving off, it seemed to Nina. She told herself that he was a trained driver and knew how to proceed in unmarked surveillance. They followed at a very significant distance and Nina guessed it was to remain undetected in such little traffic. She was waiting to see which way Gee left town. The car moved slowly down the main street and straight on. He wasn't going to Middlesborough, he was on the road that would lead directly to the university.

'He's going left!' called Jen a short while later.

Ahead of them the tail lights were disappearing down a

left fork signposted Danby Wiske. Nina knew the area well – the road could still take him to the university but it could also bring him back onto the A1M.

'Don't follow him!' shouted Nina. 'Go straight on.'

She had ten minutes to explain why she had instructed Graeme to lose the suspect. She began by agreeing with Jen that Gee had probably clocked he was being followed and was trying to shake them off.

'Did you see the way he accelerated?' she asked.

Nina told them that with the help of ANPR on the main road, Dave would pick Gee's car up again if he joined the A1M or the A66M. She then explained the tip-off she'd had from Gee's sidekick, when he was interviewed, about a building on campus.

She didn't wait to let Dave know of her change of plan. There was no time. If Gee was going to the university, they would be there in less than ten minutes. If she was wrong and he nipped off to Darlington, all well and good – Dave would spot him. If not, she had two officers with her and there was help on site. She rang the number of the campus Security Office.

'Detective Sergeant Nina Featherstone,' she explained quickly. 'I believe we might have a suspect known as Gee arriving on campus.' She looked at her watch, it was half six. 'In about eight minutes. Can you make sure that Oliver Hayes is informed and remains safe? I believe the suspect may be heading for the summerhouse on the far side of the lake. Do you know where I mean?'

The voice was gruff. 'That student place, I know it. It's locked up, they don't use it this time of year.'

'I have two officers with me, we'll keep a low profile. We want to arrest him on site at the summerhouse if he's there. If you can provide support it would be appreciated.'

His response was enthusiastic. He had two colleagues he could send. He would be staying in the control room in contact with them. 'Don't worry, I'll tell them to get over there now and take up position. They won't do anything until I order them to, just let me know when you're on site.' He added that he would find Hayes and make sure he was safely inside.

Graeme could put his foot down now. Nina gave him directions and, as they entered the main gate, she warned the security officer that they were on campus. He directed them to the car park close to his control room. Nina reckoned it was the last place Gee would choose to park his car. She didn't want him to be alerted of their presence. Their vehicle may not be a patrol car but criminals knew how to identify an unmarked police car from all the instrumentation visible on the dashboard.

The security officer was waiting by the office door to reassure her that Hayes was locked in his flat. He showed them the quickest route to "The Barbie". It would be dusk soon but for now Nina could see the path quite clearly as she led the two police officers along the edge of the lake. She was reminded of the sight of Callum's body lying half in the water and shuddered. Just keep following the path, the guard had said, before promising to let his colleagues know they were on their way. There was a blackbird singing in the trees to her left, creating the illusion of a peaceful Sunday evening. She began to worry that she may be leading her colleagues "up the garden path", so to speak. What if Mills had got it wrong? Had Roscoe been winding her up? Was Gee coming to find Hayes or, worse still, not coming here at all? The further they walked, the more anxious she became, until she had convinced herself that it was all a terrible mistake.

'There it is,' Jen whispered beside her.

Ahead of them was an ugly brick-built box. It was nothing like Nina had imagined. In her mind it had resembled a village cricket pavilion. It lay back from the path, which continued round the edge of the lake, presumably back to the far side. She couldn't imagine what use it was built for, so far away from the rest of the campus. A boathouse perhaps? She spotted two doors marked "men" and "women" at the side of the building, presumably toilet facilities or changing rooms. Nina was wondering whether this really was the "The Barbie", when a figure emerged from the other direction waving at them. He was joined by another security guard, who explained that they couldn't get inside because someone had fitted a new padlock. He indicated double glass doors with a chain through both handles. Nina, who was conscious that time was passing, was directing everyone to take up position behind the building, when one of the guards held up a hand, placed the other one over his earpiece and stood with his head on one side.

'An Audi has just parked up by the halls of residence,' he whispered.

'It's him.' Nina tried to hide her excitement at having been proved right.

'He'll take five minutes to get here from there,' the other guard said.

'Wait until he's inside the building before you make a move,' she ordered.

She told Graeme and Jen to enter the building with her when the time came, but instructed the security guards to stay back in case he made a run for it. Because everyone seemed happy to take her lead, she felt confident she had the situation under control. So once they had moved out of sight, Nina sent a text to Dave, telling him to ring the Security Office number to find out where she was and why. It seemed the easiest way to explain the situation. Then she muted her phone, before checking the others had done the same. It was nearly half past seven and it was becoming dark. She hoped there would be enough light to see what they were doing when the time came.

It was surprising how noisy the woodland was. Several times Nina thought she heard a twig snap or the swish of a branch. She could hear the others breathing heavily as if her senses had been enhanced. Finally, as footsteps approached along the path, it felt as if everyone had stopped breathing altogether. They listened to the rattling of the chain being released as the padlock was removed. Loud creaking sounds as the big glass doors were being opened. Then, suddenly, a floodlight came on at the side of the building and Nina indicated they should move in. She walked quietly round to the front and stared into the internal space that was now flooded with light.

A man in a hoodie had been crouching over a pile of small boxes in the corner but, when he heard Nina step inside, he straightened up and turned. His expression was at first surprise then irritation. He was like a trapped animal, looking first one way then the other. He made for the door, pushing Nina aside but Graeme and Jen were behind her, blocking his exit. The security guys were already inside, closing the doors, ensuring he had no means of escape.

'Mr Kadare?' Nina turned to face him as he stopped

struggling against the police officers' firm grip.

He didn't answer. He was staring ahead, presumably still startled by their sudden appearance. Jen pulled his hands behind his back and fitted handcuffs, holding on firmly while Graeme searched him. He opened a wallet and removed his driving licence, handing it to Nina. As expected, it was in the name of Getoar Kadare. While they hung on to him, Nina walked across the empty room to look at the boxes he'd been examining. The one on top contained several large packages, polythene bags full of white powder. She moved it aside and opened the next one, it was the same. Five identical boxes. If, as she suspected, this was cocaine, there was as much as fifty kilos. It was extraordinary that he would choose to leave it in this empty building but perhaps his sidekick, Roscoe, was responsible for that decision. Was Gee here to move it somewhere safer, now there was no Darlington connection? Nina turned round to find everyone waiting for her to give some direction.

'Five boxes containing what I believe to be cocaine,' she reported.

She looked forward to asking him about his bullyboy Roscoe and the deaths of the students here on campus, but meanwhile she could only realistically arrest him on the drug offences.

'Getoar Kadare, I am arresting you on suspicion of possession with intent to supply class A drugs. You do not have to say anything, but it may harm your defence if you do not mention when questioned something you later rely on in court. Anything you do say may be given in evidence'.

His expression remained unchanged, a blank stare at no-one, and nothing, in particular.

She turned to her colleagues. 'We'll take him back to the control room and wait for the patrol car to arrive. They can deliver him to the Harrogate custody suite.'

She looked at the boxes, quickly assessing whether three of them would struggle to manage all five. 'Can you take two boxes each?' she asked the security guards, judging they would agree in order to demonstrate their superior strength.

She guessed right. While they sorted themselves out, Nina checked to see if Dave had replied to her message. He and Patrick were on their way following the patrol car. She told him to meet them at Security, that Gee had been arrested. Picking up the last box herself, she followed everyone out, leaving "The Barbie" as an illuminated beacon by the lake.

Chapter 25

Mills and Simon had gone for a walk over the fell to Gunnerside Gill. He was complaining because the strong wind was making progress slow. She was glad she'd worn her woolly hat and gloves. Only Harris seemed oblivious of the cold conditions. At the top they admired the view briefly before taking the path downhill into Gunnerside. Mills was thinking how much nicer it was up here than walking round the lanes of Osmotherley and told Simon so. He had to agree but pointed out how much more convenient his place was for the university.

'When we're running the business, we'll need to get into work quickly,' he declared, pre-empting any further discussion about moving into Laurel Cottage permanently.

Mills hid her disappointment. She'd hoped that the balance between the two homes might have shifted towards Swaledale now he'd been here a while.

'It's a perfect arrangement to be over there during the week and here at weekends,' he added.

'I guess so.'

She was beginning to appreciate the impact that starting a forensic science service was going to have on her life. They'd spent hours on the business plan and finance. They'd worked into the night on how to balance the books if they employed Donna, and argued about how they might manage without her.

'D'you think we've made the right decision?' she asked, as they picked their way down the track. 'I mean, d'you

272

think we'll regret it later?'

'Of course not. It'll be brilliant once everything is sorted out. We'll be fine for two years with the support the department is giving us and by then we'll have built up the business.'

Mills didn't feel so confident. It was the frustration of not being able to get on with it during the lockdown. But Simon told her not to be silly.

'There's loads of stuff we can be doing online,' he said. 'We need to make contacts with the forensic consultancies that use scientific services like ours. They get business from organisations like insurance companies and law firms, so they'll need us. Several of them mention criminal defence work on their websites, just as you suggested. As soon as we can get back on campus…'

Mills knew she shouldn't be so negative and tried to make light of it. 'But I thought you liked staying here?'

'I do but…

She gave him a hug. 'Just kidding.'

The village was empty, there was no-one around, and the pub and tearooms were closed, of course. They chose the easy route back up the tarmac road, walking steadily with the force of the wind behind them, not wanting to stay in the cold longer than necessary.

As soon as they were home, Simon was on his laptop calling Alfie in Washington. It occurred to Mills that they could do the same to catch up with Nina and Nige, it would be fun to have a drink together over the internet. The conversation with Alfie lasted longer than usual and when it finished, Simon looked dejected. He disappeared upstairs for a while, to work, and Mills left him until dinner was ready.

'I do hope Alfie will be able to visit this summer,' Simon said when he finally appeared.

'I'm sure he will,' Mills replied without conviction.

'Not if his mother can help it, she says it's too soon. And he's dying to come here to the cottage...' He stopped abruptly. 'If that's all right with you?'

'Of course it is,' replied Mills with a smile. She loved the thought of Simon wanting to bring his son to meet her. 'I suppose I'll move back here full-time while he's staying with you anyway.'

'We'll see. There's so many things I want to show him... that we can show him, I mean.'

She understood he would want time alone with his son and suggested they wait to see what Alfie thought about it.

'Anyway,' she added, 'if it involves football, cricket, digger parks or rollercoasters, you can count me out!'

Nina ensured she was in good time to interview Getoar Kadare. There had been no opportunity to gain an impression of him before he was bundled into the patrol car and whisked away into custody. Dave had stayed long enough to congratulate her on the arrest. He'd seemed genuinely impressed with her ability to track Gee down and collar him single-handedly. She protested that she had a team of four supporting her but he still praised her enthusiastically in front of everyone. She was so buoyed up by the night's activities that she couldn't get to sleep for several hours, and was up earlier than usual. She and Nige had only managed to exchange a few words, to decide what they were eating that evening, before she left for Harrogate. He had asked, rather pointedly, whether she was sure she'd be back in time.

Nina waited for Dave, so they could discuss how they would approach the interview. Gee's charge sheet read "possession with intent to supply". Time would tell whether the white powder was a class A drug or not. If it wasn't cocaine it was probably ketamine, which was only class C, although the amount he was caught with could still see him serving up to fourteen years in prison. Dave would want to find out about the set-up, where Gee was in the command chain, who were their suppliers. She wanted him to admit that Roscoe did as Gee instructed him, so he was ultimately responsible for killing two young men.

'You do realise that he won't say a word,' Dave told her. 'And I'll bet you my pension he'll have the same solicitor as Roscoe.'

As he spoke Mr Shehu appeared, smiling amiably, stopping two metres away and shrugging to indicate they wouldn't be shaking hands.

'Good morning, I hope I'm not late,' he said, looking at his watch. 'Shall we?' He indicated the uniformed officer standing by a door at the end of the corridor, where presumably Getoar Kadare was waiting inside. They were in the same airy room where they had met only four days ago. This time there was a hand sanitiser dispenser on the table and bottles of water placed symmetrically, two on each side of the large table.

Dave's pension was safe. Gee sat motionless, staring ahead of him, not making eye contact with any of them. Despite being dressed in the grey hoodie, she was struck by how smart he appeared. Perhaps it was his thick black hair, expertly cut, and his youthful clear complexion. Maybe it was his poise, his confidence. He was fully in command of the situation. He recited "no comment" in the same flat monotone each time he was asked about any aspect of the County Lines operation.

After Dave had exhausted his list of questions, Nina felt like tearing hers up. Why give him the benefit of learning everything she knew about the murders when he was giving nothing away. She quickly decided to turn it around, asking him about Roscoe instead. Did Gee know he had killed the students? Perhaps he had a history of violence? She didn't want to give Gee any reason to think she was looking to charge him with murder if she could find the evidence.

An hour later Gee was led back to the custody suite and Mr Shehu was politely wishing them well before departing, presumably feeling it had been a good morning. Dave swore a few times then suggested heading for the canteen. Over coffee, he agreed it was no worse than expected, while he was clearly frustrated by the outcome.

'My work here is done,' he said. 'The evidence is clear: he was found in possession of about fifty kilos of illegal drugs; another few hours and we'll have confirmation it's cocaine, no doubt. He can't wriggle out of that. Although it was a shame that he wouldn't tell us why it was there and what he planned to do with it. He'll appear before the magistrates tomorrow and be detained in custody until the courts are back to normal.' He took a slurp of coffee. 'By the way, I'm getting my guys to look into that smarmy solicitor, Shehu. He's turning up with drug dealers too often for my taste. There's something dodgy about him, I can smell it.'

Nina was wondering whether there was anything more she could have done to pursue her case against Gee. Dave must've have guessed what she was thinking because he told her not to worry, with a bit of luck he would get a maximum sentence, which for that amount of class A was life.

'If only Roscoe hadn't been so scared of Mr Shehu,' she said.

'You can see why.' It was Dave's turn to go quiet. 'You know we could get Roscoe back to ask a few more questions.'

'There's no point with Mr Shehu there.'

'We could offer him a different solicitor,' Dave suggested with a grin. 'Let me go and have a chat with the custody suite. Are you all right to hang around for a while?'

She nodded. While she waited, she called Hazel to let her know what had been happening overnight. Her colleague was impressed that she'd caught the dealer with his hands on such a large haul of drugs.

'I bet the DS from Leeds was well pissed off he didn't make the collar,' said Hazel.

'He was very generous actually. Can you tell Ruby that we're hoping to interview Roscoe again, in case she has anything else on him – she was looking at his finances.'

'Will do.'

Dave was gone for half an hour before he returned looking triumphant. 'He's agreed to meet the duty solicitor, a Ms Campbell.'

'Is that OK with everyone?'

'You mean with Shehu? Probably not but it's worth a punt. I've explained it to Ms Campbell. The big interview room is free now.'

They were in position before the uniformed officer escorted Roscoe in. He looked more drawn than before, causing his face to appear hollow, his eyes sunken, and

Nina assumed he had a drug habit. The duty solicitor, a young woman with designer glasses and a ponytail, followed them. Her red suit made a splash of colour in the grey décor.

'Hi, I'm Mary Campbell,' she said brightly as she sat down, moving her chair a little further away from Roscoe, smiling at him as she did so. The contrast between them was stark.

As agreed, Dave took the lead. When he said they had Mr Getoar Kadare in custody, Roscoe looked puzzled until Dave explained he was known as Gee.

'Gee was arrested with fifty kilos of cocaine in his possession, thanks to the assistance you provided DS Featherstone.' Dave went on. 'We know he was your boss but, until you confirm it, we have to assume you were in partnership with him or even calling the shots.'

Roscoe looked at the solicitor then back at Dave. 'What's in it for me?'

'You help us, we can help you, can't we? We can keep your Mr Shehu off your back for a start.'

Nina could see Ms Campbell didn't like that comment. She kept her head down and scribbled in her notebook.

Dave cleared his throat. 'At present you are charged with two counts of murder and one of attempted murder, in addition to the drugs charges of course. They're not going away but if there was any pressure on you from Gee, that will be relevant. My only interest in all this is to shut down any County Lines operating out of Leeds. On the other hand, DS Featherstone here wants to get whoever gave the orders to kill the two students from your university.'

Roscoe was glancing nervously at the solicitor, who still had her head down. Dave waited. Nina smiled encouragingly.

'When did you first meet Gee?' she asked. 'Was that in Middlesborough?'

Roscoe nodded.

'Is that how you knew Oliver Hayes?'

He shifted in his seat. 'Yes.'

'You were all working for a dealer in Middlesborough.' It was a comment not a question. 'And you recognised Hayes when you saw him years later, on campus?'

'Yes.'

'So was Gee your boss when you worked in Middlesborough?'

He snorted. 'No, me and Gee were mates then, Hayes was just a foot soldier. It was small time stuff really. My mistake was using. Gee never did, he was too smart. He had big plans to take it over, trouble was the bosses didn't like what he had in mind and there was big trouble. That's why he left.'

'Tell me about his business in Leeds,' Dave asked.

Roscoe's eyes were alert now and he straightened up, as if he'd come to a decision. 'If I talk to you, will you make sure my brother's safe?'

Nina recalled the message from Ruby. 'Your brother is studying mechanical engineering at the university, is that right?' she asked.

'He's a bright lad, our kid,' Roscoe's face lit up. 'He'll get top marks and find a good job in London or go abroad. As far away from here as possible.'

'So what's the problem?' Dave asked impatiently.

Roscoe scowled at him. 'What d'you think?'

Nina attempted to calm him down. 'Was it your brother who helped you get into university?'

Ms Campbell had been looking at Roscoe, trying to get his attention. Now she leaned forward. 'I think my client would like a few minutes consultation,' she said with a deadpan face.

He looked at her in surprise then acquiesced. Dave followed Nina out of the room and stood in the corridor. 'If she's got any sense, she'll get him to spill the beans,' he said impatiently.

'Now he's started, I hope he'll keep going. It sounds as if he's trying to protect his brother. Do you think he's been threatened?'

'Quite likely, it's the way people like Gee get what they want, by intimidation, threats to the families, we know where they live, that sort of thing.'

They must have stood out there for at least fifteen minutes. When they finally took their seats again, the solicitor looked worried, Roscoe appeared to have been crying.

'My client wants to cooperate with you.'

This began a discussion regarding what Roscoe was prepared to divulge about the drug operation. Dave explained that if he was willing to act as a witness at Gee's trial, he might be shown leniency on the drugs charge. However, the murder charges were a different matter. There were witnesses to prove his guilt, only extenuating circumstances, such as threats to his family could reduce the sentence but he warned that duress, such as threats to his family, was not a defence in the case of murder.

'I have explained all this to my client.' Her face revealed nothing. 'His only concern is the safety of his brother. If he was to appear as a witness for the prosecution of Mr Kadare, he believes he would be putting his family in danger. He understands that he has been charged with murder and will have to leave the court to decide what is a suitable punishment in the circumstances.'

'If you appear as a witness at Gee's trial, he will be put away for a very long time,' said Dave irritably.

'I'm not going to give evidence against him in public,' Roscoe said. 'It's too dangerous, but I can tell you what I know off the record.'

Dave sighed. 'In that case we need to get a "co-operating defendant agreement" in place,' he said to the solicitor.

She looked concerned, asking about the fact she was standing in for the client's solicitor, Mr Shehu.

'No problem. Mr Roscoe can request that his legal representative is not informed of the agreement.'

'So what does this all mean?' Roscoe asked.

Ms Campbell turned to him. 'It means you have to agree to plead guilty to all charges, and to divulge everything you know in relation to the crimes. If you do that and give full co-operation, the CPS agrees to ensure the assistance you provide is placed before the court before sentencing. In other words you help the police and the judge will take that into consideration.'

'Does that mean a shorter sentence?' Roscoe asked.

Dave leaned forward. 'I've seen a sentence reduced by half where a dealer provided valuable information that shut down County Lines.'

The solicitor glowered across the table, warning her client that there was no magic formula. Nina suggested they left Roscoe to discuss the proposal with the duty solicitor while they made some enquiries of the CPS. It was Dave's turn to look annoyed. It was nearly lunchtime so Nina asked the officer outside if he could get some sandwiches and drinks while they waited in the corridor.

'We nearly had him eating out of our hands,' Dave muttered, getting out his mobile phone. 'You can see Miss Smartypants isn't happy.'

She won't be, thought Nina. Her position is at best tenuous, since she's supposedly standing in for Mr Shehu. When the sandwiches arrived, they chose a pack each and disappeared up to the offices to ask the CPS to authorise a draft agreement, in the hope that Roscoe would then comply. After a couple of hours, it was made clear to them that approval wouldn't come through until the following day at the earliest.

Back in the interview room, it was settled. Roscoe was going to sign the agreement if, and when, it was approved. He didn't want a solicitor present, Ms Campbell had already told him she wasn't on the rota for the following day so it would be a colleague, a new face. Basically he would continue to have Mr Shehu to represent him, but only after they had held the interview where he told them everything about the County Lines operation and the murder of Wilf Marriott and Callum Wallace.

'I think that's a result,' Nina said to Dave as they left.

She felt confident they would get approval for the agreement from the prosecutor. Roscoe was clearly under pressure from Gee to carry out his dirty work and once Dave had a full picture of Gee's role in the County Lines operation, he would have further intel to trace his supplier.

It was nearly the end of the day and she decided it wasn't worth going back to the office for an hour; she deserved an early finish after all the time she'd spent chasing round the university campus in the dark. She was about to give Nige the good news when she found a voicemail from her

DI asking her to come in for a chat as soon as possible.

'Do you know what Mitch wants?' Nina asked Hazel as she struggled out of her coat and placed it over a chair.

'He's complaining that you're not keeping him up to speed.'

'Did you tell him I was interviewing Roscoe today?'

'I thought best not to,' objected Hazel.

'Did Ruby say anything?'

'I haven't seen her.'

Nina went along to Mitch's office, annoyed at being late home again. He looked up and scowled at her and she surprised herself by glaring back.

'So what have you been up to today?' he asked crossly.

'Interviewing our murder suspect. He's agreed to inform on the drug dealer who we believe gave the orders to kill the students.'

'Is this something Leeds put you up to? Can't you keep it simple, Nina? We've got the guy, he's in custody, why drag it out? You know we're short of staff. And Ruby is off now.'

'Is she OK? What's the matter?'

'It's just a cough but she won't be allowed back for two weeks. All cases are to be put on the back burner now. We could be asked to cover for anyone in the next few weeks or months. Have you got that, Nina?'

'Yes, sir.'

Chapter 26

The office seemed empty without Ruby. Somehow it was normal for Hazel to be out and about, but the researcher was desk-based and it was strange for her seat to be empty. Besides, Nina relied on her for all sorts of things, including keeping confidences. She wouldn't be telling Hazel where she was off to that afternoon, for example. Dave had sent a message which she interpreted to mean that they had the go-ahead to interview Samuel Roscoe, under the CPS arrangements to keep it confidential from Mr Shehu. She waited until her colleague was out of the office before slipping out to drive down to Harrogate.

Dave was waiting with news that Roscoe had been tested for drugs when he was charged and he'd admitted he used cocaine. They weren't particularly concerned about his health, although he wasn't getting much sleep. Knowing that, Nina was surprised to find the man in good spirits when they joined him. Perhaps he was looking forward to getting everything off his chest. Before they began recording, Dave asked Roscoe to sign the agreement that had arrived from the CPS, re-iterating that it was provisional on him pleading guilty to the charges and fully divulging everything. Then he asked him to begin, and once Roscoe started, there was no stopping him.

Children as young as ten had been recruited by the dealers on his estate in Middlesborough when he was growing up, he began. If you didn't have a bike, they stole one for you. They paid better than a paper-round did and so it was difficult not to get involved. Once you were in, there was no turning back and he was still working alongside his mate, Gee, in his early twenties, organising the kids who were distributing the drugs. That was until his friend tried to muscle in on the business and he had to leave. That was when Gee moved to Leeds. He couldn't start a new operation in the city so he set up the County Lines, delivering the drugs further north.

'Is that when you moved to Darlington?'

'Yeah. My brother was going to the university. He's smart, never in trouble. He kept on at me to get a legit job, do some qualifications like him. Daft kid thought he could change things. He helped me pass this access course for mature students. Gee thought it would be a good connection to the area, so he told me to apply for a degree course.'

'Was it his idea for you to study crime and investigation?' Nina asked.

He grinned. 'It had to be part-time and we had a laugh about it.'

He'd rented a flat in Darlington with his brother at first, but he soon moved out when he discovered Roscoe was still working for Gee. By then he was responsible for moving the drugs to remote locations, where schoolkids recruited from Leeds would pack them ready for delivery in towns like Darlington and Bishop Auckland.

'What about the university?' asked Dave.

'That came later when I spotted Hayes on campus. He'd been one of our delivery boys in Middlesborough. It didn't take long for him to be persuaded to work for us, if you know what I mean. Gee knew where his parents lived in Middlesborough. Hayes recruited his flatmates, nice lads who looked after the weekend packaging teams.'

When Dave asked him to explain his role in that part of the operation, Roscoe said he would drive the drugs to the cottage booked for that weekend, along with all the equipment, like scales, bags, spatulas and the food for the boys. He'd leave the money for Hayes to pay the kids when they left. He'd get there in the afternoon and leave it ready for when Hayes arrived. On the Sunday evening he would go back after they'd gone to collect the packaged drugs and take them, with the equipment, back to his flat in Darlington. He would call Gee when that was done and other nameless, faceless youngsters would collect batches of the drugs from him for distribution. He added that he was only involved in distributing cocaine, ecstasy and ketamine, and nothing serious like heroin or crack.

Dave ignored him. 'Did you book the cottages and the taxis?' he asked.

'No, I don't know who did that, maybe Gee did it himself.'

He was asked more questions about the County Lines operation but didn't know how the drugs came into the country. They had a break before Nina began her questions, during which she asked Dave if he'd got what he wanted. It confirmed Gee's role as the boss of the outfit but he wasn't sure how helpful it was going to be for Roscoe, since he was still a key figure in the distribution of the drugs.

Finally it was Nina's turn to direct Roscoe's narrative. She began by picking up on what he'd said about keeping his brother safe.

'What did you mean by that?' she asked.

'What d'you think? Gee knows where to find him, if I

shop him.'

'We have Gee in custody now, so your brother is safe,' she reassured him.

'You think so? Yes, he's in custody but that solicitor will be visiting him. He has contacts.'

'He won't know you've been talking to us, it's in the agreement you signed.'

Eventually she persuaded him to continue.

'It all started because of the new one called Wilf. It turns out he's been looking at the ecstasy and he says it's not pure. That didn't surprise me but he was kicking up a fuss, so Hayes tells Gee. Next thing, I'm told to get rid of him. I thought he meant pay him off, but no. I tell him it's not a good idea, it will draw attention to the business, but Gee starts talking about my kid brother, in a threatening way and I know what he's saying.' He stopped talking, pressing his lips together, an anguished look came over him.

Nina spoke gently. 'What exactly happened to Wilf?'

Gee had told him exactly what to do. He would contact Wilf to arrange a meeting outside his accommodation, late at night. Roscoe was to go there with a small bottle of liquid, which he provided, and was to get him to swallow the contents. When he asked how, Gee told him to use his imagination.

Nina encouraged him to continue. 'What did you do?'

'I took the top off a can of pop and poured it in. When he came out, I said Gee was on his way but he was late, so we sat on the bench and I offered him the can. At first he said no, but after a while, when I was drinking mine, he took it and swallowed nearly all of it at once.' He shuddered. 'He went floppy almost straight away and keeled over on the bench. I left him there, hoping someone would find him.'

It went quiet. Nina was thinking of the poor lad called Lewis who had found Wilf's body. Unfortunately he'd found him too late.

'So what did Callum do?' she prompted.

'He was asking questions about Wilf. He was scared and wanted to stop working for Gee. That wasn't going to happen, I knew that, and so did Hayes, but he told the boss anyway. Next thing Gee's handing me another bottle. "You know the drill," he said, calm as anything, then asked how my brother was doing.'

'So what did you do to Callum?'

'When I heard the rumour on campus that Wilf had committed suicide, I realised why Gee was giving me the bottles. I didn't want to be accused of killing them, so I thought I'd make it look more convincing this time.'

Nina found his logic chilling.

'I told him Gee was waiting down the way. This time I poured the bottle into a can of beer. He was wary of me but even more scared of meeting Gee, so he took the beer and swigged it as we waited by the lake. It took a while to take effect but when he fell into the water I scarpered.'

'So he wasn't dead when you left him?'

A few seconds passed. 'I don't know.'

Nina could see Callum's body, curls of hair plastered across the white face. She couldn't speak for several seconds. When she did, she tried to keep the anger from her voice.

'And so we come to Oliver Hayes,' she prompted.

He shrugged. 'He came back to the boat after the cottage was raided. Gee wasn't happy. He ordered me to teach him a lesson, then we left. Then Gee says he's back at the university and wants to talk.'

Nina sighed. 'And he provided you with yet another bottle.'

Roscoe looked at the floor and muttered under his breath.

'Speak up, we need to hear you. Did Gee provide you with the lethal dose of fentanyl?' She emphasised each word.

'Yes.'

'Did you threaten to kill him if he didn't write a suicide note?'

'Gee thought it would be more convincing if there was a note. Everyone thought the others had committed suicide. It seemed a good idea.'

Nina was beginning to sicken of such prosaic talk about the ending of life and needed a break from it. She looked at Dave who nodded and took over the questioning. He wanted more information about how the children were recruited but Roscoe knew nothing about that side of the operation. Nor did he have anything to do with the actual County Lines – the mobile numbers through which drugs were ordered by customers from across the county boundaries. Roscoe was simply told to provide drugs to contacts in the North-East, who then delivered them to the customers.

When the interview was over, Roscoe asked what would happen to him now. Dave explained that he would be in custody until the courts were operating again, which could take some time. He would be held on remand locally and appear at the Crown Court in York eventually.

'You'll be tried for two counts of murder and one of attempted murder,' Nina warned. 'The fact your brother's life was threatened is no case for a change to that, but your agreement to plead guilty and give us full disclosure will be taken into account when you are sentenced.'

When he asked how much reduction he might expect, she couldn't answer. But Dave repeated that he'd seen sentences reduced by more than half, although that did apply to a drug dealing charge. It didn't appear to give Roscoe much reassurance.

Dave waited for Roscoe to be escorted away before asking Nina if she now planned to charge Gee with incitement to murder. She didn't see how she could prove it if Roscoe was unwilling to appear as a witness. No, she would just have to hope that when Gee came to trial, his drug charges would carry the maximum possible sentence of life imprisonment.

'I'll do my best,' said Dave with a smile.

Mills hadn't progressed any further with a video call to her father but instead she was planning to link up with Nina and her family. It had taken a few days to set up but finally, on Saturday afternoon, Nina invited them to a video tea party to celebrate Nige's birthday. Mills dressed in a flowery top and skirt, insisting that Simon change into a shirt instead of the sweater he'd worn all week. Her friend said she would get the children to put on their party clothes. Rosie had gone for a frilly creation with a fancy hairband, her brothers had brushed their hair. Nina was looking elegant as ever and Mills complimented her on her cashmere sweater. Typically, Nige appeared not to have made any effort, until he complained he'd been too busy getting the party food ready. He reinforced his argument by panning the camera round to the table, where Mills could see sandwiches, cakes and was that trifle? He zoomed in to show that it was.

'Welcome to our virtual birthday tea party,' said Rosie solemnly.

The announcement launched a series of quizzes from Nige and games designed by Simon for the children. Mills had to admit he had an excellent insight into what they would find entertaining. The competitions involved forfeits which degenerated into chaos as the boys became increasingly excited. Nina eventually suggested they have something to eat, in order to calm everyone down. Mills was unable to compete with their spread, having produced a few ham sandwiches, although Simon had used the last of the flour to make his special chocolate cake.

While they were eating, Nige and Simon discussed the trials of organising online lectures for the undergraduates. For once they had a topic of mutual interest that they both felt strongly about. Mills was pleased to see them getting on so well but she sensed that Nina was tiring of the topic. Undeterred, Nige kept going until eventually it was time for him to blow out his candles and for everyone to sing "Happy Birthday'. Tea over, Nina put on a video for the boys while Rosie was settled in the background with a book of word searches.

Now was a perfect time to find out about the investigation, thought Mills. 'Nina, I meant to ask you, have you uncovered what really happened to Wilf and Callum yet? Or are you still working on it?'

Nina shook her head. 'The case is finished, I'm moving on. From Monday I'm being seconded to the domestic abuse safeguarding team. You've probably heard on the news how incidents have increased during the lockdown, so it's the priority now.'

Mills had hundreds of questions but it was Simon who spoke first. 'Does that mean you know where the lads in the minibus were going and what they were doing?' he asked.

'Lads?' Nina sounded puzzled.

'We saw them arriving in Clapham, didn't we, Mills? And they were at Horton-in-Ribblesdale the week before. It was an outdoor adventure holiday wasn't it?'

Mills could sense that Nina was calculating what she could say without divulging confidential information.

'All I can say is that we have two men in custody. One is charged with possession of Class A drugs with intent to supply. In a related case, we have another who is charged with the murder of two students and attempt to murder a third.'

'I knew it!' said Mills. 'The flatmate in the big coat was a drug dealer, wasn't he? Wilf and Callum were working with him, and the man on the narrow boat was the boss.'

'So what were those children doing at the cottage?' asked Simon.

Mills laughed. 'Working for the dealers, isn't that right Nina?' Simon hadn't believed her but she'd read about teenagers working in rented places, moving around. It made perfect sense.

Now Nige was asking Nina how dangerous her new role in domestic abuse would be, while Mills was still trying to find out more about the drug ring, but Simon had run upstairs. He soon reappeared holding a small plastic vial, pointed at the closed end and with a hinged plastic cap.

'Did you find any of these when you caught up with the dealers?' Simon asked.

Nina couldn't see it properly so Mills sent her a photograph.

She peered at the image and shrugged. 'I don't know. I wasn't at the cottage when they found the drugs. Why do you ask?'

Simon told her that a large box of them had disappeared and he suspected that Callum had taken them, having found one at the cottage in Horton-in-Ribblesdale. This required further explanation, since Nina was unaware of their stay in "The Cot". Mills found herself admitting that she'd been following Callum and Hayes to find out what they were up to.

Nige interrupted their conversation to ask whether it was time for a birthday beer or a glass of wine, but Nina was busy using her phone.

'So have you been home schooling the children?' Mills asked Nige, when he returned with a pint in his hand.

He had and he was enjoying it. He was taking his responsibilities very seriously and had taught Rosie some rudimentary Welsh phrases; even the boys could count to ten in his native language. They had a structured day of learning in the morning and fun in the afternoon, with sessions of Disney film classics if he had a lecture to prepare.

When Nina was paying attention again, Mills took the opportunity to check out a few more facts. 'So the youngsters were spending their weekends, doing what exactly?' No answer. 'Bagging up the drugs?' Nothing. 'OK, so the man on the boat was organising it from that end, right?' Silence. 'The student in the black coat, Oliver Hayes, he supervised the kids?'

'It's not another quiz, Mills.' That was all Nina would

say before changing the subject. 'Simon, your son in America, he's all right, is he? Mills told me he usually comes over in the summer. I hope he will be able to.'

He looked at Mills before answering. 'Yes, although I was thinking maybe we could go over there to visit. We have a beach house in Chesapeake Bay, it's not too far from Washington. I thought it might be fun.'

Mills thought it would be too, but pointed out they had a whole new laboratory to get working once they were allowed back into the university.

'That reminds me, Nina,' Simon said. 'Did you get the results from your forensic science service eventually?'

'Not yet. There have been delays. But we now have independent confirmation that fentanyl was involved in Wilf Marriott's death. Your results have been audited by Wakefield, so the report will be submitted with the evidence when the case comes to court.'

There was a ping, she reached for her phone and read her message. 'OK, so this is a response from a colleague in Leeds. He says a box of a thousand of those plastic tubes was included in the drug paraphernalia. Apparently, the tubes are used to sell one-gram quantities of cocaine in reusable containers, because some punters don't like single-use plastics.'

'No way!' said Nige.

'That's what he says.'

'I can believe there will be students on campus who think that way,' said Mills.

Nige was still shaking his head in disbelief.

'Students don't appreciate the potential dangers of their actions sometimes,' commented Simon. 'Look at Wilf and Callum. They were bright students, possibly not even drug users themselves, and yet they were working for men who had little regard for their lives when it came down to it.'

There followed a discussion about whether the university should take more action on the use of drugs on campus. Simon pointed out that Wilf had been trying to persuade Student Services to provide drug testing kits to the students but had had no success. Nige felt it just encouraged drug use and things began to get heated. Nina brought the conversation to an end by saying that the important thing was for the authorities to ensure that the students were safe.

'We'll never eradicate the supply of drugs or the dealers who distribute them, Nige, so it's imperative that students feel they can ask for help and advice,' she concluded. 'After all, universities have a duty of care for their students, don't they? I'd like to think that will still be the case when Rosie goes off to university and I'm sure Simon feels the same about young Alfie in the States.'

He agreed. 'You're right, Nina, I'll see that the drug-testing kit that Wilf was working on is completed and ensure it, or something similar, is provided on campus by Student Services. It will be Wilf's legacy, and the least we can do to keep our students safe.'